I0693333

HIDDEN VILLAINS: BETRAYED

ROBYN HUSS

Inkd
Publishing

Inkd Publishing LLC

Copyright © 2024

All rights reserved.

ISBN - 979-8-9892810-2-2

No part of this book may be reproduced in any form or by any electronic or mechanical means, including information storage and retrieval systems, without written permission from the author, except for the use of brief quotations in a book review.

Bartholomew's Bluff Copyright © 2024 by Mike Jack Stoumbos

Daisy Chains Copyright © 2024 by Sarah J. Sover

Glimmer Copyright © 2024 by Tim Lewis

The Goddess of Crime Copyright © 2024 by Michael La Ronn

Jove Two Copyright © 2024 by Kevin A Davis

Killing Karen Copyright © 2024 by Karen A. Phillips

The Last Mermaid Copyright © 2024 by Rachel Nussbaum

Light as Air Copyright © 2024 by JL George

Manic Pixie Demon Girl Copyright © 2024 by Laura Ruth Loomis

A Mother's Pride Copyright © 2024 by Michele Stuart

A Murder in Bel Hammond Copyright © 2024 by Kareem Miskel

The Nightengale's Curse Copyright © 2024 by Patrick Dugan

Splitting Image Copyright © 2024 by Sara Jordan-Heintz

The Universe in Her Eyes Copyright © 2024 by Madelyn Lopez

Cover art © Vivid Covers | www.VividCovers.com

HIDDEN VILLAINS:
BETRAYED

IN MEMORY OF DAVID FARLAND

The inspiration for Hidden Villains anthologies.
His novels are numerous, but those he taught are beyond count.

CONTENTS

INTRODUCTION

Dear Readers,

Some of these authors are names you recognize, and others are publishing their first short story. I have enjoyed reading, editing, and compiling all of them for you.

Discovering a hidden villain is one thing, but when that involves a betrayal? Well, that just tears at your heartstrings. The betrayals in these stories impact friends, families, coworkers, and couples. Which is the most devastating? That is for you to read and decide.

Wherever these hidden villains may lurk, I hope their betrayals are worth the consequences!

Robyn Huss, Editor

* * *

Robyn Huss is a freelance editor who specializes in heavy developmental and copy editing; she is a thorough grammarian and has a good eye for inconsistencies. She is able to focus on character development, dialogue, paragraphing, sequencing of events and details, theme, and symbolism, in addition to providing a thorough review of grammar, usage, style, and word choice.

Robyn has spent a lifetime analyzing fiction and writing. Her bachelor's degree is in English with teaching certification; she taught literature and writing for more than thirty years to grades six through college, and she has been editing professionally since 2013.

To learn more about Robyn and see samples of her work, visit www.HussEditing.com

ROYAL WEDDING

KEVIN J. ANDERSON

ells of rejoicing rang throughout the kingdom. Peasants and townspeople were called away from their tasks to line up and cheer the wedding procession of Prince Derek and Princess Lilac. The people wore their finest clothes and tossed flower petals along the path to the castle. Though they had no coins to spare, they spent time and money cleaning the streets, fixing their roofs, painting their homes, and making everything beautiful for the royal couple. They cheered as best they could.

Up in the castle, Hedda had worked in the kitchens since midnight to bake wedding rolls, wedding cake, and wedding puddings. The silverware had to be polished until her fingers bled. Hedda scowled even though she was supposed to be beaming with joy for what was sure to be the prosperity of the kingdom.

"Come now, all of you!" barked the head cook. "We have to prepare a feast for the eternal happiness of our prince and princess."

"How about our happiness?" Hedda muttered.

"That is not for us to worry about."

Jack, the scruffy young serving boy, came in with an armload of wood for the ovens. "This'll take care of the last breads and pies." He winced as he dumped the wood in the pile. His hands were red and inflamed, and Hedda hurried over to the sweet young man. They had grown up in the village, known each other since they were small children, though neither of them had many prospects.

"Let me see those hands," she said.

His fingers were blistered, every knuckle swollen. "It's the bee stings. Can't help it."

"You could help it if the royal couple didn't insist on honey-drenched bumblebees for an appetizer." On a whim, Princess Lilac had asked for the treat, which meant that someone had to catch jars full of bumblebees, and bumblebees did not like to be caught. Jack had been stung repeatedly, but the appetizers were safe.

With each passing day, Hedda had grown to hate the prince and princess more and more.

"I made a salve for you. I know all the secret recipes." Hedda's mother had been an herb woman, a specialist in medicines and folk remedies, and she had taught her daughter every trick.

She gently rubbed the salve into his fingers. Hedda was sweet on Jack, and each night, the two would find a shadowy alcove in the castle and sit together with a meal scraped from the plates of the decadent nobles. Neither she nor Jack could ever scrounge the coins necessary to pay the marriage tax. The closest they would come to a fine wedding would be to hover in the banquet room and wait for the noble guests to demand more wine or another serving of broiled larks.

Hedda knew the other servants felt the same. Everyone was instructed to keep up appearances no matter how much the prince and princess were despised. But she had had enough, and she saw her opportunity with the wedding banquet.

Nobles from across the kingdom would attend, counts, dukes, barons, and other titles that Hedda didn't entirely understand, except they all had to be addressed as "m'lord" and unquestionably obeyed. Hedda was an attractive girl, but too drab and scuffed to draw any nobleman's lusty attention; fortunately, Jack found her pretty. That was all she needed with the thing they had to do tonight.

She had planned for weeks, digging through forest mulch to find the right kind of mushrooms, the orange spiky ones her mother called Death's Daggers. The head cook saw what she carried in her basket, and although the cook knew full well what the mushrooms would do, she turned a blind eye and whistled as she scrubbed a cauldron.

None of the other servants admitted that they knew of the plan, but Hedda didn't need to give them any warning. Finally, when it came time for the meal, the breads, the soup, the roasted boar and venison, every course had a liberal dose of mushrooms, minced up so small as to be unseen. When one serving girl tried to snatch a roll from a basket, the head cook had nearly screamed, swatting the girl's hand and scolding her never to taste the food of her betters.

Hedda, Jack, and the army of castle servants served the well-dressed and perfumed crowd. The handsome prince and blushing bride were too enamored with each other even to think to compliment the meal, which the guests ate with great gusto. Everyone stuffed themselves, but none of the servants tasted a bite, even though the food seemed luscious.

Princess Lilac was the first to groan and cry out in pain as she hunched over with stomach spasms. She spewed vomit into her plate. Her prince cried out for help, then he too doubled over. Very swiftly, all the nobles were retching, writhing on the floor, their skin erupting in boils, their throats constricted.

The servants waited patiently. The process was longer and noisier than Hedda had expected. Her mother had not given her all the details, but Death's Dagger was certainly effective.

Even before the victims all were dead, Hedda and Jack scurried about, pulling rings from fingers, snatching jeweled pendants, and prying rubies and sapphires from goblets. Gold coins were piled up as wedding gifts, and Jack stuffed his pockets. Hedda filled a sack with necklaces and brooches, while the other servants scavenged their own riches. They would scatter after tonight.

This castle was dead, but now she and Jack could be free. They had all the money they could imagine, even enough for the marriage tax, though she had no intention of paying it. They would be married in their own hearts and rich in their own souls.

In the dark of the night they fled the castle and the dead bodies piled in the banquet hall. Hedda didn't think about the people she had just murdered. In her mind, they were a different sort of people anyway.

She and Jack ran off, and they lived happily ever after.

* * *

KEVIN J. Anderson has published more than 175 books, 58 of which have been national or international bestsellers. He has written numerous novels in the Star Wars, X-Files, *and* Dune *universes, as well as a unique steampunk fantasy trilogy beginning with* Clockwork Angels, *written with legendary rock drummer Neil Peart.*

His original works include the Saga of Seven Suns *series, the* Wake the Dragon *and* Terra Incognita *fantasy trilogies, the*

Saga of Shadows *trilogy, and his humorous horror series featuring Dan Shamble, Zombie P.I. He has edited numerous anthologies, written comics and games, and the lyrics to two rock CDs.*

Anderson is the director of the graduate program in Publishing at Western Colorado University. Anderson and his wife Rebecca Moesta are the publishers of WordFire Press. His most recent novels are Clockwork Destiny, Gods and Dragons, Dune: The Lady of Caladan *(with Brian Herbert), and* Slushpile Memories: How NOT to Get Rejected.

BARTHOLOMEW'S BLUFF

MIKE JACK STOUMBOS

art ran his thumb along the edge of one card. His eyes flicked up at his opponents, then back down to his hand. He let his tongue escape from between his lips and bit down slightly, as if considering.

That gesture, like every other, was a performance. He appeared to make a hard decision, but he'd known the outcome since receiving two painted toad cards in the opening deal, after which, Bart had waited patiently as the pile of chips grew.

"I call," he said, after due deliberation, his guttural accent clashing against those of the other players.

The lady with the feathered hat and green veil smiled to herself, thinking she'd just picked up a pretty pot. The gent on her left, sweating through his silk waistcoat, was along for the ride and seemed relieved to end the hand; the in-for-a-penny adage would cost him much more than a gold piece today, which he still could easily afford.

"Shall we?" asked the lady, splaying her cards face-up, proudly confirming she hadn't bluffed.

The gent nodded politely, knowing he was beaten.

But when the lady saw Bart's silently spread hand, her expertly tweezed brows arched in shock. For while both players had full houses, his led with a higher-value triple: three crowned toads labeled with red or black *K*s.

"That's me then." Bart swept the not-so-modest pile of clay chips, clacking and pinging, to his side of the table.

"My stars!" The gent raised his monocle to inspect, now that no one could read his hand in its reflection. "You certainly played it cool with three Kings—"

"*Kroeters* here, Sir," corrected Bart, pointing one finger at the faded image of the toad, the thirteenth and highest-value sign, labeled with a proud *K*. "In MiddleMoor, we use *traditional* names, pay homage to the star-signs and magic therein." Though he could not speak as fancily as any of the opponents, Bart never missed an opportunity to play the expert in his own den. After all, not only was Bart at his favorite table in his home city, but he'd also been born on the thirteenth day of the thirteenth and final month of the year, under the sign of King Kroeter the Toad. Despite its association with a celestial god, the number was still regarded as unlucky, unless one wielded a deck of cards.

The gent must have been just foreign enough to use the more broadly spoken *King*, but not so far away that he didn't know better. He tried to laugh off the minor afront with an affable, "Of course! Do forgive me."

In reality, the gent may have been more religious than Bart, but it kept players on their toes to think Bart a devout astrologist — and it seemed to make them less likely to question windfall winnings.

He'd had the hand of the night, a payday pot, far more than he'd ever managed in an honest day's manual labor at the lumbermill. Promising starts all around had suckered six players to meet the opening ante, then encouraged them to bid considerably.

"Well!" announced the lady, keeping her anger in check with a forced laugh. "That was quite a coup for you, wasn't it?"

Another man, also a regular, chimed in, "I told you. Bucksaw's damn good." This fellow had folded early and lost less, having seen past power hands from the player called Bucksaw Bart.

"Well, if he's so *damn good*," said the lady, maintaining fewer niceties, "perhaps he'd play a few hands more. Give me a chance to re-inherit my money."

Her type often used words like *re-inherit*: people who thought their upbringing and education made them superior to a port-city gambler.

He pretended to consider. "Not anymore tonight. Better go out now on a lucky break." He stood, placed his cap on a nearly hairless head, and excused himself.

Bart felt the tug on his shoulders and soul as he exited the threshold around the table — a dome that restricted all magic and leveled the playing field to skill, bluffs, luck, and the odd sleight-of-hand. In a city like MiddleMoor, a prominent sea and airship port, so many were born or trained with magical talent that mundane prestidigitation served little purpose — not that Bart would ever engage in *that* kind of cheating. His methods were far more elegant.

He closed the door to the high-roller room behind him, then strode across the casino's main floor, where folks lost far less of their hard-earned wages in the name of entertainment. Bart kept his step quick, his eyes forward while passing under the many mirrors the proprietors had arranged for surveillance.

At the concierge's counter, he exchanged most chips for coins and collected his overcoat without needing to show a claim ticket. Several jackets were nicer than his; many were accompanied by bespoke rapiers or dueling canes. Holstered on the interior of Bart's coat was a simple, single-shot pistol — not quite state-of-the-science, but more effective for someone who'd never been trained with hard-to-pronounce blades.

Bart made no small talk with the lift operator but tipped the little fellow a large chip when he'd reached his high-level apartment. Bart's rented corner of the world, in one of the many interconnected buildings that made up MiddleMoor, was high enough above the sea to spot airships coming in for miles and had a glorious view of the constellations on a clear night. It had gotten much easier to afford in recent months.

The locks' mechanisms clicked in rhythm, something of a lullaby to Bart, as he let himself into the main room. Several large frames had been draped with black shrouds, and even these were only dimly lit by a small everflame on the center table. Bart touched the largest of the frames as he entered, as if confirming it hadn't fallen. The one uncovered portrait hung over the mantlepiece: a life-size rendition of a younger, prettier version of Bart, marred only by a faint scar on the clean-shaven jaw, which could have been a miss-flick of the painter's fingers or a crease in the canvas.

He trotted up the stairs, coins jangling against his hip, then bypassed his bedroom and ducked through a slanted doorway, evidence of patchworked, interlocking apartments. This back room, a storage space, also sported shrouded frames, some of which were taller than Bart. He walked directly to a regal chest, whose style matched none of the decor in this home — or much of MiddleMoor, seeing as it was bright, unsullied quartz and boasted no visible gears or even hinges. Bart pressed his palm on the rune lock, whose magic extracted a drop of blood and allowed the chest to open. Inside lay Bart's riches, carefully compounded over the recent windfall months.

While Bart emptied the newest purse, another man's voice entered the space, muffled by fabric. "Did it go well tonight?" asked the unseen gentlemen, his tone and articulation refined, despite the black drop cloth concealing him.

Reluctant to disrupt his good mood, Bart gave no reply.

"I can hear you there," said the voice, properly pronouncing the *H*s and not growling through the *R*s like Bart did. "Won't you speak to me, Bartholomew?"

Bart tensed one hand into so tight a fist he heard his first knuckle pop, but he held himself from punching through the covered mirror behind him, which was what the other man wanted, and why he used the name *Bartholomew*. No one else addressed Bucksaw Bart with this proper-sounding name, and to do so now was more mockery than grace. Even so, Bart wouldn't give the other man the satisfaction of seeing him rattled, or even imagining such a sight. Besides, if he *really* wanted to shatter the mirror, Bart could throw it over the edge of the high walkway with a flick of his finger…

By force of will, Bart relaxed into his poker face. By the time he'd turned and pulled away the shroud, he even wore a serene smile, but no such expression reflected back at him. "Evening, Leland," he said to the other, imprisoned in the mirror.

Leland neither stood nor sat, but he was clearly visible and upright behind the glass. Everything around and behind him was deeper and darker than the black cloths, more devoid of substance than a starless night. His blond hair was partially fastened back with a ribbon but was otherwise allowed to flow past his shoulders or drift in the uncertain gravity of the space. His hands were gently clasped before him, and his feet seemed to float over nothing; the bright blue coat he wore had been painstakingly embroidered with finery and, along with the pale scarf, would look more at home on the deck of a luxury airship than in a magical pool of blackness.

To some untrained eyes, the contrast of their demeanor and clothing would be enough to place the two men in entirely separate worlds, bounded by more than an extra-dimensional cell or glass partition. However, if one peered closely, beyond any signs of station, they might notice the uncannily similar eyes, ice-blue and almond shaped, situated above strong cheekbones, and lips that might have turned out identical if they had had similar care and conditioning.

One physical difference neither could change was the scar on the prettier man's jaw, set over a slight distortion where the bone had broken years earlier.

"So the game was successful?" asked Leland. "Was my prediction correct?"

Bart considered lying or at least downplaying the hand. "It went well. I let the lady raise the bid all on her own, thinking she had a winner."

"But thirteen was again your lucky number." A laugh escaped Leland, a small joy in being right, or possibly in having helped Bart, as if the gesture were out of goodwill alone. "I knew it! I saw that the two Ks would lead that hand, didn't I?"

Bart nodded, giving Leland his due. "That you did."

"Now, just think how much more help I could be on the outside. Working *with* you." Leland's icy eyes opened wider, showing more hope than helplessness.

"And risk you locking *me* up and running away," muttered Bart.

"I wouldn't — not this time. Please, Brother, you can trust me."

Bart barked a laugh, exaggerating his emotional reaction

to what was still a preposterous notion. "Trust you? Sorry, Leland, I've learned."

"I've apologized, Bartholomew, and I'm not the same person," protested Leland, but Bart was already picking the cloth off the floor.

With a practiced flourish, Bucksaw Bart had covered the mirror again, only minorly muffling the pleas from within. Placing his own face close to the cloth, Bart whispered, "When I've said we're even. When I live as noble as you got to."

Bart turned and, after ensuring the chest was rune-locked, exited his side-room, leaving his brother in a dark mirror.

Leland was still calling out, so Bart pointed to a dresser in his bedroom and redirected it to fully cover the short and slanted doorway. His right arm ached from the sudden force of moving so large an object, but that was a small price to pay for a quiet night's sleep.

* * *

NO SUN MADE its way into Bart's bedroom, but he woke to the bell ringing below. More alert than groggy, Bart spun the gear by his nightstand, moving the periscope's viewer close enough to his eye and lining up the narrow tube's reflectors.

Three people stood at the entrance, most notably the lady from the previous night, still wearing a fancy hat with a forest-green veil. The others consisted of a uniformed member of the local constabulary and someone wearing magenta but covered by a smudge on the exterior lens.

Bart held his breath to listen and was greeted with silence, meaning Leland was asleep, or whatever equivalent applied to persons trapped in mirrors.

In less than a minute, he was dressed enough to receive

company, even if not to formally entertain. He had no cap for his close-cropped receding hair and had not fully laced his cream-colored shirt, but ladies offended by chest hair ought not call on folks so close to sunrise.

Bart carefully unlocked each ratcheting mechanism holding his door shut, then opened it with a neutral, "Good morning. To what do I owe the pleasure?"

The lady's lips pinched down, then pressed their way into something insincerely genial. "Good morning, Mister Bucksaw Bart. I came to see you again regarding our game last night. First, I would like to apologize for my boorish behavior as a sore loser, and secondly," she cleared her throat, "I wish to invite you to yet another game."

Throughout her salutation, Bart sized up her companions. He did not know whether this lady intended the constable for intimidation or reassurance, but Bart did not find himself disturbed by either prospect. As a local, he would be more familiar with MiddleMoor custom than she, but local knowledge rarely managed a fight against foreign wealth unless you fought dirty. This constable — whom Bart recognized as the long-established Constable Baker — didn't appear particularly impassioned about the lady's cause; rather, he seemed to have thoughts of returning to sleep as soon as possible. He gave a nod to the constable, as a subtle sign of their shared alliance to MiddleMoor.

The magenta companion was a woman of impossible-to-determine age, due to the gold and red designs painted across her cheeks, distracting from wrinkles. Her forehead and every strand of hair was contained in a hood, like a priestess'. She stood shorter than the others, sharp of nose, and thin of lip. The magenta gown was wrapped around her in loops and drapes, a design familiar to her but a maze to anyone else.

"Would you care to come in?" asked Bart, stepping aside

from the entryway. "Forgive my poor hospitality — I haven't got tea on yet, but I can heat some for you."

"No need," said the lady, taking her entrance with smooth, gliding strides, and letting Bart know they wouldn't stay long.

The priestess followed, but Constable Baker remained on the step with the door open, a witness in case of any funny business or attempted attack.

Bart didn't flinch or show nervousness. After all, several people had seen him win fairly the night before, and an officer of the peace would know better than to let a high-profile player come to harm on his watch — unless he'd been promised a larger sum than what the lady had already lost.

She regarded the covered frames festooning the room, and her eyes eventually settled on the one uncovered portrait above the mantle. She then eyed Bart suspiciously, possibly picking up the resemblance or maybe just confused by the presence of such a well-made portrait in this man's front room.

"What a lovely painting," remarked the woman in magenta, her accent neither high-class nor from the Middle-Moor slums. "Who is it?"

"Someone I once knew," reported Bart, stiffly, "but who left here when we were boys."

Though the lady with the green veil creased her brow, sensing Bart had hardly given the full story, her companion seemed charmed by the notion and concluded, "And sent you a noble portrait. You must prize it so."

"I don't believe we were ever formally introduced," the lady cut in. "I am April Handschel, and this is my friend, Tiacel, also visiting MiddleMoor from abroad."

April did not extend her hand. She remained as upright and corseted as ever, but Tiacel reached a slender arm from under layers of looping fabric. "So pleased to meet you, Dear Sir," she said, stretching out her *Ss* like snakes.

Though rarely drawn in by flirtation or flattery, Bart found this priestess quite alluring. He could see little of her shape or figure and was attracted instead to her eyes. They were slightly different colors, not enough for everyone to notice with certainty, but Bart considered himself more observant than most. While each was some shade of purple, one had a sheen of gold around the pupil, like the glow of a wedding band she'd tossed aside.

Bart accepted the hand, which slid surprisingly smoothly into his own callused fingers. Even the *Lady* April had shown evidence of former blisters and rough layers, most likely from airship riggings, clearly visible throughout their card game. Tiacel's unsullied fingers were rare in MiddleMoor, especially rare for a logger-turned-gambler to touch, and a petty part of him wondered if Leland's hands had remained equally soft.

Pretending he was used to the gesture, the gambler lifted Tiacel's knuckles to his lips and planted a soft kiss.

"Well?" asked April, after Tiacel had withdrawn her hand.

In a glance, Bart had developed more than a hunch about what had just happened.

"He is indeed magic," confirmed Tiacel, "but not in the way you suspected."

"You brought a reader to the game!" accused Bart, dropping enough decorum that any hope of high-society diction slipped into the salty surf among pirates.

The constable seemed to wake up a little and brought a hand to the sword at his belt. He eased his stance again when April laughed.

"Hardly," said the lady, drawing her veil aside and finally pinning it on her hat. "She will not be playing today, but she is a senser, and I wanted to make sure it was a fair game.

Tiacel can tell with a touch what kind of magic you have, unless you're very, very good at concealing, and I don't think even you can bluff like that."

Bart stiffened, showing indignation, offense at being scrutinized without warning. He glared at the constable, who had been unaware and now appeared apologetic.

"Well," resumed April, "now that we've come this far, we might as well have all of it."

Tiacel chuckled to herself. "We haven't time for all of it. He was born near the cusp, either *Kroeter* or *Adler*," she mused, using the old names for the Toad or Eagle, the last and first months of the common calendar. "I'd bet he's more a *thirteen* than a *one*."

Despite her friend's interest in Bart's birth, April pressed her purpose instead. "And what does he wield, Tiacel?"

"Transposition magic."

April raised an eyebrow. "Meaning?"

Bart intercepted. "Meaning I can send you out and over the rail if I choose to."

She grinned, revealing perfectly white teeth. "Do you make a habit of throwing things when you lose?"

"Not at all. But if I'm offended, threatened, or accused of cheating—"

"I see, and could you use this to, say, move a card into your hand?"

"Not at a magic-controlled table, and not with that kind of precision," said Bart, but she didn't seem convinced. "I was employed to move logs at the lumbermill, set 'em on ships or through full-size portals — not to thread needles."

April looked to Tiacel, who offered no dispute.

Bart's next move was calculated to impress, but he wanted to appear motivated by frustration, so he practically growled, "I'll show you." He marched across the room, and tore one of the black curtains from the wall.

Both women reacted backward in fright, for, trapped in a wide, rectangular mirror, was a hulking horned beast.

The constable had drawn his sword and rushed in at the sounds of distress but paused when he saw the contained creature. This mirror, situated in a crude, wooden frame, was a little too tight for its prisoner and was made of different magics, which allowed no sound to escape.

"I transpositioned a minotaur," said Bart, "placed it in this mirror. That drew seed-money for this apartment. You remember, don't you, Constable Baker?"

Baker, roused by his name, had worked in MiddleMoor long enough to recall (or pretend to recall) Bucksaw Bart's deeds, and nodded his corroboration. Either way, the gesture satisfied both other guests.

"Isn't that dangerous?" inquired Tiacel.

"More for an intruder than me," said Bart. "If something happens here, and I break the glass, I'd know how to defend myself. Would you?" Without waiting for an answer, Bart covered the beast once more.

No one implied a threat after that.

* * *

"Wake up, Leland," said Bart, drawing away the curtain of the more ornate, free-standing mirror in the storage. "I need a read on tonight's game."

"Another?" Leland appeared drained, despondent. While he needed neither food nor drink for his non-corporeal body, he did grow weary with time.

"Yes." Bart turned away and unlocked the chest with a drop of his blood. "Same lady from last night. Wants a rematch. I need to know which hand I can win."

Leland sighed. "It's getting harder to see, Brother. If only I could leave this mirror—"

"You'll leave when I tell you," snapped Bart. Then he calmly resumed collecting the necessary coins for the night.

"Haven't I more than repaid my debt?" asked Leland.

Bart growled, "After the life you stole from me? Hardly."

Leland clamped his jaw closed.

The clinking of several gold pieces scattered their arhythmic tones through the otherwise silent space.

"What if this time buys your apartment?" asked the man in the mirror. "No more renting, no more scrounging, enough for the difference. Would that pay my debt?"

Bart paused. He licked his lips then looked to Leland. "Could you do that?"

"It would be difficult — draining. But I see the hands. Your opponent is wealthy, stubborn, and arrogant."

"Like you?" laughed Bart.

Undeterred, Leland continued. "If you play it right, you could get her to wager far more than what you bring. I see…" He faltered and brought a hand to his forehead.

"Leland?" wondered Bart, rushing to the mirror, putting both hands on the metal frame, with the closest thing to compassion he'd shown since Leland's return.

"Sorry. I just… Too many possibilities. It's hard to sort." He closed his eyes. "But what it all hinges on, whether you walk out with a modest sum or a bankroll, is whether you lose on your first promising deal."

"Lose?"

"Hear me out: Early in the game, maybe third or fourth hand, you will be dealt a pair of *Adlers*." Eagle cards, the first card named for the first month — Leland's month. Whereas others might call them *As* or *Aces*, Leland used the proper, old-world name, like they'd done as boys, before he left. "But that hand won't end strong enough for you. If you bet high, go in overconfident, it will set them up to fall thereafter. And I can tell you every winning hand from then on."

Bart pointed one shaking finger at Leland. "If this is a trick, I set you in a vault where no one ever finds you."

"It's not a trick," said Leland. "It will make the difference. And if it does, will you let me leave?"

* * *

BUCKSAW BART WORKED a precarious balancing act as he unlocked his front door, but was laughing joyfully when he shoved it open. He'd barely lugged the bags of gold in both arms and a backpack and now let them fall on the main floor. He continued to chortle while he hung up his jacket then schlepped his payday to the storeroom bag by bag.

"I see the scheme was successful," observed an uncovered Leland.

"You could say that."

"How much?"

Bart finished emptying the first bag into the chest and could see that the coins would soon overflow. "More than enough for this place. Maybe even something better."

"So will you live up to your word?" asked Leland, a note of optimism in his articulate voice. "Will you release me?"

"Hmm." Bart put a finger to his lips, which smelled of metal, traces of copper and silver. "I think not, little brother. I'll just put you away for a while. Long enough that you'll tell me *anything* for a bit of company."

"But Bartholomew!" Leland was still sputtering protests when Bart headed down the stairs again to collect the next bag.

When Bart returned, Leland resumed his attempt at persuasion, with more desperation than ever before. "I made you win! I helped you cheat people. I've more than covered my debt."

"You think so? Because what you stole from me, I

measure in years, Leland. You may have locked me in a cupboard for a night, but you stole my entire future."

"You forget how *you* used to treat *me*?" asked an appalled Leland. "That was my one chance to get away from—" The younger brother gasped, stopping himself.

Bart scowled. "Well, now you're in that mirror. You're going to stay until you've missed *your* life, brother, until you're the one people scorn and pity. *Then* you'll be free."

"But I returned to MiddleMoor to make amends! I came to beg your forgiveness."

"And maybe you should have foreseen my wrath, mighty soothsayer, for I will never, *ever* forgive you."

Leland mustered all the indignation he could from behind glass and demanded, "How can you stand to look at yourself?"

Bart finally dropped the façade; any guise of humor or anger was replaced with somber resolve. "That's rather the point, Leland," he said to another's face in the mirror, "I don't."

A sound from below startled both, and they looked to the opening, to the bedroom, and the stairway at the far wall. Quietly, Leland observed, "You left the door unlocked."

Bart raced out of the small room, ready to fend off a looter. But the woman standing in his front room seemed to take no interest in the coins.

"Tiacel," said Bart, but could think of nothing else just then.

The small, sharp-faced Tiacel gave a small wave. "Hello, Bart. Congratulations on your game."

Bart descended the last few steps warily. "Why are you here?"

"Curiosity. And confirmation." She smiled to herself, then indicated the portrait. "You know, April actually thought you had that painted with *yourself* as a noble. But this is someone else, isn't it?"

The gambler side-stepped between her and the mantle, just below the painting. "You oughtta leave."

"Such a miraculous evening, odds you see once in a hundred lifetimes, but you knew it would happen, Bart." She did not take her eyes off the painting. "See, I've traveled the world, but you've never left the city of MiddleMoor. You might not realize that for a senser like me, a prominent soothsayer is recognizable. And it's noticeable when he goes missing."

Bart's eyes darted to his jacket where the pistol visibly hung, next to which resided a covered minotaur he could free in an instant.

"I'm not going to turn you in to April, Bart," said Tiacel, taking a slow, smooth stride forward. "I just want to know. Is Leland the Soothsayer your brother?"

"Was," muttered Bart, his accent thickening as his heart raced. "Got himself adopted. Locked me away and left me behind. Saw opportunity and took it."

"Yes, but he went missing, just a few months ago. Where is Leland now?"

From up the stairs and around the corner, Leland took another opportunity, shouting, "Help!"

Tiacel started to the stairs, but Bart acted faster. Reaching up, he ripped a wide slash of the painting, revealing an unused mirror. Then, with a quick point of his finger, he placed Tiacel securely above his mantle. She appeared to be yelling, pounding on the glass from within, but the mirror would not relent for her and could only be broken from the outside.

Bart knew he didn't have much time. Once again, he sprinted up the stairs. Seizing the mirror by its frame, Bart hauled his brother with the strength he'd honed working a bucksaw through sturdy trunks.

This time, Bart would hurl the mirror off the balcony — better to cut his losses now. Leland's shouts of protest went ignored, but then they stopped. Leland, suspended sideways, gasped and said, "Brother! She's coming."

The remark slowed Bart at the top of the stairs. "What?"

"The lady in the green veil will come through your front door next; she will try to kill you."

Bart uprighted Leland and saw the man's fear through the glass. He wanted to doubt, wanted to call *bullocks*, but instead, he hesitated.

And when the door was forced open by two constables, Bart pointed to each one and repositioned them, high enough they'd fall hard, but each reposition weakened and wearied him. The lady brushed aside her green veil and aimed a revolving pistol at Bart, which he batted away with a last desperate flick of force.

No other assailants poured in, and Bart sagged against the banister.

Then, Leland warned, "She'll take *your* pistol!"

April, noticing the jacket on the wall, seized the exposed weapon, ready to put down the gambler who'd cheated her.

"Duck!" said Leland, and Bart dropped to his knees at the right moment.

The one slug coursed over his head and shattered the glass behind him. Bart shielded himself from spraying shards.

Suddenly, a heeled boot kicked him from behind, sending him tumbling down his own stairway, cracking his forehead on one step and crunching his shoulder on the lower landing.

Then, sounding closer than it had in weeks, Leland's voice said, "It's a single-shot, Milady, nothing else to fire."

The heels clicked down the steps toward the crumpled and gasping gambler. "Your winnings are upstairs, in a chest I can open with a drop of my blood."

Possibly in shock, April did not respond. The constables who'd dropped from ceiling height were gradually finding their feet again.

Bart lay on the floor, aware of the damp sensation on his forehead and pooling around his cheek. A beautiful face entered his field of vision, as the blond man crouched before him, sporting a reminder of where Bart had broken his jaw when they were children — mere street urchins in Middle-Moor, with budding talents for both magic and trouble.

"I saw *all* of this, Bartholomew. Everything that would happen if you grew too greedy and couldn't keep your promise."

Bart snarled something wordless.

Leland scoffed. "You're just upset I called your bluff." The last thing Bart heard before he fell unconscious was, "You should have forgiven me when you had the chance."

* * *

MIKE JACK STOUMBOS is an author and educator, living with his wife, parrot, and puppy in Virginia. He is best known for his space opera novel series This Fine Crew *and as a 1st-place Writers of the Future winner (2022). His work appears in anthologies from Zombies Need Brains, WordFire Press, and Camden Park Press, as well as the previous* Hidden Villains *installments from Inkd Publishing.*

Mike Jack is the lead editor of WonderBird Press and the Unhelpful Encyclopedia Anthology series, which include Murderbirds *and* Murderbugs, *and will soon add* Murderfish. *In addition, he teaches fiction writing and mindset workshops for teens and adults and enjoys collaboration and cooperation ventures with other independent publishers and author support groups whenever the schedule allows.*

You can find him at MikeJackStoumbos.com as well as Virginia and DC area conventions. You might even spot him in the wild with a microphone in hand on a karaoke stage.

DAISY CHAINS

SARAH J. SOVER

The pony's sticky blood warmed Eagan's throat as bones splintered between his mighty teeth. The pitiful creature had quit screaming minutes before, but a horse, trapped in the flames engulfing the barn around them, whinnied and bucked somewhere nearby. Eagan considered putting the poor beast out of its misery, but then, when had life ever shown him mercy? The smoke went to his head as it poisoned the animals around him, and he was nearly giddy.

"Them's the breaks, bud," he grunted through chunks of pony flesh. The horse fell silent. "At least I spared you the abuse of men. You're welcome."

As if on cue, shouting from the main house drifted down the hill. It would take the humans hours to get the blaze under control, but the warning bells in the distance cut Eagan's meal short. The infamous dragon hunter Zed had been tailing him for months, and he didn't care to add another scar to his collection. Licking the blood from his lips and snout, Eagan stretched his wings and pushed himself from the ground with a mighty heave. He burst through the hole he'd made in the roof of the barn just in time to see a flurry of mortals organizing a bucket brigade. One brave soul was running toward the barn door.

It's amazing what they'll risk to protect their investments, thought Eagan. *And they say dragons hoard wealth.*

He looked to the sky to gauge his angles perfectly so that he would be silhouetted against the moon, a trick he'd developed to chill the blood of those who would hunt him. The advantage gained might mean the difference between continued existence and a crossbow to the gullet. His wings beat air downward, battering and fanning the flames below as the people grew smaller and smaller. They would be too concerned with the inferno to come after him in the moment, but by morning, Zed will have learned of his presence. It was the same story in town after town. He paid for his meals with a hasty exit.

Eagan headed west, toward the mountains, flying just below the cloud line. He'd crossed over the first of the rolling foothills when an arrow struck him in the hindquarters. *Not again!* Eagan roared in pain, his fire illuminating the ground below where a band of tiny men had formed a line stretching for miles. Another arrow whizzed by his snout.

"Hunters already? For heaven's sake, it was just a little pony," he said to the empty air, swooping low to barbecue a few of his assailants before flying beyond reach of their weapons. Zed wouldn't be among them, not yet. He'd left his nemesis back in Lutgar, three days south, and even on horseback, it would be dawn before the famed hunter would make it this far.

Eagan wished he could take delight in the screams of his attackers as he flambéed them one by one, but the throbbing in his backside urged him to find refuge. Besides, he had no way of knowing how many more hunters hid higher in the hills, and he hadn't lived for two hundred and twenty-three years by investigating such matters.

By the time he found a cave large enough to hide a full-sized Archanian dragon, the pain was nearly blinding. He spent a restless night sheltered by rock and dirt, thankful he'd at least had time to feed. By morning, the pain had morphed into a dull throbbing — the kind that doesn't let you forget it's there — and his legs and wings were stiff.

He stepped into the warm sunlight and surveyed the valley below for signs that he'd been tracked. If he didn't find a place to clean his wound, infection was sure to set in, but first, he needed to remove the arrow. Stretching his neck backward, he was just able to grasp the feather-tipped end in his front teeth.

All right, here goes, he thought. He gave a tug.

The arrow didn't budge. Eagan teetered, lightheaded, on the edge of the cliff. Perhaps it would be wiser to deal with his wound at a lower elevation. He spotted a field below bursting with wildflowers and spread his wings to glide down in search of a source of water. He nearly landed on her.

A girl, no older than seven or eight, was sitting in the grass. She dropped the daisy chain she'd woven and gaped openly at him. Under normal circumstances, Eagan would be thrilled at the chance to pick up an easy breakfast, but the pony sat heavy in his stomach, giving him wicked indigestion. All the same, he couldn't let the girl scurry off for help. Lingering to wait for hunger was out of the question — he hadn't put nearly enough distance between himself and the horde of dragon hunters just over the ridge, not to mention Zed, who would surely be hot on his tracks by now. This girl was a complication Eagan didn't need.

"What are you looking at?" he snapped as he recovered from his less-than graceful landing. The grass and dust his wings had kicked up settled around him, the screams of startled birds retreating into the distance.

The girl's eyes were huge as she took him in, as blue as

the sky above. And her flaxen curls the color of the wheat humans so painstakingly raised framed her sweet face. Her bottom lip trembled for a moment, but then she scrambled to her feet to face him. Well, that he could respect.

"P-p-pardon?" she stammered.

"I said, What. Are. You. Looking. At?" Eagan did his best to ignore the pain in his haunches as he decided what to do about the child. He could kill her and save her for later, he supposed. He needed to find new hunting grounds, and it would be wise to keep a snack on-hand for the journey before him.

The child stood stock still for such a long moment, Eagan wondered if her brain ceased all activity. Finally, her face blossomed into a huge grin. Yep, she'd gone plumb stupid.

Then, a deluge of words spilled from the child's mouth.

"You're beautiful! I've never seen a dragon before. Not a real one, anyhow. That's what you are, isn't it? Pa says dragons are dangerous, and there's a bounty for one that's been spotted near town. There are hunters everywhere talking about how they're going to take down an Archanian. Is that you? Are you an Archanian? What is that anyhow? You're sure big enough to be what they say. But you don't look dangerous to me. You look hurt."

A bounty explained the ambush. So, the humans were organizing, were they? That meant the danger was more than an overzealous hunter and a pack of farmers waiting in the foothills with arrows and pitchforks. These were merce-naries. If the arrow in his ass weren't enough to convince him that it was time to move on, a pack of greedy mercs certainly was. As he was considering his next move, the girl bounded around him, wrapped her tiny hands around the arrow protruding from his hide, and gave a mighty heave. The offending arrow came loose, and blinding pain washed over Eagan. Head turned to the sky, he roared, fire shooting into the air.

The girl didn't seem to notice. She kept on talking. "That's better now, isn't it? Let me gather some nettles, and I'll make a salve so it doesn't get infected. How'd you get that arrow stuck there anyhow? I suppose somebody shot you. I shouldn't like it if someone shot me in the caboose with an arrow—"

Smoke wafting around his head, Eagan turned on the child. "Enough!"

She paused, curls dancing in the air, big blue eyes staring into his own. Eagan reared up and opened his mouth to devour the helpless child, but as he did, he processed her words. If the girl could ward off infection, she might be worth keeping around for a bit. A wound like this had been known to end dragons stronger than he. As if reading his mind, the girl said, "Infection is the number one killer of man. That's what Pa says. By the posters in the village, you'd think it was dragons."

"Don't you ever stop talking?" asked Eagon. He settled back into the grass. The child looked pensive for a moment, and he was terrified she was gearing up for another bout of acute logorrhea.

"Pa says I babble when I'm excited. I was just so excited to meet a real life dragon. Imagine it! Little me talking to the likes of you!"

Eagon's chest puffed up just a little. He was so accustomed to people screaming and running for their pitchforks, it was nice to have someone admire him for once.

"And just where is this pa of yours?"

The girl's face fell. "He died. And I never had a Ma, at least not one I remember."

Something moved inside of Eagan. Was it the pony? No. He distinctly remembered dismembering his prey before swallowing this time. He'd learned his lesson last spring with an inconsiderate goat. But if that wasn't it, what was this feeling? Pity? For a human? All his life, humans had hunted him. That's why he never had a cave of his own once his own mother was slaughtered. He kept on the move from town to town along the mountain range's edge, ever moving to keep from being taken by an arrow or blade in the night. Humans made his existence a constant state of misery. He should just kill this one and be done with it.

What was she doing now? The child was wandering off, collecting nettles. She was trying to help him. Maybe he could let her live for just a while longer. Besides, if he killed a child, that would only incense the villagers.

"Pa taught me to always be prepared. 'Allara,' Pa said, 'life is tough, so you've got to be tougher. Keep everything you might need close at hand, and never turn your back on a stranger.' But you're not a stranger. You're a dragon. Hey, I still don't know your name." The girl was talking long before she was within hearing range. As she approached, she took a sudden turn and disappeared behind a large boulder. Eagan strained to look after her, only for her to pop back around the rock, all smiles and bounding curls. In one hand, she clutched a cloth full of nettles and in the other, a waterskin. This kid took being prepared to new heights.

"I'm Eagan, Scourge of Mankind, Flayer of Ponies and Wreaker of Terror."

He'd expected the girl to cower. Instead, she crinkled her nose as she used some kind of stone to crush the nettles against the boulder. "What's with all the titles? We've got lords and kings and all, but what does a dragon need them for?"

"I earned my titles, unlike your mealy kings and lords. King or knight, peasant or farmer, all your bones break the same."

"And don't yours?"

"Well, I suppose. But dragon bones are made of tougher stuff."

Allara looked doubtful. "But they still break, all the same, so why waste your energy on listing all those titles? If a king and a farmer crunch the same, then who gets to say which is which? You gave yourself titles, so I will too. I'm Lady Allara of the Meadow, and you are my knight, Sir Eagan!"

Eagan's mouth fell open. Not only was the girl insufferable, she was incorrigible. He should save himself a headache and just eat her on the spot.

Sir Eagan, what a laugh. Still, he'd often wondered what his life would be like had he been born a different kind of creature — one that wasn't hunted from the time he hatched. Imagine, him a knight. As Eagan looked down at young Allara, warmth spread through his veins. The only time he'd felt that way was just after hatching when ma would baste him in flame before bed. What was wrong with him? How had this little snack brought back such long-forgotten memories?

"If you please, Sir Eagan," said Allara, standing straight with outstretched hands, "I am ready to apply the poultice." As she spread the mixture on his scales, it soaked into the place where the arrow had penetrated, sending first a stinging then a cooling sensation through his tender skin. Eagan groaned, and Allara smiled. "There, now, doesn't that feel better?"

It did, but he wasn't about to let the child know it. Instead, he turned and stretched his wings in preparation for departure.

"Sir Eagan! Where are you going?"

He turned back, and the child's eyes were imploring.

"I must be on my way. The hunters who skewered me will be searching, and then there's Zed."

"The famed dragon hunter?"

Eagan saw a spark in Allara's eyes, and it was no wonder. Zed was a legend to the humans. He'd downed more dragons than any hunter alive. Eagan had always been a loner, ever since his mother was killed, but he used to cross paths occasionally with a young dragon named Frisk. That was before Zed.

"The same," he replied, schooling the anger from his face. "He's been on my tail for months."

"How do you know? Did you see him? I heard rumors back in Dyersville, but I've never laid eyes on him, though the bounty was a lot last I heard. Is that why Zed is after you?"

Eagan sighed as he considered which, if any, question to address first. "I narrowly avoided a trap he set back in Lutgar. It was far too sophisticated for merchants and farmers, and I heard Zed's name called out as I feasted on the villagers."

At that, Allara's face paled. Eagan turned again to leave, expecting that she'd be glad to see him off, but she called out.

"Wait! Take me with you!"

What was it with this child? Eagan's confusion must have shown in his countenance, because Allara dropped her gaze as she took a step forward. "You can't leave me. There's nothing for me here. My parents are long dead, and I've no friends. I spend my days in the fields making daisy chains, fending for myself. I can help you."

Fighting back laughter, Eagan replied, "How can you, a little snack of a human child, help me, an Archanian dragon who predates your tiny village?"

She raised her eyes to meet his. "You may be ancient. You may be strong. But you are wounded, and that makes you vulnerable. I can care for your injury and provide you with food until you are healed."

Hours later, Eagan flew through the air with Allara on his back, wondering how he got in this position. Tiny arms clung to the back of his neck, and the girl squealed and giggled when they dipped and dropped through the clouds. He told himself he was taking her along for when he got peckish. He expected she would be shit at hunting, but she did have a point about him being vulnerable, and she would make a fine meal tomorrow.

The cave he found that evening was low in the mountains but far away from any human settlements. It would do no good to be spotted by villagers who would sound the alarm and bring Zed and the mercenaries. As soon as Eagan's claws touched earth, Allara bolted behind a nearby tree to relieve herself. After a quarter of an hour, he began to suspect the girl had run away.

Oh well, he thought. *It saves me the trouble of offing her myself.*

He was drinking from a little creek when Allara returned. She was skipping through the trees holding a fistful of daisies in one hand. Something else was tucked beneath her arm. The smell hit Eagan first. Blood.

"I got you a present," chimed the child as Eagan rose from the stream, all senses on high alert. She held out the carcass of a rabbit. Its head lolled to the side, neck broken, and it was plump. "I found it in a field just over yonder."

Eagan cocked his head to the side. "I thought you ran away so I wouldn't eat you."

Allara grinned wide and bright. "No, I brought you a snack so you wouldn't eat me."

"Why would you do such a thing?"

"Well," said the girl, taking a deep breath as blood dripped from the carcass to the ground at her feet, "I thought about running away, but where would I go? You might kill me, of course, because you are a dragon and that's what they do, but if I go into the woods alone, something else certainly will. I figured that if I find you something to eat, you wouldn't want to eat bony little me."

Eagan felt his mouth drop open once again. The kid was right. He'd intentionally chosen a remote location, far away from human civilization and the threat of dragon hunters. She didn't stand a chance out there alone.

"What keeps me from eating you tomorrow?"

"Nothing as far as I can see except your honor, Sir Eagan."

With an exasperated, smokey sigh, Eagan snatched the rabbit out of Allara's hands and swallowed it in one gulp.

"Fine. But you sleep out here, little snack."

With that, he retreated into the cave and wedged a boulder over the opening. He would decide what to do about Allara in the morning if the forest didn't take care of her first.

Eagan slept like the dead, and when he awoke, the pain of the arrow was a distant memory. He pushed the boulder out of the way. Allara was still asleep, her back to the rock and a pile of leaves covering most of her body. If he didn't know she was there, he would have missed her entirely. For such an annoying little girl, she really was quite clever. He stood over her for a long moment, watching her eyes flutter in her sleep. How sweet her blood would taste.

As he was about to close in on her, those baby blues popped open. "Good morning, Sir Eagan," she said, a smile blossoming on her little face.

Damn, thought Eagan. He didn't know why, but the thought of harming her while those eyes were on him killed his appetite. He sighed and walked away.

They passed the day in relative quiet, Allara on Eagan's back as they flew along the mountain range. Around midday, she asked to make landfall so that she might find some food and a place to break water. Eagan's own stomach growled, so he agreed. It was finally time to end this charade and feast on the child.

But when they landed, Eagan also had the need to relieve himself. When he was finished, Allara had already caught and killed a goose. It was just enough to take the edge off his hunger.

"I told you I could hunt for you!" said the girl as Eagan crunched the brittle bird bones to a pulp.

"Mmmph," he replied before coughing, the force sending a plume of feathers into the air. They rained down on Allara, who giggled and danced as they fluttered around her.

When Eagan did speak, it came out sulkier than he intended. "You would taste a lot better, I reckon."

"Perhaps, but you need me to re-dress your wound," she replied, giving a last twirl before sitting on the ground to pull supplies from her bag.

That night, Eagan didn't sleep at all. He perched on the edge of a cliff, high above the resting place of his baggage, looking back the way they had come for telltale signs of pursuit — campfire smoke or movement in the distance. He saw none. In the early hours of the morning, he drifted off. He woke when the sun warmed his scales.

Below the sheer cliff he could just make out the movement of the girl as she bustled around a fire she must have lit herself. He gave a stretch, then swooped down and was immediately met with the divine smell of roasting flesh. On a skewer wedged between stacks of rocks was a wild pig.

Eagan went for it.

"Stop right there, mister." Allara's voice, the only sound in the silent forest surrounding them, startled him. He turned on her, warmth in his throat, but she didn't seem to pick up on the threat. "That's breakfast for both of us, and it's not done cooking yet."

Eagan opened his mouth to answer or flame, but nothing

came out, so he closed it again and went down to the creek for a morning bath. When he returned, the skewered pig was waiting for him, minus a small slice off the hindquarters. He ripped the morsel in half and was delighted by an explosion of flavors. It had been decades since he'd tasted seasoned meat.

"What is that flavor? Oleander?" he mumbled with a full mouth.

Allara's eyes got big at his mention of the death flower. "Oh, no! I hope not! The flowers were pretty and they smelled so sweet. I thought you would like it!"

Eagon narrowed his eyes as he looked her over. She wasn't pale or shaking, so she must not have used the poisonous blooms on her own meal, at least not in the amount that flavored his. Pity. She would have made a fine second course. Her surprise caught him off-guard. Most village children were taught to avoid poisonous plants from an early age. Was the girl making an attempt on his life?

"You didn't ingest any, I take it?"

She shook her head and bit her bottom lip. "No. I was so hungry, I tore mine off as soon as it was cooked. I didn't have supper last night like you did. Once my belly was full, I thought it would be nice to spice yours up a bit seeing as you're my knight. I saw you looking over me as I slept, and I wanted to take care of you too. Please forgive me!"

"Your pa never taught you how to identify oleander?"

"My pa worked so hard to care for me alone. He did the best he could, and now he's gone. I can't lose you too."

Allara looked as if she were about to burst into tears. No, she couldn't be trying to kill him. If he died, she'd be alone in the forest, and they'd already talked about how dangerous that would be. Eagon laughed and sucked down the rest of the pig as Allara watched, her tearful gaze morphing into a look of pure horror.

"No harm done, little snack," he said once he finished chewing. "Dragons are immune to all poisonous plants — the ones in these parts, at least. Oleander is a delicacy."

Allara's giggles of relief were enough to make the hardest dragon smile.

After breakfast, she reapplied the poultice to Eagan's wound, and they resumed their journey. Eagan was in less of a hurry now that he'd put some distance between himself and the dragon hunters, and there hadn't been any sign of Zed's clever traps. So, they walked through the forest, side-by-side.

"What do dragons do when they're not razing villages?" asked Allara after a while. Their feet crinkled the leaves of the forest floor, a comforting sound in the silent woods.

"I don't raze villages. I eat."

"Oh, I know, but you must realize how it looks to us. We toil away at the land, build communities, then one of you comes through, and it's all gone in an instant. Our food, our livestock, our families."

"A dragon's got to eat."

"And a village has got to defend. I guess that's just the nature of it." Allara picked a rock from the ground and tossed it into the woods. "Why don't you eat forest animals?"

Eagon stopped walking. He stood as still as death and Allara waited.

"What do you hear, little snack?"

"Nothing."

"That's right. It's the same no matter how far I go. I can take to the skies and drop suddenly into the woods, but by the time I break the tree line, the animals have all fled. Hunting is possible for younger dragons, but when you get to be as old as I, survival depends on finding easier prey."

"Oh." Allara didn't say anything more for some time.

Then, she placed a small hand on Eagan's haunches. "Don't you get lonely?"

The dragon snorted and began walking again, Allara's hand falling to the side. She had to jog to keep up.

"Company is overrated," he puffed, but the smoke belied his words.

What is wrong with me? he thought as he tried to leave the girl behind. *Lonely? I'm an Archanian dragon, the oldest of my kind. I need no one.*

Later in the day, Eagan flew with Allara on his back until he found a suitable cave. This one didn't have a boulder to shove into place, and the girl took up residence in a crevice near the entrance, weaving her daisies together.

"I'm going to stay with you, Sir Eagan," she declared as he settled in for the night. "Not just tonight, but forever. Then you won't be lonely anymore."

"And what about when I need to eat?" he replied. "When I raze a village, as you say. What will you do? Will you help as I devour their ponies and burn their crops? Will you watch as I slay your people?"

"You won't need to. I will hunt for you." The girl beamed up at him so eager and full of life, he couldn't help but smile back. He didn't have the heart to tell her he couldn't live on rabbits, geese, and the occasional wild pig. His stomach was sated for now, but feeding him would take all her hours in the warm months and, when winter came, it would kill her. No. He would have to eat her or send her away. He looked at his little snack, curled up in the corner, her head cushioned by her bag. She shivered.

Carefully, Eagan blew fire at the pile of sticks Allara had gathered. It ignited and warmed the space. Once he was sure she was comfortably asleep, he sunk to the ground, face turned toward the entrance of the cave, and drifted off.

Eagan dreamed he was tied up. He thrashed and smacked

his head on the wall of the cave. The force of the collision caused him to bite his tongue. Blood filled his mouth as he struggled to move.

"Shh, it'll all be over soon." The voice was familiar but it held an edge he didn't recognize. Eagan blinked in the darkness until his eyes adjusted to the faint light filtering in from outside. The air was moist with dew of early morn, but the sun wasn't yet in the sky. He was bound, back legs to front, and there was no give in his restraints. A rope around his neck pinned him to the dirt floor.

"Little snack?" he wheezed, smoke filling the cavern.

"Yes, you are," replied the girl.

On one side was the rock wall and on the other, he could just make out movement in his periphery. A moment later, he felt her clambering onto his back. Then, the cold steel of a blade pressed to the juncture where his wings met his body.

His wings, his salvation in a world that wanted him dead, the only thing keeping him out of the reach of his enemies, were laid bare before this girl, and she was merciless.

Eagan screamed, his fire bathing the cave in orange as Allara hacked through his scales. One wing, larger than the girl by double, fell to the cavern floor. Blood ran down his sides, and he thrashed again, but it was no use. She was carving him alive. The pain was unbearable.

"Oh, Sir Eagan, you weren't so tough, after all," hissed the girl. "Over two centuries no hunter could touch you. They said you were unkillable. But all it took was one little girl."

Eagan's breathing was labored, and his body spasmed against the restraints. His mind reeled, and his vision blurred. None of this made any sense. His mouth was dry, and he croaked out her name. "Allara."

"I prefer to be called Zed, the final letter in the alphabet. I'm the last of my line, my family laid in the ground by your kind. And mine is the last face you shall see before you die."

A wave of nausea made Eagan heave as the child slid down his back and walked around to face him. She stood not ten feet from his face, clothes soaked through with dragon blood. If Eagan had any fire left in him, he could have roasted her on the spot, but his throat and heart were empty. The world around him grew dim as darkness creeped inward, but Zed's unrelenting blue eyes never wavered from his face.

"I thought — you were — my friend," he gasped. He knew it was pathetic, but he didn't care. "But you — just wanted — revenge."

The girl laughed, a cruel sound reverberating off stone walls. She batted her baby blues. "And money, of course. Your bounty is a thing of beauty. A girl's got to eat."

Then, she stepped forward and drove her dagger into the side of his throat.

When the dragon hunters arrived, Zed was long gone. Sir Eagan, Scourge of Mankind, Flayer of Ponies and Wreaker of Terror, was nothing more than a rotting corpse still bound in a shallow cavern, bloody nubs replacing magnificent wings. Leftover cooked dragon flesh marked the place where Zed had feasted, and the ground was marred where she'd dragged his wings, her trophy, into the cover of the forest. Around Eagan's bloodied neck was draped a daisy chain fit for a knight.

* * *

SARAH J. Sover is the author of fantasy crossover novels, short stories, and nonfiction articles. Sarah writes the Urban Fantasy Fractured Fae *series (*Fairy Godmurder, Faed to Black, *and the forthcoming* Pixie Dusted) *for Falstaff Books. She calls it Jessica Jones with sparkle. Her comedic fantasy* Double-Crossing the Bridge, *about a group of drunk trolls pulling a perilous heist, originally released in 2019 and was re-released by Falstaff in 2022* *with a sequel,* Trolled, *slated for 2024/2025. Her short fiction has appeared in anthologies, and she's written articles for* Writer's Digest *magazine,* WritersDigest.com, *and* Dan Koboldt's Putting the Fact in Fantasy. *Sarah has a degree in Biology and a background in animal care, which she uses to thoroughly gross out readers. She spends her time raising two little forces of nature with her husband Alex in John's Creek, Georgia. In addition to writing, Sarah enjoys bingeing all SFF media, blues dancing, painting, and pretending to play guitar. She can frequently be found pillaging Hades or Hyrule while sipping on a good IPA and pinned beneath her rescue pup Gandalf the Grey.*

GLIMMER

TIM LEWIS

1

No good story ever started with someone eating a salad, I thought, as I flipped through slivers of rehydrated egg, faux ham, and simulated avocado paste that swam in a veritable sea of algae strips impersonating a Cobb. My instructions were explicit about what time to arrive, where to sit, and what to order.

The lawyer said this was the way their client would know me and initiate contact. The elaborate intrigue didn't bother me too much; there are a lot of paranoid people in the private investigator business, but my skin crawled when I had to deal with a pettifogger. Not a decent one among the bunch, which includes the rotten bastard my ex hired for the divorce five years ago. That was when I retired from the military and left Earth to find a new life on the orbital station.

I had heard of this lawyer before, or rather their firm. The shysters were damn near celebrities here in Newer Orleans, and just as soulless and money-grubbing as their Big Easy twins. I only considered this job because I was told the client was friends with Sam Schippe, my old partner. Whoever this prospect was, they had to have some money to afford anyone in that law firm, so that was fine by me.

I forked the salad, turning insubstantial pieces over each other just to keep my hand busy, and realized how similar my life was to this agglomeration. I scanned the beveled glass French doors that led into the main restaurant and the other Creole brick archway that served the patio, for any person out of place. Painstaking work had been achieved to create the look and feel of a spring day on the space station to make guests feel they were in the sister city on Earth 250 miles below.

As if to announce her, the high note of a trumpet punctuated the end of a smooth jazz number played by a four-piece band in the corner. The patio doors hissed open, and the slow rat-tat of a snare drum on the next song was muted as the cacophony of the promenade outside enveloped the area. The woman stepped in, her chin in the air as she scanned the restaurant, more to be seen than to see.

It was mid-morning, and the artificial image of a sky created a dull, overcast sun. The hazy light accented the colors of a pinafore red dress, punctuated by the deep crimson lipstick of a brunette with loose curls that fell past her shoulders. She tilted her eyes toward my stare without turning her head, and a slight smile rose from her pouting lips. Her walk was the deliberate slide of one foot in front of the other so her hips would swing as she oozed across the simulated brick path of her catwalk. The band seemed to use her movement to keep time as they stepped into their bridge.

She approached and looked down at me as her gait slowed. She grazed a single polished Bordeaux nail along my forearm and walked on past. I watched her over my shoulder as she slid into a seat with another woman, then both started to giggle.

"Colonel Markson," said a voice, followed by the scrape of a metal chair across the imitation concrete patio. I turned back to see a woman make herself comfortable in the seat across from me. She was middle-aged with blonde hair pulled back in a ponytail, narrowed eyes that were intelligent but suspicious, and an oversized Tulane University hoodie that looked like she was expecting company to join her inside. Her attempt at anonymity in this place made her stand out more than the woman in red.

"It's just Markson now," I said in a level tone. "Miss Scarlett, I presume?" I used the moniker I was instructed, noting not a stitch of red on her. Even still, I liked a good mystery; plus one point.

"Thank you for meeting me." She extended her arm across the table. Her grip was solid, confident. She did a quick double-pump and pulled her chair up to the table. I liked her already.

"Nice ring," she remarked with nod to my hand as she let go.

"Um, thanks. My old business mentor left me his signet ring when he retired." I turned my hand over to look at the bauble. "So, I usually just have a client meet me in my office," I said.

"Welcome to The Bower. Can I get you anything?" asked the young waiter.

Waiters were like wraiths, the way they showed up without notice, and only when your mouth held a forkful. Although, I have thought about a part-time job as a server just to hone my own clandestine skills. The kid looked comical, trying to appear professional in an ill-fit dress shirt and slender black tie knotted too high.

"Double Glenlivet 18," said Miss Scarlett.

"On the rocks?" asked the waiter, not taken aback at all by a 10 a.m. drink request. Or perhaps, he just expected her to order in kind since I was already on my second tequila — my second here.

"Neat, with a water back." She picked up a menu, and the waiter took the cue to leave.

"I hear they're known for their salads," I offered in attempt to turn up the charm.

"Only the orbit moms order salads," she said, and scanned the daily specials side of the menu. She looked across at the two women, who were giggling again, then saw my quizzical face as my fork hovered over the trough of greenery. "Sorry, I knew they served them in big bowls to make you easier to pick out."

Nice. I like a person who knows how to plan; another point.

In my single days, my academy friends and I had a point system to determine whether we would ask a girl out. We had this arrogance that a girl had to have ten before worthy of our consideration. The scorecard was a little misogynistic — okay, maybe a lot — but we were young and oh, so dumb. It was ironic, as none of us would hit even halfway if those same women had a similar scale. I don't date much anymore, but I still score people as a measure of being worth my time. "So, why all the cloak and dagger?"

She looked around for the waiter and recognized the boy might be a while, then picked up my tumbler, smelled the amber reposado, and drained the contents. "A person of my station needs to keep a low profile when they're planning to murder someone."

2

The brunch with Miss Scarlett was two days ago — the day before she disappeared. My contacts in the other rings scoured Newer York and Newer Delhi, but she had some skill in not being found; tally a point.

I thought about searching the core pillar, but it is all contracted support staff and Space Force oversight. A civilian would be as odd as a vegetarian Po Boy.

Scarlett and I had worked together to get her off station because, as she put it, she had *exceeded her usefulness to her husband.* The simple plan was to fake her death and put her in a body bag for a drop ship to Earth before she ended up in a bag for real.

She had turned up missing yesterday without my help.

I rolled out of bed accompanied by the chorus of creaking joints and straining muscles. My head swam as my mind fought to balance itself from the previous night's revelry and the exacerbated effects of the insubstantial gravity of the station. I picked up a hip flask from the wall alcove and gave it a shake. *Empty.*

The window, which was nothing more than a display panel in my steel coffin of an apartment, told me it was late morning. A stock photo gave the impression of looking out a window on Royal Street with deep blue skies.

I trudged across the small studio that sat on the spoke leading to the French Quarter of the Newer Orleans ring. The well-off live in the full gravity of the ring proper. The rest of us make do, hoping to get to a place at least halfway down the spoke where gravity feels somewhat normal and we're not in a constant state of nausea. My place was a quarter way from the core.

The station used to be *the* spot. It was the first orbital platform that had three tiers and was built solely for the purpose of indulgence. The builders tried to mirror each of the three rings after a city on Earth in its heyday, before they all went to rot. Odd that something created for the opulence of adults looked more like a 1,500 meter-wide child's top.

They had a fancy name for the station that was too long to remember, something about The Grand Oasis with some other fluff words. Soon, everyone started calling it Glimmer because it shone so brightly in the sky when viewed from Earth. Fifty years later, they still called it the same, but it had become just a glimmer of its former self.

The rolling chime of an Amazoogle call came over a speaker, and the image on the display changed to a business logo. I hit the accept icon to receive an upscaled video of my ex-wife's lawyer. The video enhancement to make a weak signal look clean made him seem more AI than human, which was appropriate since they were all soulless. The slight haze in the video frequency matched the shiver in my spine.

"Good morning, Ben," said the jovial shyster. The unmistakable double-take told me he saw the eye bags and the worn look on my face. "Is it morning there?"

"It's mid-morning," came the garbled sound of my voice trying to force out the first words of the day. "This turnip is dry. What else do you want, John?" His name was Jonathyn, with a Y. He hated people shortening his name, but I thought it was more polite than the other things I wanted to call him, and I enjoyed the innuendo.

"Looks like the paperwork finally caught up with the system. Your pension check from the military came in at zero."

I retired from the military, but on my last day I took a poke at my boss. He had a nasty habit of getting a little too friendly with the newly enlisted. Caught him in the hallway preying on a young cadet, giving her a choice to *enhance or hinder* her military career. His stalking, the divorce, and being forced to leave the only real family I'd ever known necessitated a release of pent up frustration.

I heard his nose still has a wheeze, so at least the kids can hear him coming. I guess in his last act of retribution, he got my honorable discharge overturned to dishonorable for striking a *superior* officer. There was probably a letter buried in the in-box I never checked.

"Well, that sucks for Emily, but like I said, this turnip is out of blood."

"Oh Ben, I'm not calling to ask." The joy in his voice hissed like the snake he was. "This is a courtesy call to let you know that I have updated your digital records for additional garnishment from your accounts." There was a snicker in the background, which was likely Emily, since she had moved in with him.

"That is kind of you. Please advise the ex-Mrs. Markson —" then I hit the amber icon and hung up on them both. *Good fucking luck garnishing zero.*

I walked into the bathroom and enjoyed the cold aluminum tile under my feet as I stared at a stranger in the mirror. Three-day stubble grew in patches of brown and gray like weeds on an old sidewalk, and bloodshot eyes hung over a pair of dark bags that had seen too many years. I had been someone when I was on Earth. When I left, my dignity stayed there along with everything else, including my dog. I was in exile because the constant legal demands of my ex couldn't make it through the extradition courts, which prevented my Earth-bound past coming to throw me in jail.

My eyes dropped to the bottle of muted yellow and brown antiseptic mouthwash on the edge of a rust-stained sink. *It's better than nothing.* I slugged a mouthful to stave off the shakes and get my day started.

3

Vacuum pressure carried me down the spoke to the French Quarter. It was just past eleven, and the stagnant air amplified the soft groan of the massive station's spin in weightlessness to simulate gravity. I'm told in its prime, they pumped in the scent of jasmine and Angel's Trumpet flowers to mimic a fresh spring day in the ring's namesake. Now the place had a mild stale scent of urine and liquor, recycled through ancient air filters, which was more on par with the scent of its sister city during Mardis Gras. I guess the magistrate stopped their attempts to correct this unintended authenticity.

I went down the simulated sidewalk and passed my office. No point going in since Miss Scarlett wouldn't be there waiting for me, and Hector would just be there at his desk to remind me he still hadn't been paid for a week.

Hector was a meager replacement for my old partner, but his enthusiasm made up the difference. I thought about including him on the Scarlett case to indoctrinate him into the PI world, but he's still best suited for surveillance of a wandering spouse or photo evidence for a business who doesn't think their employee's medical claim is legit.

I made my way through a few throngs of people. The simulated ambiance created a late morning sun as some locals with bags of supplies started their day and tourists drinking from half-yard glasses started theirs. One woman, a familiar brunette with long hair and pouty lips, gave me a sidelong glance, and I was not sure if it was because of my appearance or smell.

I stepped into Tujague's Too, my usual watering hole, and sidled up on a stool. The place attempted to have the look of the bar from its days in the 20s — the 1920s. The walls had the textured look of bone white plaster, and a barrel-valuated ceiling was probably re-purposed insulation foam from the heavy lift rocket that brought the pieces here. The floors had the irregular spans of aged boards, at least a facsimile of wood. At one time they even had sensors that would make the boards squeak as you walked in, but the piezo speakers fried out a decade ago and left the odd clang of metal on a faux wood floor whenever a heel walked across.

I palmed a handful of soy imitation peanuts from the community bowl. Everything used in the station was just a faux fabrication of everything planet-side to save weight and cost. I brushed away anything that didn't look like a nut as I plucked a few in my mouth.

"Those are for paying customers," said a baritone voice from the end of the bar.

"Hey, Charlie," I said. "Got anything that won't give me dysentery?"

A woman he was serving dropped her handful of nuts back into the bowl.

The bartender, a massive wall of a person, walked down the length of the imitation oak, his pace and demeanor never changing an iota. I still insisted he was an AI, but he assured me he was as much of a bastard as I was.

He pulled a shot glass from below the bar with a set of sausage fingers, along with a bottle of unlabeled brown liquid that swirled with fragments. Anything that wasn't soy was hard to come by on the station, so people were inventive in filling the gaps. His eyes didn't steer from me as he filled the shot glass to the brim without spilling a drop.

"Nice trick," I said.

"No trick," he said. "I can just *hear* when the glass is full."

Definitely AI.

"So, I don't get the good stuff?" I asked.

"You do, when you pay." He slid the shot forward a few inches and set the bottle down next to the jigger. His eyes were impassive, and then I caught the faint hint of a smile that the average person would confuse for a twitch.

I watched the liquid swirl in the shot glass as flotsam hovered in the hooch before spiraling to the bottom to be forgotten or ignored. The glass and I were a lot alike.

"Seen her?" I asked, then knocked back the shot in a single pull, and tried to ignore the miasma that burned in my nose.

"Nope." He wiped the bar with a towel that had seen a hard life. The tattered rag, barely visible under Charlie's club-like hand, left more behind than what it picked up. He tucked it in a back pocket and then sauntered toward another group of customers who had come in. "Oh, but I did get that address," he said as he nodded to the bottle where a slip of paper stuck from under the edge. I never saw him place it there.

I pulled out the crinkled note, and written in a perfect cursive script, not a skill you would expect from a behemoth like Charlie, was the address 17-4G Freret.

"That's the last time," he said over his shoulder.

"I know. I'll get you square." I owed him, for more than the shot and the information. I got him out of a serious jam when I first arrived on station, and he said he was indebted to me for life. However, in just the last year, I burned off his debt and then some. I used to have a lot of people who owed me, and now I'd called in every marker.

The slip of paper was Scarlett's home address. Or rather her second home. A few inquiries, along with a few credits, told me she tended to stay there most nights. She didn't feel safe at the townhouse with her husband, even though her husband was the Chief Constable for all of Newer Orleans.

4

A SINGLE WALKWAY OF ALUMINUM, contoured and textured to look like an asphalt street, traversed each ring for five kilometers. A few alleys and side streets were squeezed in here and there, but they were more for show. To maintain the feel of the Earth city, the main road was renamed each eighth of a radian to help with location. The builders also changed the theme of the architecture to look as if you were moving through each neighborhood. There was even a Streetcar named Desire that would ferry you between each eighth. Actually, there were four of them, equally spaced through the ring, and each of them was named Desire.

Addresses were ordered and easy to find, and told you a lot about a person's caste. The numbers were buildings and floors, and the letters told you the apartment. Some of the well-off had letter A and no other letters followed, and some, like me, got into double letters.

I stepped off the maglev streetcar midway down Freret in Uptown, and the automated system admonished me: *please wait for Desire to come to a complete stop before departing.* My knee, from an old battle injury, gave me a similar reproach.

The Rogier Building at 17 Freret wasn't high class, but one month's rent would still cover my place for a year. I pushed through the turnstile door into a mosaic lobby and headed straight for the elevator.

"Welcome home to the Rog— Sir, . . . *Sir*, you need to request a rendezvous." The concierge over-pronounced the last word with a fake pompous French accent. Everything is *soy.* He hesitated too long trying to place me as a resident, and I was in the lift before he could waddle around the front desk to stop me.

The doors slid shut and I pressed the retro-style button for four, rather than a proximity or voice control. Why they insisted on aesthetic features that you still had to touch to interact with was beyond me. Just another breeding ground for disease in a city that had gone to filth. But I figured if I hadn't already died from hanging at Tujague's, then I was immune to everything.

I walked to the last door facing streetside. A stylized G marked Miss Scarlett's door, and just to avoid a surprise, I knocked.

As I expected, no answer. I knelt and admired the pricey Kreckler proximity sensor on the door. Nice security upgrade; I gave her another point.

The system used a fob like a watch, ring, or some people even had them embedded under the skin, to activate the door lock. I had a similar one for my office, but this model was SHA-2048 encrypted and linked to a person's biometrics, so not anyone could use them, and that made them nearly impossible to bypass. But, people didn't hire me because I did the possible.

I pried off the sensor panel to reveal a series of microprocessors across a silicone board. I kept watch on the elevator, expecting the concierge to come up, but I guess his duties stopped in the lobby. After a few failed attempts, and wafting away a little smoke, the lock gave a satisfying *clunk* and I pushed.

The door crept open and unveiled a sparse apartment with high ceilings, aglow with light from gossamer-draped windows. The layout told me this was not a place for entertaining but a place of solitude where a person could have the basic comforts of serenity.

Standing up, but still in a crouch, I pressed my head past the threshold. The room was quiet but had that stagnant sense of being too quiet. I inched a little bit more and heard a faint squeak of a shoe across the wood-paneled floor.

"Oh shit," crept across my lips as a hand reached around

an accent pillar and grabbed the back of my hair to force me face-down to the floor. I could feel the smooth end of a standard Parish issued ceramic and carbon fiber barrel pressed to the back of my neck.

5

AFTER A FEW SOMEWHAT POLITE requests spoken through clenched teeth when I first arrived, the situation escalated to more physical questioning.

"I'm only going to ask one—" the word was punctuated by a fist to my gut. "More—" another punch to my side. "Time." The last hit was a knee right below my sternum, and this would have dropped me to the floor if the second guy, Guidry I think, hadn't held me up with my arms locked behind my back.

I had tightened my stomach for the telegraphed knee, but I still wheezed and hacked to put on a good show. No point inviting more abuse from a dissatisfied assailant. The hit still fucking hurt, but I wasn't spitting any blood — yet.

The man who threw the punches was named Pourciau. I didn't know him personally, but in my business you learn to recognize the cops. You can have the best security, but cops can get a bypass code from the manufacturer if there is probable cause. There always seemed to be probable cause.

Pourciau clenched my cheeks with one hand to hold my head up, "Where is Chief Gains's wife?"

"Pi—" and I coughed again. A little spittle hit the cop in the face. "Pi—let." I forced out through a face squeezed together by the vice-like grip.

"What?" Pourciau asked, removing his hand so I could speak.

"Piglet," I said, as a rough translation for his last name and also appropriate for his chosen profession.

His face cycled through shades of red, and his jaw tightened. Pourciau telegraphed the punch, like all his others, and when the haymaker came, I bowed forward, dragging Guidry's head along with me.

Pourciau's fist crunched as it went into his partner's head. Guidry dropped me and staggered from the impact, while Pourciau stepped back and clutched his wrist.

"You stupid, fu…" Pourciau groaned, as he pulled his gun from its holster with his off hand.

I pushed his damaged wrist to his body. His face went sheet-white, and he dropped the gun to protect his wrist. He stumbled over the back of a chair and sprawled across the floor with a litany of swear words.

Guidry shook his head, probably trying to help stop the room from spinning, as I made my way to the front door. He pulled his own weapon and centered the sights on me — and fired.

The shot tore through the door frame, where my head would have been had I not leaped into the hall. I scrambled to my feet and down the corridor as the second errant shot hit the wall where I had been lying.

"I know your face. You can run, but we'll find you — and the girl!" Pourciau's pained voice echoed through the hall as I ducked through the fire escape door and down to the lobby. I knew they would come after me hoping to get some answers, I just hoped they couldn't place my face.

Onlookers jumped as I burst out the front doors of the Rogier. Cops in Newer Orleans were just organized crime with badges. They took care of the occasional public indecency and the drunks who used the sides of buildings as urinals, but that was the closest thing they did that resembled upholding the law. The city was a profit machine for a few of the elite not hindered by morality.

I raced about two blocks down the road, then slowed my run to a normal pace. I shrugged out of my coat as I checked over my shoulder for a tail, and then turned it inside-out. My sport coat went from black to a simple tweed as I pulled it over my shoulders.

That's a little trick I picked up from my business partner and mentor, Sam Schippe, may he rest in peace. I tried to help him, but some people just can't handle the loneliness of space. When we met, he was estranged from some girl who married someone else, and the depression took its toll. She was a relative or something, but he never really talked about her, and I never asked. Maybe I should have cared more; maybe I could have stopped him, but I tend to stay out of people's personal business so they don't feel obliged to dig into mine.

I heard the commotion of the shocked crowd in front of the building as two men brandishing weapons raced from the tenement. I moved across the street, just before Desire passed, to cover my movement from the cops. The simulated staccato of steel wheels on iron tracks echoed off the buildings from speakers on the virtually silent maglev streetcar; another *soy* thing in this *soy* world. As it passed, the noise reduced to the hum of conversations from crowds of people. When I hit the sidewalk, I sidled into the crowd and headed back toward the Rogier. My chin was kept to my chest and fists shoved in my pockets as I moved to keep pace with the murmuration of people on the streets.

Relentless drills and training made the cops formidable but predictable. They split up in opposite directions, barreling down the street, looking into stores and at the backs of people for someone fleeing. They would never look at a person's face who walked toward them. From the corner of my eye I could see Guidry pass along the curb, gun held low at his waist, scanning the flock of people ahead of him.

When I got back to the Rogier, the crowd of gawkers had moved on. The concierge stood in the street relaying his harrowing role in the escapade to whatever passerby would listen. I moved past his back without notice, *like a waiter might,* through the front doors and into the lift.

6

PIGLET and his protégé wouldn't come back to the apartment for a bit. They had been doing a search of Scarlett's place and were staked out either for her return or an idiot like me to come by. The pair would search the street below for an hour or so and interview a few people. Maybe onlookers would have some information, but nothing that would keep them too long.

In my brief visit earlier, when not clouded through the pain of blurred vision, I could tell the room had been turned over. It wasn't torn apart like a scene in a bad movie, with drawers strewn across the floor and the wisps of stuffing from cut pillows and couches floating through the air. This was a methodical search, with obvious stacks of books and papers in the defined places of a person who organized their hunt as they moved items to track what had been reviewed and what was remaining.

I stood in the center of the room and circled to admire her cozy little getaway. A digital fireplace was against the streetside wall, framed by windows on either side. An ornate painting with silver filigree hung above the mantle, which I imagine was supposed to be a fleur-de-lis, the symbol of New and Newer Orleans, although the abstract piece looked to me more like an ace of spades from a deck of cards. "Art's in the eye of the beholder," I said to no one, while tilting my head at the painting like a curious dog.

The mantle had a few knickknacks on top, but they were decorative rather than personal, and the uneven placement told me they had already been rifled. A view screen hung on one wall, but the position of the furniture told me this was not the centerpiece of the room. Scarlett didn't come here to watch movies, and I turned my focus to the opposite wall where a set of shelves brimmed with books and boxes. Some of the titles were pop culture, but there were classics mixed with biographies and nonfiction.

She had some substance; I gave her a point.

Several groups of books toward the top had been stacked on each other, rather than placed with their spines vertical. Someone had started their search through the pages for a note, cut out center, or any information regarding her whereabouts, but had not yet finished. There were a few picture frames interspersed among the books, but they all held postcards from Earth before the Gray Days, when people would photograph the natural wonders. On the bottom were a series of boxes, all board games, with some newer versions and some timeless ones.

One caught my eye in a polished mahogany box with *150th Anniversary* in stylistic letters etched across the side. I pried the heavy box from under a few others, set the board game on the coffee table, and settled in a plush velvet blue chair, where she might have sat for hours poring through books. The lid had an old mansion sketched on the front with images of cards inlaid around the edges that portrayed the various characters of the mystery game: Professor Plum, Mrs. Peacock . . . and Miss Scarlett, the *femme fatale*.

I opened the lid that revealed a folded playing surface displaying the study and a few of the rooms where a murder would take place. I levered the board loose and expected to find the collection of cards and game pieces. Instead, the hollowed out box contained a stack of credits, some pieces of jewelry, a few ivory envelopes — and a ceramic carbon-barreled Parish-issued pistol.

7

I HELD the pulse weapon in my hand, and its size and weight felt insubstantial compared to its destructive power. Possession of a projectile weapon on the station was grounds for immediate exile, not to mention a fine that would put your family into crippling debt for generations. In untrained hands, an errant shot would be catastrophic; pressurized vessels in the vacuum of space do not respond well to holes.

Despite the risk, someone convinced the magistrate of the requirement for police to have them *for the indelible safety of the citizens and guests of Glimmer.* Morons. Perhaps knowledge the cops carried them was enough of a deterrent, since one had never been used in an arrest on record, but many knew they had been used plenty of times off-record.

The contents of the box must have been her getaway stash. She wouldn't be in need of it any longer. I picked up the credits and slid them into my coat pocket when another slip of paper caught my attention at the bottom of the box. A sheet ripped from a notepad resembled parchment. I turned over the paper and recognized the game tally sheet that listed all of the characters, weapons, and rooms. Along with various notes from a game play, circled in red were Miss Scarlett, Poison, and the Lounge.

I chuckled as Mrs. Gains, or Miss Scarlett, laid out her escape based on the board game; I had to give her a point for whimsy. That put her up to six; impressive.

When we sat over brunch, she spoke of her need to get

away, but Chief Gains, a good Catholic, would never permit a divorce. Gains struck me as the type more concerned about the public humiliation of having his wife leave him than he would be for the eternal salvation of his soul.

Her only means of escape was murder, but of herself. She had an associate who could drug her and give the appearance of death, leaving her body to be found at their home. Very Shakespearean of her; a point for invoking the bard. She was earning a high score.

The station wasn't equipped to handle severe medical issues or bodies. Scarlett made sure she had an advanced directive to be buried, which would put her on a drop ship for a quick run to a planet-side morgue instead of an air lock to be cremated on reentry. A simple payment, or payoff, and a record of DOA could be filed before Chief Gains was the wiser. She talked about growing up in what was once Germany, before Europe became a single country. Gains would be so preoccupied with absolving himself that she could flee to any parcel of land on Earth before he could even see the body, which would be buried long before he could get a transit flight to Earth, or at least that's what the records would say.

My role in all this was simple. I was the red herring, the person who would report she had come to me for protection out of fear of her husband, and I'd sow the seeds of murder to give her time to tie up any loose ends.

During our brunch, she had slid an ivory envelope across the table with a small retainer to seal the deal. She placed some credits for the bill and walked out of the restaurant; that was the last time I saw her. I gave it ten minutes before I left to start my part, and I picked up the tip as I walked out to help offset my expenses, of course. Making her vanish had been a perfect plan — until she disappeared.

I still had no clue where she was, and the cops, well at

least Guidry, would be back soon to finish their search. Since she was gone, and I knew the other half of the payment was now gone, I grabbed the jewelry and went to put the box back so it didn't look like I'd been there. I hesitated, then took the gun, too.

8

My desire to find the truth, as well as Desire, took me back to the French Quarter and to my office. I stopped by the little bistro at the bottom of my building to pick up lunch to go. When it came time to pay, I must have misplaced my identification card to scan the credits, but Marie knew me and accepted a rain check. Maybe I did still have a few favors left on this station. I could have used my signet ring to pay, but who would say no to a free lunch.

This case was perplexing and had too many loose ends. *Why did she disappear before we could execute the plan? Did Gains catch on and she had to scatter? Why didn't she reach out to me for help? Why did she leave her nest egg at the apartment?*

I climbed the stairs to the third floor since the lift in my building had been broken for six months. The door to my office was standard metal with the faux glass stencil on the front that read Benjamin Markson, Private Investigators. There was adhesive residue of a name that used to be above mine, but it had been peeled off a year ago when Sam left. I passed Sam's old signet ring over the proximity sensor, and the door slid open to a room lined with imitation oak panels and inset bookshelves on every wall. Two desks sat facing one another on either side of the room with a pair of club chairs in front of each for clients. The back wall carried more bookshelves and a little wet bar with a coffee maker. It was a comfortable room and where I spent most of my time when I wasn't sleeping one off.

"You owe me for two weeks," said Hector.

I walked further into the room and looked past a pile of books hiding a young man slouched in his chair with tight cut hair atop an olive toned face. "Good morning to you, too."

"Ben, I can't keep doing this. I have bills." Hector came on board after Sam decided he couldn't handle the heartache anymore and walked out the station's back door, literally. My new associate was a young guy wanting to learn the trade, but I didn't have the heart to tell him he lacked the soulless grit necessary for this line of work.

"I thought I owed you a week?" I stepped over to my desk in the snug office and collapsed into my chair with an exaggerated sigh.

"Two weeks ago you owed me for two, then you paid me for one, but now you owe me for last week too. That's two."

"Math is hard. That's why I let you handle the business side." I reached into my inner jacket pocket and felt the jewelry, switched to the other, pulled out some of the credits, and estimated the amount. "Here, I got an advance, so that should cover your back pay and this week as well." I pushed the pile to the edge. Hector came around his desk, but before he could grab the stack, I pulled off a couple credits. "A little for petty cash."

Hector narrowed his eyes, but swiped the stack and went back to his desk. "You know I don't even drink that swill you call coffee, so I don't know why I have to chip in."

He counted the credits, laying them out in stacks by amount, then entered some information in the system; accounting I guessed. I slid my chair over and hit the button on the *swill* generator. The room was filled with the sweet smell of Arabica and notes of mold and burnt wood. Maybe I did need to change the filter.

"So where are you with that red girl case?"

"Hit a wall. We were supposed to initiate the plan yesterday, but she turned up missing. I went by her place, but a pair of Newer Orleans's finest thought her location might fall out of me like I was a piñata."

Hector dismissed the beating reference. He might have become as used to it as I had in this line of work. Maybe he could cut it. He didn't look up from his spreadsheet and commented, "So they don't know where she is either, but they also believe her to be missing."

The realization slapped me harder than my ex when I told her I was leaving. "Son of a . . ." My mind swam as I put the pieces together. No perfunctory would risk signing a DOA, or keep it silent, when they found out who the husband was. Gains had too much clout and ego to let a woman be his downfall. If she didn't want to get drug back into this life, Scarlett needed an out that left Gains free of blame and her free of him; she needed a scapegoat.

"Fucking eight points," I muttered under my breath.

Hector perked up hearing the count. "*Hmm*, so has anyone ever gotten a ten on your exclusive scale?"

"There's one other girl who has a nine." My mind went through the events. The public meeting with her. My search and questions around the rings for her whereabouts. My visit to her apartment. These all added up to a possible lover, not a business associate; *another point*.

"Really? I'm intrigued. Who scored that high?" He asked, shutting off his monitor and leaning back in his chair. "Was it your wife?"

"No, my dog, Sierra." That brought a chortle from Hector. "She was at a ten, but then she went with my wife in the divorce."

Hector was holding his sides. "So I take it the wife is what, an eight or a seven now?"

"Ex-wife," I said. "And she never got above five."

"Ouch."

"Nah, I was lucky to get a person that high." She was a good woman, but I wasn't the type that could flourish around good. "I'm a two on a good day, and there aren't a lot of good days anymore."

Hector shook his head and got up to leave. "I'm out for lunch and taking the rest of the day off." As he stepped out the door, he nodded at an ivory envelope on the corner of my desk. "Oh, Mrs. Gains came by and dropped off the envelope for you yesterday."

"Miss Scarlett came here?" I asked, genuinely surprised. "A middle-aged blonde woman?"

"No, Mrs. Heather Gains is a tall brunette bombshell." He shrugged like there was no other way to describe her. "She also left a bottle of tequila with the note. A Clase Azul Reposado, 2142. Nice tip." He nodded his head downward toward my desk as he made his way to the door. "I put it in your drawer, as a bottle of liquor doesn't scream 'professional office' sitting out on the desk." The door slid closed behind Hector, leaving me alone, gobsmacked.

9

I DON'T KNOW how long I sat there staring at the missive on my desk as my mind swam though each moment over the past few days. With a sigh, I opened the ivory envelope and poured the contents on my desk. There were two items in the sleeve: a playing card of a woman in red with Miss Scarlett in printed script at the bottom, and a postcard with an old picture of Neuschwanstein Castle before the Grey Days. I flipped the postcard over and written in crimson lipstick was a single phrase, *Für meinen vater. Lebewohl.* I did a quick translation on my console: *For my father. Farewell.* Below the valediction was penned a flowing upside-down heart — no, a spade.

I emptied my pockets on the desk. The other credits, the jewelry, and a pistol lay next to the rest of the clutter around the leather blotter — simple physical evidence that would make a case for even the worst lawyer to hold me culpable for the missing woman.

She knew she would be followed, always. She made an effort to connect with me at the restaurant by running her finger up my arm as a seductive gesture that could be witnessed. Her friend, pretending to be Miss Scarlett, did the actual meet to set me on the path so the chief's lackeys didn't drag me out right then and there for a tryst with Mrs. Gains. Damn, they've known I was part of this all along. All that was needed was supposition that Scarlett and I were connected.

If I had just left things alone when she disappeared, they might have hassled me for a bit, shut down my business, and left me for destitute. The contents of the box were meant to be found, not by me, but as an indicator she disappeared without her stash, assumed dead rather than a runaway, to keep Gains from looking for her. But then I hit a cop and had items from her apartment.

Well, they might not require proof of her body since all the bins emptied into space burn upon reentry. On Earth I might have seen a trial, but up here I would never make it to court before I found myself in a dumpster.

I pushed the items around on my desk and noticed the ring on my finger, Sam's old ring, with an ebony embossed spade — or a schippe in German; Sam Schippe. I pulled up a query engine and searched for *Newer Orleans + Gains + Marriage.* The fourth hit was a news article from eight years ago. "The station spun a little faster with excitement as people celebrated the union of Chief Gerrard Manuel Gains and Miss Heather Iva Schippe."

My personal hell grew a little larger. Her father was my old partner who killed himself because of an estranged daughter. Now it looked like a bitter washed up PI was seeking revenge for his dead partner, when it was really Scarlett who blamed me for her father's death.

I threw the gumbo I had planned to eat for lunch in the trash and pulled the bottle Miss Scarlett left out of the drawer. The gift could represent some guilt for what she had done, or as a final toast to my demise. I admired the white ceramic bottle with hand-painted blue agave design, and thought I should save it for a special occasion.

Failure is a special occasion.

I popped the silver capped cork off the bottle, filled a tumbler, and a tendril of amber sloshed on the table in an arc to be wiped up and forgotten, just like me.

"Plus one point, Miss Scarlett. A perfect ten," I said, as I toasted her and downed the aged tequila. *Maybe things could have been different if she had talked to me herself*, I mused.

My lament was interrupted by a fist against the door. "Benjamin Markson. By order of the magistrate, you are compelled by law to open the door!"

I refilled my glass, palmed the weapon, and admired the smooth lines of the pistol. *Am I the type to go out fighting, or just disappear in a glimmer?*

I picked up the tumbler, cocked the pistol's hammer, and whispered in the glass before I slugged the spirit, "Colonel Markson, in the study, with the revolver."

* * *

TIM LEWIS MANAGES *rocket programs by day and collects hobbies by night. Writing has been the longest running hobby, going back to middle school and first place in a Halloween story contest. He took creative writing at Purdue, but his public works have all been scholastic and technical. In the years following, there has been an accumulation of short stories and scenes brewing that few have seen beyond his laptop. Tim leans toward Sci Fi, Urban Fantasy, and Noir, where each contain an element of humor and sarcasm from a life spent as a smart ass. He published his first fictional story, "Switch," in 2019 and additional short stories in various anthologies. He continues to write and submit as he aspires to his favorite quote by Benjamin Franklin: "If you wou'd not be forgotten / As soon as you are dead and rotten, / Either write things worth reading, / or do things worth the writing." For more on Tim and his work, go to LewisVenture.com*

THE GODDESS OF CRIME

MICHAEL LA RONN

*H*ere's what happens when you're about to get mugged:

It's nighttime, usually some blackened hour when you should be rolling over in your toasty bed. Your only excuse for being out so late is your vanity. You're one drink away from drunk, but you've still got your judgment.

The streets are deserted and rain-slicked. In the dark valley of buildings through which you walk, every window has its curtains drawn, like children covering their eyes while watching a horror movie.

A distant car horn blares as if trying to warn you. You see your reflection in an inky puddle under a flickering street-light amid a background of pinwheels of light.

Above, the stars glitter like Turkish lamps, but they are not your compass home. Their beauty is a temporary distraction that pulls your eyes upward to marvel at the strangeness of the city that you've lived in for years but never stopped to admire.

You will be so busy staring at the breathtaking sky that

you will not see the hooded man waiting for you in the door-well two buildings down.

He saw you the moment you turned onto the street. You don't see him until you're a few feet away. When his hooded shape slinks out of the shadows, Mother Nature kicks in.

Your heart rate accelerates.

Your breath runs shallow.

Beads of sweet bloom in places you didn't know you could sweat.

That alcohol buzz burns away, and you get as sober as if you never had a drink in your life. His shadow looms larger with every step.

If you run, he'll grab you. If you turn your back, he might hit you. He's got you right where he wants you.

If you have a knife, it doesn't matter. If you have pepper spray, it doesn't matter. It is too late. All those videos you watched on the internet about self-defense were just your imagination fooling you into thinking you could be your own hero.

If you were going to avert disaster, you would have done it seconds earlier.

The only thing that matters now — the only thing that's real — is your fear.

First, he'll ask you politely if you have the time. You'll look down at your wrist and find yourself on the ground, tasting cement as he grabs your things. Your watch. Your ring. Your phone. Your wallet.

You will feel light as his hoodie swallows your things. You will feel as if it has swallowed your soul. The urge to vomit will well up in your stomach, but somehow you will hold it down.

You will struggle, but he will be ready. You will hear the metallic click of a gun cocking and stare into the depths of its barrel as he continues his pillage. His gruff voice will tell you to stay down.

If you're lucky, he will strike you on the head as his getaway act.

If you're unlucky, he will shoot you and you will die.

* * *

As for me, I will live. No harm will come to me tonight.

I invented the ancient art of mugging. It hasn't changed in five thousand years. The first man standing in a stone doorway in early civilization waiting by firelight to accost the first unlucky passerby — that was my design.

I hovered behind history's first mugger in an ethereal mist, whispering in his ear and telling him exactly what to say and where to strike. His every move was a prayer to me. When that innocent pedestrian in a toga stumbled by smelling of dry wine, I guided my subject's hand into the back of the fool's bare head. A few silver coins and drops of misery later, my offering was complete.

Any time a criminal inflicts misery upon the world, I grow richer and stronger. Yet, there have never been any shrines to my greatness. No one has ever painted a mural in honor of me that I know of. No one has ever uttered my name because history has never bothered to record it, and it is just as well. A goddess like me thrives best in the shadows.

As misery grew in the world, I didn't need the same foolishness as the rest of my brothers and sisters. I didn't need larger-than-life shrines on grassy hilltops to flatter my ego. I didn't even need blood. All this goddess needed to thrive was misery.

Now, the eons pass like a film on long exposure. Humanity has crawled away from its pagan origins, and most of the old gods are dead. No one prays to them anymore. My dead brothers and sisters live on in paintings and myths that praise their lives. They live forever in the zeitgeist but will never breathe again.

Yet, I am here, but only because my subjects continue to grace me with executions of my inventions: crimes of every kind. I don't live on a hallowed mountain or in sun-drenched clouds. I live among humanity. I have a familiar but forgettable face. I blend easily in a crowd. You see me, then you forget me. Lovers throughout the ages have known me, and I have had to forget them.

Being a goddess in a world that has forgotten about your kind is a private existence, and lonely. You take your tributes where you can and keep living. No one you meet will last, and you cannot risk being found out, so you must always keep moving.

My travels brought me to this gray, sunless city covered with wet surfaces and shadows. I feel at home here because the unrest is palpable. The crime is also exceptionally bad. I wear this city like an old warm blanket that I've forgotten but am oh-so-glad to have rediscovered.

While walking these streets among my faithful subjects, I sense her.

My sister is here.

It has been four thousand years since I've seen her. I sense her presence like a parched tree senses rain.

Walking through the shadowed streets drenched with fear and loathing, I use the stars as my map, my astral tea leaves. It has been ages since I've stared up at the night sky, but feeling her pulls me out of my usual drudge.

I stand in a darkened street and stare at the cosmos from whence I came, marvel at their everlasting radiance, and reorient myself in my sister's direction.

I must find her at all costs.

It just so happens that my path tonight has brought me

into the path of our dear mugger. This one's an amateur. I can tell by his hesitation in stepping out of the doorwell.

This isn't the first time I've been assaulted with my own method. Even my godly, forgettable face doesn't mean I don't get targeted every now and then.

Any other person would have frozen. Instead, I walk right to him, let him think that I'm playing his game.

I glance around. We're the only ones dancing tonight.

Then I meet his face, which I can't see but know all too well. The mark of innocence. A teenager? Perhaps a child forced to become a man too soon. Dark hoodie. Stiff frame ratcheted back to seem taller than he really is. Except there's no menace. This noir street is doing all the menacing work for him.

"I don't have the time," I say, taking him off guard. He steps in front of me. I still cannot see his face.

"I don't give directions to strangers, if that's what you're asking," I said. "And if you think about following me, you will be following me for a long time before you regret it."

He studies me. Any mortal would be perplexed. "I've got somewhere to be, so if you're going to make a move, let's get it over with," I say, balling my fists.

One of the man's hands slides into his hoodie.

I smirk. "Okay, I'll let you strike first."

He draws a serrated blade. Military-grade. Curved, with holes in the blade for a deeper, smoother cut. The kind that can disembowel someone without too much effort.

"Come on, honey," I said. I don't take my eye off the blade. I hold up my palms to let him know that he'll have an easy freebie. "Strike fast and strike hard, my love."

Yes, most definitely an amateur. He hesitates, but not the hesitation of a criminal before deciding whether to do a deed. His hesitation is about where to strike.

If you want to strike someone to kill, aim for their collarbone. With enough luck, you can hit the subclavian artery and send them to the underworld in minutes. Only amateurs go for the abdomen. It's a myth perpetuated by bad movies.

He goes for my stomach, but I sidestep.

I grab his wrist and shove it forward, hyper-extending his arm. The knife clinks to the ground. I give this brave subject a sucker punch to the nose, then a sweep to an ankle. He's on the ground groaning and spitting out blood before he knows what hit him. I stand over him. "This is the part when I'm supposed to be on the ground and you're supposed to be taking my things," I say.

He coughs across me into the street, but I don't let him get away. Even an inch.

"If you were really good," I say, crouching and leaning in, "you would have killed me. But goodness — it seems that you are on the ground instead. Let's find out who you are."

I draw a little snub-nosed pistol I carry with me for protection and jam it into his chest. With my other hand, I snap my fingers, sending ragged orbs of light that color the street tungsten as if someone flipped a light switch.

I roll back his hood.

A tangle of black locks falls to his shoulders.

Staring back at me is the bloodied and bruised face of a young girl.

Women worship me from time to time, but the vast majority of my subjects are men.

I stare at this girl in disbelief. I thought I knew this city, but it turns out there are still things that even a five-thousand-year-old goddess can learn.

"Who are you?" I ask. I press the gun even harder into her forehead. "Why did you attack me?"

The girl wipes a streak of blood from her cheek. "I have my reasons."

The fragility in her voice tells me she's not a threat. She

can't be older than twenty-one. She's as thin as a stick, with rips in her jeans. In the moonlight, her face is a quilt of cuts and scrapes. Probably from street fights. This girl isn't winning any hand-to-hand fights, that's for sure.

"Your technique is terrible," I say. I holster my gun and extend a hand.

I sometimes forget that I can break a mortal's mind with my actions alone. She's got to be the most confused girl on the planet right now. She doesn't take my hand. Instead, she doesn't take her eyes off me.

"You're right to be suspicious," I say. "You're probably thinking how crazy I am to be here talking to you and not running away."

I wiggle my hand again and soften my voice. "Don't worry, you're not in danger, unless you want to be."

The girl's eyes widen, and she reaches up. I pull her sweaty hand, then she's standing next to me, smoothing out her hoodie. She takes a step back to keep her distance and raises a hand to nurse her cheek.

"I could ask about your situation, but the story is always the same," I say. "Down on your luck . . . hard times . . . troubled childhood . . . you're only doing this because you have no choice, but you'd stop if you could. Sound familiar?"

She takes another step back, but I take a step forward, like a wolf stalking its prey. "I asked you a question, and I expect a response."

"You — you don't know me at all," she says.

I laugh in my condescending goddess way. "I know you better than you know yourself. You just don't know it yet. Don't back away from me. I'm not done with you yet."

I pause to see if my goddess charm is still working. It is. She can't look away.

I hold out my hand. The knife she used to attack me zips into the air and into my palm.

"Curious weapon choice," I say, holding the blade up to the starlight. "Not what I would've chosen. You should have used something more discreet. If you're going to go through all this trouble, why not just get a gun? Better protection, especially for you."

The girl's face hardens. "Why are you mocking me?"

I puff. "I don't mock. I speak truth. You're not exactly winning any street fights, are you?"

My words hit her hard. Her face contorts from vulnerable to the-wanting-to-prove-themselves look that young people are so good at putting on.

"No need to get defensive," I say. "You see, you remind me of a younger version of myself. I ran the streets too, you know. I've been the woman in the door. You know how that feels: lying in wait for some innocent sap to pass by. Surely you understand the fear running through your body the moment before you strike, don't you? Let me guess — you've only done this about a dozen times."

She shakes her head. "How do you—"

"Must you insist on asking questions I've already given you the answers to, girl?" I ask.

I hand her the blade hilt-first. "You must never hesitate. Even easy prey can surprise you. You must strike the same regardless of whether I am frail or a fierce soldier. You will never know who I truly am until you reveal yourself."

I point to the doorwell where she had waited. "That was a bad choice. Even a drunkard could have spotted you standing there. Your only saving grace was that I was preoccupied with the stars. Next time, I suggest you inhabit a building slightly closer to the corner. That will give you the illusion of surprise. Then, you don't even have to ask them for the time. Strike and seize your spoils."

I'm breaking the girl's mind again. I hope she can take it. Her brain is one step short of a cognitive malfunction.

"I don't know who you are, but I'm done," she says.

I hold up a hand again. An invisible wall springs up behind her, but she doesn't know it yet.

"Sure, run away," I say. "But maybe I'm who you've been waiting for all along. Maybe I'm just what you need."

I grin as she turns, runs, and faceplants into the wall.

"Listening is another critical criminal skill," I say. "You would do well to try it."

I tilt my head at her as she rubs her other cheek. "Shall we continue your lesson?"

The girl glances over her shoulder. My senses sharpen.

Hurried footsteps are coming from half a block away.

"You've made a grave mistake," I say.

"Katrina!" someone cries.

A man.

Two men, actually, both wearing hoodies of course. They round the corner, their blackened shapes running at me.

I shake my head and cluck my tongue. "Katrina, why didn't you tell me you were working with a team? That's a misrepresentation that's liable to get one killed."

I will her knife to slide out of her hand and back into mine. I laugh as the two goons launch their ambush.

The one on the left side of the street is lean, the kind who looks like he needs to rob people for money. If he had been the one who jumped out at me from the shadows, I wouldn't have thought twice about it. I would've taken pity on him and given him something. He needs a sandwich — better yet, a three-course meal at a buffet.

The one on the right is the leader. More muscular, slightly overweight, with a peach fuzz mustache. A proper deadbeat. He's the first to reach for his gun.

I like to play a game when I get accosted on nights like this. In the few seconds I have before these goons light me up in a blaze of glory, I predict that the first is a leech and the second is a lover.

I expand the invisible wall to encircle both me and the girl. Their bullets don't stand a chance.

The girl covers her head with her hands and crouches down. I detect a slight smirk, like she thinks this is the end for me.

I don't flinch as the bullets race toward me. My wall flashes red with each impact, holding the bullets in place for a few seconds before spitting them to the ground in a metallic rain. I wait until these fools empty their guns. My ears ring like struck gongs. I yawn as I wait for the first trigger to click.

I flick my wrist as if shooing away a fly. Both men rise into the air and crunch into each other before collapsing into a pile on the asphalt.

"You have a poor choice of a boyfriend, and your boyfriend has a poor choice of friends," I say. "Let me guess: Mr. Boyfriend is the one with the mustache."

The girl stares at her friends incredulously. I know I'm right — my instincts never fail me.

"Before this unfair ambush, I was giving your precious Katrina a lesson in true criminality," I say to the amateurs. "Would you like to join this private lesson, or shall I finish you?"

A twinkle draws my eyes upward. The constellation of stars on which I relied to point me toward my sister is fading. A few minutes ago, they had been as bright as distant planets. Now, they glow like the embers of a dying campfire.

My sister is leaving the city. If I don't do something drastic, she will escape me. The thought of missing this precious reunion makes a knot catch in my throat.

I level my gaze at the woman. She keeps backing away from me, and the two men lie groaning.

"The crime in this city is to die for," I say sharply, "but the education is lacking. I asked you three a question."

Silence.

"Answer me!" I shout. My voice echoes off the walls and slick surfaces and multiplies upon itself on its way to nowhere.

Mr. Boyfriend with the mustache rolls over. "Go screw yourself."

"Bad choice," I say. I close my fist, imagining his heart in my palm. He screams and writhes like a wounded animal as I squeeze.

"Okay, okay!" he says.

"Much better answer," I say. "Now stand up. You're going to make it look as if I'm having no mercy on you."

I will the invisible wall to disappear, though they can't see it. I glance up again at the stars. My time is running out.

"Before you three tried to ruin my evening, I was on my way to somewhere important. Because you interrupted, you will now be responsible for getting me there. In exchange, I will teach you about your craft so that your next plunder will be successful."

Mr. Boyfriend puffs. "Yeah, like you're a—"

I squeeze again, bringing him to his knees. "I'm a what?" I ask.

Mr. Boyfriend waves me quiet.

"You're catching on. Which one of you knows the city the best?" I ask. Katrina's and Mr. Boyfriend's eyes drift toward Goon Face, who is coughing out a tooth. I note that he has an extremely punchable face.

"Very well," I say. "You. Have you ever stolen a car before?"

Goon Face jumps back as if I tried to punch him. "Hey, lady, I don't know who you think you are, but—"

"This city and its aversion to answering questions," I

mutter. "Looks like you don't have the guts. That leaves Katrina or Mr. Boyfriend. Who wants the honor?"

The three look among themselves like terrified school-children upon receipt of the worst assignment ever.

I snap my fingers. "Katrina, you're up."

She shakes her head. "I've never stolen a car before. That's not exactly the safest thing to do."

"Now you're worried about safety," I say, walking away.

I don't look back. They will follow.

"Fortunately, I'm an expert at this," I say. "Follow my instructions, and I will be with you every step of the way."

Stealing a car isn't hard. Technically, it's easier than robbing someone. The trick is to get the setup right. My preferred carjacking method is the good old note under the windshield wiper. Preferably, it should look like a parking ticket. It should also be in a place where there is an irregular trickle of people, best if the parking lot is poorly lit.

The marks stumble to you like clueless animals. They wander through the dark, jangling their keys and laughing at a joke that one of them tells. Usually a couple. The passenger never sees the note; the driver sees it immediately and leaves the car door open as they inspect it. Then, my subjects strike. Forcing the passenger out of the car is just a formality.

I would love to use my favorite method tonight, but I don't have time. Tonight requires a more brutal method.

I stand in the doorwell several blocks away from the place where Katrina assaulted me. The leader stands in an alley directly across from me, his back against the brick wall in a darkened alley. Goon Face hides behind a parked pickup truck a few yards to our left. Katrina stands on the curb, ready to follow instructions.

I have no shame in what she is about to do; that is, if she follows instructions. The way I see it, by teaching what these three need to be more loyal subjects, I will grow stronger.

The headlamps of the car sweep across the street.

Across the alley, Mr. Boyfriend stiffens. He's ready.

Katrina shambles into the middle of the street, screaming and clutching an arm.

"Help!" she cries. "Somebody help!"

It's always a man who gets out. That sense of chivalry and the remnants of a bygone era always compel them to pump the brakes and get out to help a pretty young girl.

This man is no different. Why he's on the road at such a godforsaken hour and what he's doing in this godforsaken part of the city isn't my business, but his car is. Goon Face sneaks up behind him as he tries to comfort Katrina from her fake hysterics. He doesn't see the pistol crack into the back of his skull.

The four of us are in his car and driving away in seconds.

I sit in the back passenger seat. The car has comfortable leather upholstery and blood-red lights on the dashboard. A deep-voiced DJ plays late-night jazz; a lonely trumpet serenades us as a gentle rain begins to fall.

Goon Face drives. Mr. Boyfriend sits in the front seat, and Katrina sits in the back with me. I roll my window down and angle my head out of the car to see the stars. I close my eyes and let the drizzle wash over me.

I give Goon Face turn-by-turn directions.

I have no idea where we're going, but the stars do.

They ask who I am.

Because I want to play with them, I tell them an elaborate story. I tell them I worked as a special ops soldier in a distant country. They ask me what it was like, and I tell them they can never know.

"That where you learn to steal cars?" Mr. Boyfriend asks.

I take pleasure in the customs of this city by not answering his question. Instead, I glance wistfully at the endless fire escapes, dilapidated buildings, and helices of steam rising from subway vents.

Every street in this damn city is the same. Perhaps one day I will take up residence here. I could hide here for a long time and grow so powerful.

"That guy back there looked important," Goon Face says, wiping his nose. He drives the car like he is going to crash it. Stop lights are just a suggestion, and I get the sense that he has never used a turn signal in his life.

"If you want to do this for a long time and not get caught," I say, "do yourself a favor and obey traffic laws. It wouldn't hurt you to slow down."

"But you said you needed to be somewhere in a hurry," Goon Face says.

"In a hurry, not in a split second," I say. "You three truly are amateurs. Only amateurs drive like maniacs and wonder why they get pulled over."

Goon Face takes the insult personally.

I let him have more. "But you've never stolen a car, just like you've never properly robbed someone, so what do you know? The techniques I showed you tonight — do them every time and you'll be just fine, as long as you obey traffic rules."

I check the stars again. We are getting closer.

I imagine my sister and what I will say to her. Where will we meet?

Perhaps she will be sitting in a graveyard when I steal upon her veiled figure and announce my presence. Or, she'll be entangled in a lover's arms in a late-night tryst. I've never wanted to see her so much in my immortal life.

"Where exactly are we going?" Katrina asks.

"You shouldn't ask questions," I say. "Besides, I'll make sure you get a nice payday when we arrive."

"That's definitely a bonus," she says.

Goon Face lets out a little laugh and shares a quick look with Mr. Boyfriend.

An alarm bell rings in my head. These three will betray me before the night is over. Even I'm not that stupid.

The rain mists the air as our destination reveals itself. Through shrouds of vapor and empty street after empty street, it rises up like a mountain in a dense jungle.

A hospital. I spot its neon sign from several blocks away. It's at least ten stories tall, a great fortress in the sea of drab. It reminds me of brutalist buildings I've seen in my travels. With bars over the windows, it reminds me more of an insane asylum than a hospital.

"You sure you want to go there?" Goon Face asks. "Who's at the hospital? Hubby?"

Katrina and Mr. Boyfriend laugh.

"I was thinking I would visit you after I finish what I started earlier," I say.

In the rearview mirror, I see Goon Face frown.

"Pop quiz," I say. "What do you say when a patron hires you to drive her somewhere and then tells you that she'll pay you a bonus if you wait however long it takes?"

"Depends on how much she's paying," Katrina says.

"Very good," I say as Goon Face pulls into the portico, which looks like the mouth of an angry dragon. The word "Emergency" is burned out on the neon sign in the stone facia, and only the "Y" flickers like the light of a dying firefly.

"So," Katrina says. "How much?"

"Ten thousand if you don't complain," I say.

I'm not going to pay them anything by the end of the night because they will betray me. That is also a lesson they must learn. There is a time and place for loyalty, but you better be damn sure who you cross. I look forward to teaching them this valuable lesson as I step out of the car.

"You two boys can wait for me in the parking lot," I say.

Katrina repeats my words and curses under her breath.

I curl my finger at her. "This lesson will be special."

She gets out of the car and follows me reluctantly, a puppy dog afraid of her shadow. But I desperately need her; the distance to my sister is not yet a straight line.

We stand gazing at the uninviting building. Somewhere, an ambulance wails. Above, the clouds drift in, covering the moon.

There are no more stars. I'm on my own now.

* * *

"Ma'am, we've got a backlog. It's going to be a long wait."

Katrina and I have walked into the hospital separately, two minutes apart. I stand, shaking my head at the green pastel walls and black and white checkered floor, leaning against a corner as I listen to Katrina argue with the late-night nurse.

The place smells like old plaster and sweat. A maddening hum from the overhead lights underscores the sad silence of this place. There are no windows here — probably by design as a reminder of your misery. You're in for a godawful night if you end up here. In a hospital like this, you walk in hurt and leave worse than when you came in.

A dozen injured people sit in the waiting room like sad statues. A man with a gash on his head. A woman with an arm bent like a chicken wing. I wonder what brought them here. Probably my subjects. The misery in the room is like electric energy. I breathe it in, and my resolve hardens.

I fold my arms and listen to Katrina.

"I need to be seen right away," Katrina says. "If I don't—"

"Four-hour wait, ma'am," the nurse says.

"I can't wait four hours!" Katrina cries. "I— I—"

Thud.

This girl learns quickly. I can't see her, but she's pretended to faint just like I told her to.

The nurse calls someone frantically. An automatic door swishes open. Another nurse. Both women hover over Katrina.

I use the opportunity to slip past and into the elevator bay behind the security desk. No one sees me slip through the golden doors into a stuffy elevator with a single fluorescent bulb. I'm on my way to the upper floors before Katrina even thinks about turning off her act.

I love subterfuge.

My sister and I share a special bond. She's the only goddess I respect. The only one I call my equal, and my opposite.

Our mother loved us, but she never showed me the same affection she showed my sister. I blame it on the fact that my sister was more dutiful than I was.

My sister pleased the other gods, always likable, always laughing, and always ready to do any bidding asked of her. She was a natural ambassador of our kind.

No one ever came to me. No one ever regarded me or asked me what I thought about anything. Whenever I accomplished an impossible oddity, they would just sneer at me instead. "What kind of goddess dwells in such darkness?" they would ask. Even the gods of the underworld received more respect than I did.

I hated them. I even grew to hate my mother, the goddess of night. The only place for a goddess like me is by herself.

I'll never forget the day I walked out of the pantheon forever. I surfed on a wave of shadow, rising tall over the gods. I told them that one day they wouldn't ignore me anymore. I cursed them all, even my mother. I wished them darkness and told them that one day I would be more powerful than all of them.

I was just a girl then. I never thought I would regret my words, but I've lain awake at night wishing I could take them back. All those gods I cursed are dead. My wish came true, but at the cost of being alone forever.

I didn't curse my sister. I couldn't. I loved her. She stood up for me when no one else would. I could always count on her to do what was right and just.

As the elevator hums to a stop, I sense her energy at full tilt. The elevator dings, and the doors slide open. We are now on the same floor.

I'm in some kind of ward. It smells of antiseptic and disease. I look for signs, but they are all scratched out. I have no idea where I am or what kind of sick people rest here.

Then it dawns on me that my sister could be among the sick. Nausea overtakes me as I sleepwalk my way down this white hall sorely in need of renovation. The rooms are empty. Each bed is perfectly made, and the window in every room is open, curtains flowing in a gentle breeze. I taste the rain in the air.

My intuition leads me to the end of the hall to a closed door. I don't want to open it. I know she's in there, and I know I may not like what I see.

After four thousand years, I'm finally going to see her again. I'm finally going to reclaim a part of myself that I've lost.

Part of me wants to run away. Another part of me wants to destroy this place in a rage, if what I think I'm about to see is true. I place my hand on the door handle. The iron is warm to the touch. I take a deep breath and push the door open.

The sparse hospital room is a tidy square, no bigger than a bedroom. The window is closed, and the lights are off. A glowing rune of my sister's mark is burned into the wall — a golden scale with both weights balanced.

The first thing I hear is the gentle sound of the television.

A late-night soap opera. The television speakers don't work very well, and the characters speak in voices that remind me of staticky snow.

The only light is from the changing frames on the television.

Then I see her. She's lying on the bed. A labyrinth of wires and catheters connects her to an ancient apparatus that shows a stable and steady heart rate. She lies breathing slowly, her long dark hair pooled on the pillow under her. She is sleeping.

I survey the room. We are the only two here. There is a worn cloth chair sitting next to the bed as if it had been placed there for me. I take a seat and gaze upon my sister's sallow, sickly face.

How long has she been here? Who did this to her? This is not a state befitting a goddess. Anger wells within me as I take her hand.

She opens her eyes. An easy smile drifts across her face. I tell her to conserve her energy, but my sister was never one to obey me.

"I knew you'd come," she says weakly. "I knew you'd come for me."

"What happened?" I ask.

"What did you think would happen in a place like this, my dear sister?" she asks.

I look away. "I'm sorry."

"Tell me about your travels and the wonders you've seen," she says. "You were always the more successful one."

I don't want to tell her anything. I just want to hold her.

"There is no place in this world for a goddess like me anymore," she says. "I have failed. What do you think life will be like in the next phase?"

"Don't talk like that," I say.

"Will someone paint a mural of me?" she asks. "Will you make sure that I at least get that?"

"Just a painting?" I ask. "There are other ways to live forever."

"I think a painting would be nice," she says. A terrible coughing fit seizes her, and I squeeze her hand, tell her to take her time.

Her voice goes hoarse. "It was your subjects, you know," she says. "They put me here."

I wince at the thought of my sister being accosted in a dark alley. This is my fault.

She takes my hand, and a tear jumps into her eye. "I've held out long enough. I can finally rest. But, Sister—"

She holds out her other hand and motions me closer. I lean in.

"You won't let your dear Goddess of Justice die without justice, will you?"

A devilish smirk spreads across her lips as I recoil. My ears buzz as she laugh-coughs.

"In the name of all those you've harmed throughout history," she says, rolling back her bedsheet. Her body is covered with dynamite.

I run for the door and scream as fire erupts around me.

* * *

THE ONLY WAY a goddess can die is to be forgotten by her subjects, but it doesn't mean injuries aren't inconvenient.

The explosion destroyed two floors of the hospital. No one died. My sister made sure there were no patients on the floors. Her blast was aimed at me and me only.

I spend a few minutes heaving in a stairwell, my body blackened and broken. I am just burnt skin and bone.

I tap into an ancient spell I learned from an old god.

Shadows swirl around my body and regenerate my skin. Every cell in my body still burns as if I'm on a grill.

I cry for my sister. She always knew how to make my life difficult when she wanted to. She is gone now, forgotten to the ages.

Weakened, I climb down the stairwell and out of the lobby as firefighters rush in and begin evacuating the place. I wave them away as they ask if I'm okay. Of course I am.

I stagger like a zombie into the parking lot amid rain, mist, and swirling siren lights.

Katrina, Mr. Boyfriend, and Goon Face are in the car, watching curiously.

"What the hell happened up there?" Katrina asks.

"Drive," I say.

"When do we get our money?" Goon Face asks.

"As soon as you drop me off," I say, directing him out of the parking lot.

We ride in silence for a while. I can't get my sister's broken body out of my mind.

Suddenly, Goon Face turns down an alley, against my directions. I sigh. Here comes the betrayal. "This is the part where you attack me for real and take my money," I say.

Katrina raises an eyebrow.

"I told you that I know you better than you know your-selves," I say. "As you ought to know, your betrayal means there is never going to be any money."

I reach up, grab Goon Face's head, and snap his neck. His foot lands on the accelerator and the car zooms ahead like a racecar.

We crash into a dumpster.

I punch Katrina and drag her out of the car, wrapping my arm around her neck.

Mr. Boyfriend tears out of the car, but I pull out my snub-nosed pistol and shoot him in the back. He crashes to the ground and stops moving.

"No!" Katrina cries. She struggles against me, slipping out of her hoodie. She overpowers me in my weakened state. Katrina is wearing a white shirt underneath her hoodie. She backs away from me, shaking her head.

A reflection on her shoulder catches my eye.

A tattoo. No — a glowing rune.

Of a scale.

"How did you get that?" I ask.

Katrina grabs her shoulder and says, "She told me you'd be a bitch."

I aim my gun at her, inching my finger toward the trigger.

"Kill me if you want," Katrina said, "but she'll avenge me. I'll have my justice."

"That explains why you were such a bad criminal," I say. "You're a warrior of the light, then. Why didn't you just say so?"

"Thanks for the advice," Katrina said. "If you're going to do it, do it."

Now I'm the one hesitating. I lower the gun.

Even Katrina is surprised. I can only watch as she turns and runs. She disappears around the corner, and I wonder if I'll ever see her again. For her sake, I hope not.

I cast my gun aside.

Above, the stars are shrouded by the clouds. The rain drenches me, and the red taillights of the car cast me in a diagonal beam of red.

The only way a goddess can die is to be forgotten by her subjects, and it seems my sister is not so forgotten.

Her laughter reverberates through my skull, a mockery that she'll never let me forget. She'll be reminding me of this night a thousand years from now. But in this moment, she's got a lot of explaining to do.

I stalk through the rain, back to the hospital to finish what we started.

* * *

MICHAEL LA RONN, *also known as M.L. Ronn, has published over 80 science fiction and fantasy novels and self-help books for writers.*

His fiction includes the urban fantasy series Good Necromancer, *the dark fantasy series* Last Dragon Lord, *and the futuristic science fiction series* Android X. *Currently, he writes primarily urban fantasy.*

His nonfiction books for writers include the bestselling Be a Writing Machine, *which teaches how to beat writer's block forever, and* The Pocket Guide to Pantsing, *which explains how to confidently write a novel without an outline.*

Michael also runs the award-winning YouTube channel "Author Level Up," with over 40,000 subscribers and 2,000,000 views. Writer's Digest *voted the channel one of the "Best Resources for Writers" in 2020.*

Michael devoted himself to the writing life in 2012 after a near-death experience, and writes 10 to 12 books per year despite working a demanding full-time job as an insurance executive, raising a family, and attending law school classes in the evenings. His productivity methods are so effective that his YouTube subscribers have accused him of being a cyborg in disguise (he pleads the fifth).

For more information about Michael's books, visit his fiction website at www.michaellaronn.com and his resources for writers at www.authorlevelup.com

JOVE TWO

KEVIN A DAVIS

The claxons of Jove Two station rang of betrayal, heavy boots thudded on metal plating, and frenzied red lights lit the gray walls of the corridor.

In my ear, my comms crackled. "Captain Lewis, confirmed holes in the *Testament* and *Iraldi*." The young, high-pitched voice of my ship's new communication officer, Dane, echoed his worry. "What do you want us to do, Ma'am?" This was his first tour on my transport ship of the past six years, the *Constantine,* and not at all what I'd promised him. It wasn't the casual lunch at port that I'd expected, either.

I grimaced at his panicked tone and kept mine level as I ran. "Tell them to keep up our defenses, but don't fire if you're not being attacked. Stay moored unless someone starts shooting at the *Constantine* or the docks are compromised." It wasn't easy sounding calm in my haste. "I'm bringing refugees." *One at least.*

Running beside me was dark-haired Kaya, an employee and resident of Jove Two and my long-time friend. Behind us, my interpreter droid Traz, short for TRZ3028, ran with silent grace. In the halls around us were a hundred or so frantic inhabitants of Jove Two.

"Refugee." Kaya repeated the word breathlessly as if tasting it. Her usually pleasant features screwed tight with worry and the strain of running. "Who's attacking us?"

"I'm assuming terrorists from the Lunarni Rebellion." The wars had long ended, and no pirates had this kind of firepower. There had been a time, long ago, when I would have joined the defenders instead of searching for a way back to the docks to save my own skin.

Over a delightful lunch, I'd been joking with Kaya about her garish red, yellow, and blue coveralls. When missiles holed two docked ships, the explosions rocked the table. Within seconds, the station's alarms interrupted our expensive cheese appetizer. I'd contacted the *Constantine* immediately, and the subsequent volleys ventilated sections of the spokes which connected to the central docks. I wouldn't be keeping my 1430 meeting with a potential new client.

"Are they going to destroy the station?" Kaya asked. Present media made out the Lunarni to be violent.

My chest was tight from exertion and concern, but I still managed a grim smile. "No, I don't think so." We'd likely be dead already if the attackers wanted to vent the station. The corridor we ran down was one of six in the single outer ring of Jove Two. Shaped like a wheel around an axle, the spin of Jove Two simulated as much force as Mars's gravity. The station supported its inhabitants in the wide outer rim, and ships docked at the stationary central axle. The spokes provided transport between the two sections. We needed a greenlit tube to access the center of the station.

Once the attacker had taken out the defenses, they could have punched enough holes into the hull or the power plant to finish us off. We'd been running for a couple of minutes, and it hadn't happened. Instead, we'd heard gunfire, but that could be security and a panicked mob. The scrubbed air stunk of burning electrical fumes. I tensed, hoping the new hire didn't lose it. I had a good crew; they just needed to hold it together for a few minutes. One working tube and we'd be at the docks and away from Jove Two.

The people ahead of us faltered, then doubled back to run toward us in a panic.

Above the clamor, the pop of small arms sounded, echoing on metal walls. "Crap." I grabbed Kaya's arm, pulling us to a stop. Far down the curve, people were stampeding recklessly. This part of the station held administrative offices, and they wouldn't be opening their doors for anyone. Some people tried anyway.

A dozen rounded archways on the corridor walls were within a quick run, but only three were marked with screens, possibly cross passageways to other corridors on the outer wheel of the station. "Traz, access maps. I need the closest public door, doesn't matter where it leads."

Wiping the light sweat from my brow, I swept my hands over my peach fuzz scalp and finished with a pinch at my neck. I'd shaved my black hair to a buzz cut, partly to ignore the gray strands that had popped up in the past few years.

"Gamma-78 leads through a meditation garden to the next Alpha corridor." Purposefully made with only the remotest likeness to a human, Traz had no distinct eyes or mouth, just vague shapes and indents in their silver head. Still, they motioned as gracefully as a human would toward one of the arches. I'd grown fond of the useful droid over the years, and always brought them to ports whether or not I expected to need their translation services. Traz pointed an articulate finger at a doorway on our side of the wide corridor, three doors closer than where everyone was running from.

"Damn." I tugged on Kaya's arm and raced in the opposite direction of everyone else, toward the danger.

We'd passed the first door when I slowed at the sight of three gray uniformed security officers who backed down the corridor firing their bean slings, crowd deterrent guns that did little more than sting and welt. One of them had a dark splotch on her side which she favored; the wound screamed of a more potent weapon than the station security's standard issue. A collo bullet, a colloidal pellet with a post-fire boost, was the most likely culprit. Military grade weapons meant the intruders had come prepared to breach. The station security had to have some real armaments somewhere.

As we passed the second door, one of the security team took a bullet to the throat and dropped, and another turned and ran, leaving the already wounded woman firing in a frenzy. I ran at full tilt as Kaya puffed alongside. We just needed to make it to the door for now.

Dane's high-pitched voice crackled through my comms. "Captain Lewis, someone tried the docking hatch. Should we leave, Ma'am?"

Crap. "Did they get into the airlock?" I reached the third door and slapped the vid screen. This kid had not joined up for a battle. I'd be lucky if my crew didn't take the *Constantine* and leave me behind.

"No, Ma'am."

I gestured Kaya inside. "Probably just a frightened dock-worker. I'll be there soon and clear the entry." A lie, but it might hold my ship docked for a few extra minutes. Pushing Traz behind her, I stood at the opening and peered down at the defending security officer. The feet of her attackers were in view below the curve. They wore heavy, white magboots. Military planning would have them breach the hull rather than come through the spokes and get pinned in an airlock against defenders. The attackers wore full, white EVA suits, confirming my suspicions.

The other female security officer went down, and I stepped back, letting the door slide shut. I wasn't here to fight the battle of Jove Two. We'd get Kaya back to my ship and putter my transport back into space.

I wasn't Corp anymore; I'd discarded the battle red and blue over a decade ago. Unarmed, I wore a jumpsuit from my transport, gray with the company's blue insignia designed into the upper right arm. The *Constantine* shipped hydroponics and spice out of Earth and brought ice and rare metals back.

The meditation garden was clear of people. Fresh, earthy growth and floral scents drifted in the air. An indistinctly lit dome from ceiling to floor encompassed a central round of grass and an encircling garden of flowering trees and groomed pines. Past the branches stood the arch of the door leading to the next outer rim corridor, a duplicate of the one we'd just left, hopefully lacking the gun-wielding attackers.

"Traz, check the opposite corridor. Try not to be seen."

Ingrained training warned me that the sanctuary, with only two exits, could turn into a trap. Options hadn't been at a premium. I had left military life behind, but the old reactions sprang to life. I studied the curved walls and floors for an opportunity. The lights were seamless, and the scrubbers were small, unobtrusive stacks among the plants.

Inconsiderate of any danger, Traz strode across the grass toward the opposite door while I settled Kaya in the thickest of the tightly trimmed pines. "Wait here." Jove Two security didn't allow weapons on the station, and I sorely missed my holster.

I jogged the thin trim of metal walkway surrounding the garden and found no hatch allowing access into the inner crawlways of the station. It had been an idle hope.

The door ahead protruded, cutting an arch in the curve of the dome with the phrase "Inner thoughts; outer peace" scrolled in five languages at the top. Traz approached it with a confidence I didn't feel. They could handle a few collo shots, but they weren't indestructible. The door hissed open at Traz's instruction. I heard a yell outside and tensed as Traz quickly tapped the panel to close it again. "I am afraid I have been spotted." They spoke with only the slightest emulation of emotion, as if they'd spilled wine on a customer's carpet.

I launched into a run for Traz. "How close? How many?"

"Eleven meters. I only saw one man standing in an EVA suit to the right of the door. The corridor was empty." Their head tilted as if they were about to apologize.

The arch over the door had a deep lip, so I ran and jumped in the low g to scramble over the doorway. I leaned against the curve and spoke just loud enough for Kaya to hear. "Everybody stand visible, hands up as if surrendering." I had no idea what the orders were for the attackers, but they had no qualms about killing security. My experience had not been positive in these kinds of situations. Too many times we'd found the cargo bays floating with corpses.

My tenuous position on the archway wouldn't have worked in Earth's gravity, but I'd never battled on Earth.

Traz calmly turned to face the door as they raised their arms. Kaya looked unsure, but popped out of her thin cover and stood on the other side of the meditation garden in her bright array as if an oversized flower.

There would be two soldiers. There were always two. They would see Traz first, then Kaya, keeping their focus on them instead of above their heads. At least, I hoped. I had a very slim window of opportunity, and a lot depended on how they reacted when they came inside.

As the door slid up, a gun-wielding hand pushed inside. The man's white EVA suit had splatters of blood on his left side that continued up to his chubby, stubbled face. He was quick to point his collo pistol at Traz's forehead and step inside with barely a glance around the room. The colloidal bullet would dent the droid and could potentially foul a sensor, at most.

"What are you doing?" the man asked Traz. His EVA helmet was attached sloppily, indicating that this soldier had never been in battle before today.

I strained to see a second man, and though I heard footsteps and a distant gunshot, I spotted no other boots heading toward the door. Out in the main corridor, there were a few bodies on the floor, one dressed in security coveralls. Releasing my magboots, I folded at the waist to begin my fall.

Belatedly, our attacker spotted Kaya and shifted farther away from Traz. Surprised, he swung his weapon back and forth between them.

I adjusted with a slight shift of weight from one foot to the next, then flipped off the archway and grabbed the man's wrist. He sucked in an audible breath as I shifted into his view.

The second man, bursting tight in an EVA suit, puffed the last few steps toward the door. His eyes widened, and he stopped as I dropped down on his comrade.

I twisted my target's wrist using my momentum. We landed on the floor together, and I snapped the back of my head into his fleshy face. I kept him firmly on my back as cover. His second, were he military, would have taken a shot before then, but he hadn't fired. My victim's gun clattered to the floor without him ever firing. I could feel his body tense from his twisted arm.

A collo could pierce an EVA and a body, but rarely exited the meatier parts. However, my arms and legs were viable targets, so I jumped to the side, twisting the first man's arm in the opposite direction. Blood flowed out his nose as he grimaced with an open mouth. His weapon waited just behind my left boot. His huffing partner still watched from outside, his gun drawn but pointing toward the floor as if too heavy. Sweat beaded on his shaved upper lip.

I slapped against the curve of the dome, exposing only my arm. "Close the door," I told Traz.

The pinned man tried to leave as the door hissed closed. Lifting his arm up, I kicked him low enough in the chin to snap his head back. He relaxed and I let him go just as the door sealed. He folded to his side, back to the door. These men were inept, or untrained at least, but I didn't have time to feel sorry for them.

Scooping up the weapon with my right hand, I checked its load then dropped to the floor. Using the unconscious soldier for cover, I nodded to myself. "Door open." With the muzzle in the crook of the man's neck, I aimed where the second man's head had been. As the door slid, I fired and pinned a red hole in his forehead. "Get the body," I said to Traz.

Traz moved quickly to comply. My blood raced, and a shiver of guilt ran down my neck in an almost giddy satisfaction at my survival. Part of me reveled in the action. I'd caused a scene and noise, so I should be focused on getting back to my ship, but a tiny sliver of my former self wanted to join the defense of Jove Two.

"You killed them," said Kaya. She had to speak from across the garden as she hadn't moved, and I barely heard her over the ringing in my ears.

I took a deep breath, holding my position while Traz grabbed the dead man's feet and glided back toward me. There were no sounds of retribution, gunfire, or even a yell, so I relaxed slightly. "I did."

I now had two EVA suits that matched the invaders. Most importantly, they might offer the ability to cross any holed sections and get to my ship in the center of the station. I had no intention of joining the defense of Jove Two.

I dragged the unconscious man to the edge of the garden and checked his sleeve readout. He had forty minutes of oxygen left. Traz reached me dragging the heavier man. "Close the door. Then, get him out of his suit."

The Lunarni Rebellion had followed the footsteps of the Galilean freedom movement, but upped the stakes. If these were those terrorists, they weren't very well trained. I had agreed with the Galileans as they moved for a peaceful separatist cause. The Lunarni had begun by blowing up the Marsnad security building on Io after the Dome 42 incident. I'd lost a distant cousin working for Marsnad security and based most of my opinion on her death and the difficulty it might cause my present contract. Evidently, I'd been correct about it affecting my job.

"You killed them," Kaya repeated her observation, closer behind me.

Technically, I'd only killed one. "Yes. Pick a suit, or wait here and hope they're taking captives." I winced at the cold comment. In my time as merchant captain of the *Constantine*, I'd grown easy-going, affable, and relaxed. This sudden return of my martial training didn't bring any subtlety or diplomacy. "I don't believe we have a lot of choices here. I'm going to rely on my instincts to survive. They might be a little brutal, in your opinion."

Kaya didn't approach as Traz and I carefully removed the EVA suits. She might decide to wait it out here in the meditation garden. The same desire to defend the station pricked at me to protect her. People had to make their own choices.

I'd just freed the unconscious man's suit when the opposite door, the one we'd originally come through, hissed open. Without thinking, I crouched with the collo in my hand and aimed just to the right of Kaya's brightly colored hip.

The man who trained his gun at me I hadn't seen in just under a decade. He and the man behind him wore the EVAs of the intruders with deep brown splatters of dried blood.

Johann's stern features always managed to charm the ladies, were they so inclined. I'd met him as a cadet when Mars threatened Earth and all the young and foolish had run to join the Corp. The skirmishes had taught us how to fly and eventually captain ships. He'd served as my First when I commissioned the cruiser *Rompo*. Tense, deadly moments, long hauls, and close survivals had cemented our friendship. We'd kept in touch, more so in the beginning, and less so this past decade when the war was just a tale told at the bars.

He didn't seem as surprised to see me as I was to find him here. "Anne?" he asked in an almost casual tone.

"Johann. What's going on?" Neither of us lowered our guns.

"I'm trying to get to my ship. How about you?"

"Same." I wavered. If he'd come in two minutes later, I would have been dressed the same as him. "What's your ship?"

"*Testament*. Yours?"

I didn't answer. "When was the last time you talked with your ship?"

"Lost contact just before the explosions." He lowered his weapon and gestured to his man. The branches of a finely trimmed pine covered the other face, but I saw his weapon lower. "I'm holstering. Let's plan to get back to our ships. We're docked near each other. You were contracted with the *Constantine* the last I heard."

Kaya had blanched where she stood, and sidled closer to me as they approached. Traz had paused initially, but continued removing the corpse from the EVA suit.

"The *Testament* was holed." I watched his expression. A cruel, hard test on my part, but he staggered mid-step.

His face tightened. "Confirmed?" A confirmation indicated no life signs, not that the ship had been fired on or its hull and shields pierced.

I nodded. "I'm sorry."

He strode quietly across the grass, followed by a thin-faced man with overly large eyes that gave him a wild, out-of-control appearance. The whites of the man's eyes dominated his face. I didn't trust him.

Johann glanced at Kaya, then to the two suits. "I see we still think alike. I might need your help, if your ship survives." He patted his holster. "Six rounds left." He jerked a thumb over his shoulder. "Malcomb has three left." He returned his glance to Kaya. "Four of us and the droid?"

I stood up with the EVA suit and nudged my chin. "That's Kaya. She works on Jove Two." My introduction left her the opportunity to decide what she was going to do. There was a spare magazine on the belt, but I didn't offer any to Johann or his friend, not yet.

Kaya was tense, but she fluttered a smile. "Used to." Her voice sounded close to breaking. "I suppose my best bet is with you."

"Traz." I motioned them to give her the EVA suit. "Have you suited up before?"

"Every six months we have a mandatory class." She reached out and paused at the sight of blood, dried on the outside of the suit.

"It'll have to do. Don't panic, and you'll be fine." I kicked off my boots, sighed, and hoped that my trust of Johann and his man wasn't bad judgment on my part. Even just Johann and I would have a better chance getting through untrained rebels. "Lunarni?" I asked Johann.

He offered to help as I stepped into the stiff EVA. "That's my guess. Any word from your ship? It would be nice if the Corp still patrolled. Best we have out here is Marsnad."

"My comms hasn't relayed any contact, and my Chief officer would certainly send news of Corp or Marsnad ships." If my crew hadn't deserted me already. I gestured for him to help Kaya, who moved too slowly for my taste. I slid my newly acquired gun into the holster on the side of the EVA suit. My mental mode had switched quickly once I'd been in the skirmish, and it was hard to turn it off. "We need to get moving while they are still clearing station security. Is that corridor clear?" I nodded toward the entrance where we'd originally come in.

"No. But we were able to move freely in the EVAs. Security is on the run." He gestured toward the nearer door. "We think we can reach a spoke back to the docks closer to the center of the outer ring. Which is that corridor."

I had my arm in my right glove and motioned for Traz. "How near is the next tube back to the docks?"

Traz tilted their head slightly. "We were almost there. About where we spotted the fighting." Once we suited up and the helmets were properly stored at our backs, Traz opened the door.

Gunshots sounded in the distance. I grimaced at the taint of electrical fires coming from the air scrubbers. I led with my weapon drawn, Johann followed with his, and we scanned the corridor. My suit hung badly at the waist, too tall for my frame. Kaya's was worse.

The corridor held more bodies than I'd noticed during the skirmish. One on the far wall had been moving at first, wounded, but lay quiet as we exited in the white EVAs of the intruders. I picked up the extra weapon when we passed it. Traz wouldn't touch it and Kaya didn't have the training, so I tucked in my thigh pouch. I still hadn't offered Johann or Malcolm any extra ammunition.

The corridor was empty. Residents were finding places to

hide. Without any apparent threat, we holstered our weapons.

I jogged the long strides of low gravity beside Johann. "Sorry about your people."

He didn't respond, obviously upset.

Traz worried me. I didn't guess that many of the intruders had an interpreter droid in their party. We'd have to talk fast if we came upon anyone. They seemed to be sweeping the outer ring, badly, or perhaps just looking to engage and kill off the station's security. I watched the distant edge of the curve for company. There were clusters of security bodies; most had secondary shots to the head. I tried not to fall into protector mode at the sight. It took several minutes to reach the next tube leading to the central part of the station.

The tube light was red, indicating a closure. The most likely scenario was that the corridor had been holed by the terrorists. We had the EVA suits, so we could try and work around it. "Traz, can you find us access ports to get us into an airlock?"

Kaya paled. "Can't we just try the next one? The corridor is empty."

Johann nodded. "I agree. One more. Traz can work on alternates if we get there and find a problem."

I'd talked Kaya into coming with us, and didn't want to risk leaving her. I agreed, opened my comms, and offered a cheerful tone. "Dane. Things have quieted down here. Security appears to be gaining control. I'm still bringing in a few refugees, just to be safe. How are things there?"

"It's over?" Dane asked. His voice pitched high and hopeful.

"Not quite. Keep the doors locked 'til I get there. Just to be safe." I cut the connection, satisfied that the *Constantine* hadn't left without me. "Let's hurry." Jogging, I let Johann catch up and keep a step ahead. His man, Malcolm, led the way down the corridor.

"Do you get the itch?" I asked Johann quietly. "To jump in and join the defense?"

He took a breath in and out, then shook his head. "I can't say that I have."

I frowned. Either Johann had softened even more than me, or I was missing something. They'd killed his crew. There were station residents lying among the security bodies.

Malcolm, Johann's shady friend, spoke quietly to himself, as if on comms. It couldn't be their ship he was talking to. They could have friends on the station, but my mind jumped to more nefarious possibilities.

I needed some sense of what Johann had been up to since we last talked, just over five years prior. We had sat at a bar together a year after Aram, Johann's son, had died leaving a wife and child, Jojo. "How's the grandkid?" I asked.

"Bitter and wild. Gives his mother a hard time. I tried to get him into what's left of the Corp. He blames them for Aram's death." Johann trailed off.

"You did too."

He nodded. "Probably where the kid got it from."

Malcolm dropped back, and Johann strode ahead so they could talk without me hearing. A cold hollow spread in my chest. Their EVA suits fit too well. If he were one of the terrorists, he'd know which ship to mention to get my sympathy. He wasn't the level of the chumps I'd taken down; he would be an officer.

I stopped, forcing them both to turn and face me. "Are you involved with these terrorists? Are you even captain of the *Testament,* or was that a lie?" My hand dropped to my holster. I had a clear view of Johann and Malcolm and kept Kaya behind me.

Johann stopped, wiping his face, and studied me. His hand flicking to the side, commanding Malcolm to stand down, told me everything. "This whole mission has gone sideways. The men are untrained and out of control. We've taken the station, but some squads have begun hunting administrators. And you're on board. I didn't expect that. Let's just get you and yours to the dock."

Rage burned in me, mostly from the betrayal. "If you know this, then stop it."

"My lieutenants are bringing the men in line." Johann pointed his thumb over his shoulder. "Malcolm knows the objectives and is relaying my updates."

Kaya choked behind me. I heard her scuffling footsteps, but I couldn't take my eyes off Malcolm or Johann. "Why?" I asked. Her echoing footsteps built up speed as she ran away.

"I could ask you the same. Last time we talked, you supported the Galilean freedom movement. The United Earth and their corporations would never give up without a fight. The Lunarni are that fight."

"They're terrorists." I bristled at the implication I should sympathize.

Johann touched his lips in thought. "In the newsfeeds, yes. Do you realize we've taken Io? The feeds don't mention that. The people have thrown full support behind us." He motioned to the bodies. "Though some of them are a little fanatical."

I stiffened, knowing he was trying to recruit me. "A little? You can't expect me to condone the murders."

"No. I don't. We expected to have to kill some of the security, but the residents were to be corralled and held peacefully. We could use calmer heads in the organization, those who have been trained to follow a mission to the letter."

I grimaced and wanted to spit in disgust that he'd even consider recruiting me to his madness. "You haven't told me why *you* needed to be a part of this." We'd be at an impasse soon. I wouldn't survive the two of them, even if I got off both shots. I'd aim to wound Johann. I couldn't kill him.

He shrugged. "Wasn't much. Brought a shipment of food out to Callisto. When there was a shortage in the return cargo, I was told to jettison half my load. People would go hungry, maybe starve because it fit the corporate scales. The Lunarni rebels aren't terrorists, they are freedom fighters."

I'd heard similar stories of corporate corruption and greed, but it didn't bring me to murder. Sweat had started earlier with the jogging, but now rivers ran down my sides. We'd either come to an agreement, or I'd have to consider shooting an old friend, or him me.

When the gunshot rang out from across the hall, my gun was in my hand. The collo bullet thudded on the wall behind Johann.

A pair of his own soldiers stood in the opening of a door. They could clearly see us. Smoke drifted in front a shaggy-faced man. The second, stained already with blood, raised his weapon toward us. I had assumed wearing the intruder's EVAs would avoid this. Traz couldn't be as easily camouflaged.

I fired a split second before Johann. My bullet caught the man about to fire in his shoulder. The foam of his EVA suit puffed toward the door frame.

Both of Johann's men went down. The one I shot crawled to the side.

The Johann I knew from the Corp growled at Malcolm. "I wanted this corridor cleared." The trappings of gentle talk and politeness were gone. He snapped a glance at Traz, then at the gun in my hand. The façade dropped over his expression once again. He lowered his weapon slowly. "Can we just get you out of here?"

Malcolm, though he did not point at me, did not lower his gun.

I might have just saved Johann, or Malcolm. My instinct had been self-preservation. This left us with three guns drawn, and two different sides. I was grateful Kaya had left. For the first time, I believed that Johann truly meant for me to escape.

"Why did they fire?"

Johann swore. "I don't have many ex-military to work with. They aren't trained, and most are hot-heads. I haven't met with them all, and they need training." He pointed an accusing finger at Traz. "The droid is going to cause suspicion and confusion. Leave it here or at least make it find its own way back to your ship."

I had a fondness for Traz; we were getting out together. "Not happening."

Johann frowned. "I've outlined a path back to your ship, and the cruiser there will not fire on you. Take whomever you want." His tone had dried out. He no longer attempted to recruit me. Johann holstered his gun and flicked a hand toward Malcolm in a signal to do the same.

With the standoff and attack over, my racing pulse sounded like steel drums in my ears. I'd spent years dulling my life into simple, safe routines. I'd become a rusty knife. This afternoon I'd found I could still cut, but for self-preservation, not a cause such as Johann held. I lowered my gun to the floor and took the safer path. "What is the route?"

"I can show you." Johann sighed and nudged his chin toward his dead men. "It is safer if I go with you." He gestured toward Malcolm. "I can leave him."

I couldn't trust Johann. On the most immediate level, he appeared to want me to survive based on our years of friendship in the Corp. That perception of him didn't coincide with the corpses strewn across the floor, which confirmed what I had known of the Lunarni terrorists. I still had the nagging desire to join the defense, despite the odds. I didn't want to walk beside him with those conflicts at my back.

"I'll take my chances alone," I said. The response was automatic, and I couldn't be sure it was the right thing. I'd become so soft in my merchant ship role that I questioned my decisions.

Johann nodded. "Understood. I'll send you the cleared path. The tube ahead is vented. They all are. We needed to keep security away from the central core. They have orders to blow the reactor if we seem like we'll take the station. You can access the airlocks and get back into the spoke. From there it's a quick run." He raised his arm console and tapped in commands.

Mine beeped and vibrated in receipt. "Why is this station so important?"

"It's a symbol. When we alert the other moons that we've secured it and divvy up the food, they'll see the rebellion as viable. We need ships, supplies, and trained fighters. The media outrage will make sure we get that."

"You really think security is going to risk their own lives and kill thousands?"

"There are military personnel on the station. Scorched earth is their specialty. We did worse when we were in the Corp."

The flash of memories stiffened my jaw. I glanced down, waiting for him to leave. "Goodbye, Johann."

As they strode away with quick steps, I sent Traz the route. "Traz, analyze this for potential issues." I both trusted Johann, and didn't. His men would shoot me on sight with an interpreter droid following.

I jogged toward the redlit tube entrance and opened the emergency hatch beside it. The air inside had been badly scrubbed and stunk of electrical fire. Beyond a maintenance airlock, metal rungs disappeared into the dark. I put my helmet on.

Traz spoke through comms as we took turns in the airlock. "I'm unclear about the airlock security at two points. Station maps mark them as code access only, but the received route shows them as open."

I began climbing. "Air requirements without deviation?"

"You will use ten minutes."

My pulse relaxed as I focused on a quick climb. "Optional routes if we're unable to get through airlock security?"

"None with our present equipment."

I was risking a lot on Johann's goodwill toward me, but I couldn't come up with a better option. Airlocks were supposed to have emergency access, but corporations didn't always play by the rules if they suspected sabotage or espionage.

I opened my comms to the ship. "Dane, things are looking good here. A couple of the refugees are going to stay after all. I'll be there in a few. Put on a pot of coffee for me, okay?" I'd likely be breaking out the good whiskey if I made it before they gave up and left.

"Oh, good. Will do, Ma'am." Dane's pitch was still high, but he sounded enthused. The crew would be pushing my officers to leave. They were good people, but not fools.

The next airlock Johann had routed us to opened easily and led me out of the wheel section into the spoke that connected the outer section of the station to the core. I sighed and hoped the airlock at the other end would be as trouble-free. Traz didn't vibrate on the rungs, and I had to glance behind to make sure they followed.

Metal debris floated inside the tube, and I easily found the head-sized hole that bent the hull to the inside and its corresponding exit. The ladder vibrated with the magnetic drives that kept the outer rings of Jove Two in motion.

By the time I reached the inner core, centripetal force had no semblance of gravity. I sensed the vibration and imagined the motion. I had only one obstacle between me and the docks. Any fantasy of joining the defense had evaporated as I neared my ship.

The airlock didn't open.

I tried a second time, glancing back at Traz and opening comms to them. "Options?"

"I've located an external airlock." They gestured toward a smaller maintenance lock that would barely fit the width of the EVA suit. "But I show nothing unlocked leading back inside. There are ships, of course."

My fingers tapped a plea to the airlock console a third time. "The *Constantine*?"

"Not the closest, but the system still shows it docked."

I pushed lightly to launch for the maintenance airlock they'd indicated, a circular hatch with a small video display. I'd never done an EVA with Traz, and though they had some magnetic pads on their feet, they weren't made for outside a ship or station. "Can you make it to the ship with me?"

"Most likely."

"Options?" I paused before activating the airlock.

"None."

I leaned my head toward them, incredulous. Traz could compute thousands of strategies.

They floated toward me. "None that are available within twenty-seven minutes of air."

I glanced down at my arm console. "Dammit." The airlock opened and I slid inside.

My boots clamped onto the metal hull of the spoke as it rotated lazily around the core of the station. The central cylinder with the spoked wheel spinning about it had a short end with three docked ships there, which gave the only hint of movement, while the other end formed the bulbous engine section with thrusters that still puffed out corrections. The EVA suit adjusted its temperature and dimmed the bright disc that was Jupiter.

The closest ship was either the *Testament* or the *Iraldi*, as a massive hole gaped in the fore section close to the dock. The farthest away was my *Constantine*. The only other ship between them was a hauler as well. Traz stepped out beside me. The rest of the docking ports were empty. They'd been half full when I docked. At least some had gotten away. I wasted a quick glance around, but didn't see any other holed ships. The hull vibrated through my boots.

I pointed to where our spoke slid inside a stationary lip at the core. "We cross over there." The speed differential would make the hop to a stationary surface tricky, but it was a shorter jump than from where we stood.

"The engine there will create magnetic instability." Traz followed me easily.

"Options?" I smiled and breathed easier as the *Constantine* swung back into full view.

"We are on the best course."

Stopping at the end of the spoke, my pulse rose. The jump would have to be timed to the release of my magboots so that I could counter the motion. I had a wide surface to hit, but I wasn't some rockhopper who spent most of my life in suits. The white-coated hull showed dents and chips giving more definition to the surface. We suddenly appeared to be moving much faster than I'd assumed.

Traz waited behind me. I had no doubt they would calculate the exact amount of thrust and angle needed for their hop.

I focused on the curved wall ahead of me. Because of the moving spoke I stood on, the central core appeared to turn away from me at its right side. I would aim for the edge of that surface and my own inertia would pull me to the center.

My heart leaped when I launched. I moved too fast and spun so that my back began to face my destination. Spasming with a flick of my left arm, I tried to turn. The spoke sped away, and Traz followed me gracefully with their arms out as if they were flying.

I coughed and sucked in a breath when I spun back to the core and saw my trajectory. I'd overcompensated. My jump would miss the hull of the core. Panic raced in my heart. I kicked on my magboots, straining to stretch them toward metal.

The gap between me and safety closed, but I'd miss by bare inches. Beyond the core, the massive wheel spun against blackness. I'd last a few minutes with the air I had. My chest tightened and my lungs refused to release a breath.

Traz pushed lightly on my shoulder, and I floated to the stationary surface. My boots clamped down, and I let out a shaky breath as they held. In my new orientation, the ships no longer spun along the axis; the spoked wheel churned above me.

Traz drifted away.

"Traz!"

They'd pushed me to safety and destroyed their own chances in doing so. "A calculated option," they said quietly in my comms. They likely had made their own jump with my imperfect launch in consideration. They were rolling away, reflecting Jupiter's cold light. Their voice continued calmly and smoothly. "No, there are no options. You have twenty-one minutes of air. I calculate navigating through the ship below to the airlock will take sixteen. You should start now."

I swayed at the loss, but nodded to Traz and took a step. Anger flared, as I blamed Johann and his rebels. I wouldn't waste Traz's sacrifice. My focus flicked between the ship ahead and the dwindling reflection from their metallic form. "Thank you." The words weren't enough.

Traz didn't reply.

My console read eighteen minutes when I reached the ruined ship.

Stenciled blue paint marked the *Iraldi* at the nose. I transitioned to the hull of the ship with ease. The docking clamps were secure, and Jove Two had green lights on the seal. When I walked down to the breach it proved to be three shots, grouped to make a hole still barely large enough for my EVA.

The galley had a dead woman floating inside. The lights were off, but I wasn't surprised with the amount of damage. I kicked on my suit lights and found the forward hatch closed with a yellow indicator light proposing caution. Considering the size of the hole in the hull, the pressure loss would have been so instantaneous that the hatches wouldn't have been able to close in time for the rest of the crew.

The next compartment showed as unpressurized, but the controls wouldn't override the safety. I opened the hatch manually and found three more bodies floating just inside with a cloud of debris. Two women and a man had been caught in surprise and sucked from their bunks or the table of their rec area along with whatever else that wasn't attached. The last compartment, the communications and helm area, held a single man, the chief according to his merchant ship insignia. Lights and equipment were lit. Alerts flashed on every panel.

I had eight minutes of air according to my console. If the airlock didn't work, I'd have to search the ship stores for a recharge. Beyond that, I didn't have a plan. I pushed off a chair's back to float to the front entry at the nose.

I sagged in relief when the airlock opened. The last leg of the trip would be easy, if I could trust Johann. If the core were manned by rebels, then Traz sacrificed themself for nothing.

The docks were empty except for a slew of floating droid tugs that awaited a task. Oxygen was good, but I left my helmet on. Ramps circled the walls and dropped to the next levels as if there were some sense of up or down in the zero gravity. A single cargo bin sat at a hatch above me, its drone patiently waiting for access that the station would not be giving any time soon.

"Anne, where are you?" Johann's voice crackled in my comms. His tone was tense and desperate.

I paused, scanning the empty docking area again. I couldn't see any danger, but his men were out of control. "What's wrong, Johann?" I held back most of the bitterness.

"Station security got to the core. We've lost the four men guarding it. It'll take them six minutes to disable the over-rides. Two of my patrols aren't responding. I can't get anyone there in time. Forty-five minutes after they get into the system, the core will cascade. I'll have to evacuate as many of my men as I can and let over ten thousand residents die out here. I've only got a light cruiser and a scout. They'll blame the Lunarni like before."

"They won't risk their own lives." I didn't want to believe station security would exterminate the residents.

"They don't have to. Once the system begins to cascade, our ships will ignore them and move in to evacuate us. They'll have time to get off station with whatever contingency plan they have. If we were in their place, we'd have a plan. They can't let us appear to win. At all costs."

I wasn't going to argue his politics. Kaya would die, along with other people I'd come to know on the station. The airlock to my ship was a half-minute run down two ramps. I could be long gone before the cascade began and out of range before the core blew. Anger burned hot on my cheeks for the station's security sabotage and at my own guilty consideration of self-preservation. "Dammit." I couldn't leave these people to die.

"Send me the coordinates," I told Johann. "Out." I knew where the reactor was and looked up the long stretch of the core. Elevators and ramps cluttered the view, but I could see the bulbous curves from where I stood.

I closed my eyes and switched over to my ship's comms. "Dane, have the chief get the *Constantine* out of here. The station's going to blow."

"Ma'am?" His voice quavered as if he might cry. "Yes, Ma'am. What about you?"

"Get my damn ship out of here." I closed the connection. As my arm console beeped and vibrated with Johann's data, I typed in a command to the closest tug, renting it for an hour. The droid responded and puffed thrusters to reach me, and I let out a slightly mad chuckle. I'd gone from considering joining the defenders to siding with the Lunarni.

The droid had a bar on the underside meant to link into cargo bins. Everyone in the Corp had taken spins across the hanger with them. I held on with one hand and set coordinates with the other. "Johann, any idea how many I'm dealing with?"

"Nope. I lost the two men inside when the doors were breached."

I could likely be dead before everyone else, if the team sent to blow the station had any numbers or skill. It was still the right thing to do.

I found the first of Johann's men floating in the core with a shot to the temple. A second drifted near an opening someone had blasted into the doors beside the ramps. The interior of the curved room was dark, so I approached the corpse closest to the door. Like the first, the shot entered the side of the head, so I guessed sniper.

My air timed out, so I loosened the seals on my helmet. The station air smelled of chemical blasting and electrical fire. Clamping my boots quietly onto the wall, I grabbed the man's leg and shifted him headfirst across the ruins of the doors.

A bullet tagged through his head and the body tried to tug away from me. Still, it gave me a direction for the shooter. Steadying the body, I removed my helmet and took a step closer to the shredded edges of the door. I swapped mags for the fresh nine bullets and took a spare moment to breathe.

I tossed my helmet with enough force to bounce off the inner deck. The sniper inside got off a shot, but missed. With my hand under the body's armpit, we leaned forward and I fired. My shot far off the mark, the sniper's bullet tore into the corpse's EVA and body. My second shot made the man flinch as the bullet bit into the railing of the high ramp where he hid, and my third collo took him through the chin.

My gunshots echoing in my ears made me realize the first man had been using a silencer. I released my boots and rolled inside. Part of me expected a meteor swarm of bullets; the other assumed they were elsewhere setting the station to explode. Did they have a way off the station, or was this suicide on their part? The latter meant people as fanatic as Johann's.

A whiff of chemical explosive hung in the air. The man I'd just killed wore a black EVA suit, as did a second corpse floating a few meters to my right. Two of Johann's people drifted higher up. At least they'd taken out one of the intruders for me.

My helmet had continued to ricochet off a wall heading toward a cluster of equipment near the center. A dark shape lifted an arm up from behind a console, aimed at my decoy, but didn't fire.

Pushing off the wall with both fists, I launched horizontally for the ramp that led toward the consoles. Skimming feet first over the metal grates that acted as a floor, I rolled over, aiming for the raised weapon.

A head rose from behind cover, slightly off from where I expected. I adjusted and fired, breaking my momentum. I caught the top of a shoulder, and he spun. If he'd gone down, I'd been lucky. I couldn't count on it.

My feet bumped the bottom of the ramp and I activated my magboots, straightening with the sudden stop. I guessed on the layout of the control consoles above me and raced up in a crouch.

A shot grazed across the left shoulder of my EVA, and I automatically dove, disengaging my boots. My console flared warnings, but I felt no pain. The bullet only caught the stiff outer suit.

Punching the floor, I rolled with my head up and arm out. A gunshot echoed as a muzzle flared, and I aimed at it, hitting a woman in the chest. She'd been the one who'd nicked my suit. I swore her last shot buzzed my hair shorter just behind my right ear. The recoil from my gun spun me. Spent gunpowder seasoned the air.

A dark silhouette hunched over the controls, dooming us all. I twisted to aim a careful bullet in the back of his head, not wanting to damage the equipment or screen where he sat.

When a bullet sank into my left magboot, my shot went high and missed. I grimaced at the pain, but the doomsday coder never even flinched.

My course pulled me to the left, both from impact and recoil. The shooter was the man I'd winged earlier. He was spread low on the metal grate, just below a chair and behind its pedestal. I could make the shot, but he might get me at the same time. That would end my troubles quickly and still mean a big problem for everyone else.

I kicked the floor with my good leg, and the bastard put a

second bullet in the same boot as I rose. My bullets were low, and I had a more pressing objective than returning his fire. The entire station's survival rested on the man working on the controls. If he succeeded, nothing else mattered. A flick of my left arm slowed my tumble, and I aimed.

My shot dropped the man sitting at the console. The recoil left me drifting backward at a tilt to the floor. Blood leaked from my boot in red globs. I'd risen high enough that I couldn't see the other shooter, but with a little shift on his part, I'd be fair game. With my second-to-last bullet, I fired for thrust. The recoil shifted me just high enough that the man on the floor missed me with his next shot from under the chair.

Rising out of any chance for control, I aimed where I expected him to pop up. Sweat pooled along my sides, and blood droplets trailed behind my foot. I took slow and steady breaths while I kept my aim.

A shape moved, and I foolishly fired into a soft, empty, EVA helmet with my last shot. I'd already thrown my gun in a side pitch, before the man rose. The toss rolled my side to him. A look of surprise flashed on his face as he dodged.

He was even more shocked when he popped back up and found I had a second gun. I caught him in the clavicle just above the heart. His shot went wide before he died.

My shoulder bounced against the curve of an outer wall.

I pushed myself toward the grates below and scanned the room for some last member of their team. If there had been one, I likely wouldn't have survived.

I holstered my gun and fumbled for the med pack in the back pocket of my thigh. When I reached the control deck I spoke on my comms. "Johann, clear. At least, they're dead and there are no lights flashing as if we're all going to vaporize." I unlatched my boot and stuffed medicated gauze where my middle toe used to be. Almost fainting at the pain, I squeaked, "Out." I couldn't be sure I'd hear him over the ringing in my ears.

His words were dim and distant, but clear. "Sit tight. My men will be there in two minutes. I'll be right behind them. We might have liberated some Glen Scotia 1992 that I'll bring with me." I could hear a familiar smile in his voice.

I shoved a compression wrap over my mangled foot, activated it, and screamed inside as I leaned back. I nodded in response, though he couldn't see me. "Kaya?" I asked. How would she feel to find out her employers had scheduled a small nova at her expense? Or, that I'd technically joined the Lunardi?

"I've got her and a score of admin stored away nice and safe with two of my best men." He coughed. "I also had my scout crew pick up something else. Luckily, they checked in with me before firing the ship's point defense."

At least Kaya was safe. My eyes closed and I felt exhausted. He had already offered whiskey, what else did I need? "What'd they pick up?"

Johann chuckled. "Did you happen to lose a droid?"

* * *

Kevin A. Davis is a fantasy author with two published series set in modern settings: the Khimmer Chronicles, featuring the lively assassin Ahnjii, and the AngelSong series, centering around the indominable Haddie. A multitude of his short stories have been published in anthologies. His newest series, the DRC Files, features Kristen, a witch with exceptional skill in magic, as the new agent on a secret team that tracks down the worst to seep through the realms.

Kevin resides in north Florida and attends conventions throughout the year either as a vendor, speaker, or a fan. As Inkd

Publishing, he publishes anthologies including the Hidden Villains *series.*

Visit his website at www.KevinArthurDavis.com, on Facebook at www.facebook.com/KevinArthurDavis, Twitter at https://twit ter.com/KevinADavisUF, or Instagram at https://www.instagram. com/kevinarthurdavisauthor/

KILLING KAREN

KAREN A. PHILLIPS

Something was wrong.

"I wonder where the other hikers are?"

The week before, I'd signed up for this outing with Join Up, an online meeting app for individuals with like-minded interests. I'd recently moved out of my ex-fiancé's house after a dramatic break-up worthy of an opera score — a crescendo of violence, building to a climax, then a sudden free fall into the crashing finale, leaving me stunned and disoriented. I found my own place and settled in. Weeks later, my emotions were still raw, but I was done with guilt. Done with regret. Like the phoenix rising from the ashes, I was ready to start over and meet new people.

"Any ideas?" Although concerned, I remained calm, while Sam, a Join Up member I'd only met an hour ago, stood next to me checking his phone.

Trusting in my previous experiences with Join Up, I'd agreed to carpool with him. Another member named Martha was to accompany us, and we chose a shopping center parking lot to leave our cars. Sam insisted on driving, so I buckled myself into the passenger seat of his luxury Range

Rover and looked around for Martha. That's when Sam informed me Martha had found other transportation.

"Do you still want to go?"

What were my options? Go home and beat myself up for all the bad choices I'd made in life? The failed marriages. The doomed relationships. The lies and betrayal. I decided to take my chances. We discussed the directions and agreed on a course. During the thirty-minute drive to the destination we made small talk, careful to avoid anything too personal.

Sam took a freeway off-ramp in Auburn and headed east across the Foresthill Bridge, the highest bridge in California and a popular destination for those who could no longer bear their unbearable lives. The American River, a ribbon of blue-green, wound through the canyon 730 feet below.

That's one helluva jump.

"Did you see the movie xXx with Vin Diesel? That scene where he drives the stolen car off the bridge? It was filmed here." Sam turned left onto a side road just after we crossed the canyon. He made a U-turn and parked under an oak tree facing out. "I want to make sure I don't get blocked in when the others get here," he said.

A man who planned ahead. Nice.

I slid from the leather seat and breathed in the fresh mountain air. I was eager to stretch my legs. We put on our backpacks and walked toward a nearby green metal gate that marked the entrance to the trail.

Birds chirped in the trees while the Friday commuter traffic roared by, en route to Interstate 80.

"What time is it?" I asked.

Sam checked his phone. "Eight ten."

I rooted around in my pack for a snack bar. I saw the knife I always carried on hikes — a useful tool. I finished eating, twisted the wrapper into a tight wad, and stuffed it into my pocket. I removed a canteen from my backpack and took a drink. It seemed like hours passed while we waited for the others to arrive.

"What time is it now?"

Sam glanced at me, a small frown on his lips. "Eight twenty."

Was he becoming impatient with me? "Wonder why they're late. You'd think the leader, at least, would've been here by now."

He looked back at his phone. "I don't have any new messages. I'm sure we're in the right place."

Sam pointed to the opposite side of the main road. "Look at that!"

A doe stood at the top of a bank overlooking the blur of cars rushing past. Her ears flicked back and forth, assessing the situation.

"I hope she doesn't jump," I said as I pictured the accident, the blood and gore, the mangled vehicles, the dead and dying.

As if sensing danger, the animal retreated into the brush and disappeared.

I turned to face the metal gate. Just beyond, the trail vanished into a thick forest of oak and pine. I needed to move. Staying in one place was not good for me.

"Thanks again for driving," I said, remembering my manners. "I have cash to help pay for gas."

Sam shook his head. "It's no problem."

I pulled the sleeves of my fleece jacket down over my hands. "Cold this morning."

He gave me one of those quick, top-to-bottom, looks. "'S'-posed to get to eighty degrees today. In Sacramento."

I suddenly felt self-conscious, my white legs covered in goosebumps. I wished I'd worn capris instead of shorts.

"I have a thing for Karens," Sam said.

I froze. A thing. For Karens. *Seriously?* "Oh?" I managed.

I was so OVER the Karen meme — the stereotype of a middle-aged, middle class, white woman who acts like she can get whatever she wants. My ex constantly goaded me about the Karen meme. He thought it was funny — until I finally snapped.

"My son's mother was a Karen," Sam said.

"Your son's mother?" I did my best to keep my tone neutral while taking a step back.

Sam watched me. "We never married. Then I was engaged to a Karen, but we discovered we weren't compatible."

I avoided his eyes. "What are the odds," I said, my breath catching as if a python were squeezing my chest. *Was he making fun of me?*

Sam grinned. "I told her once, 'I pick Karens so I can't mess up and say the wrong name.'"

I ignored the sick feeling in the pit of my stomach and smiled brightly. I looked around, annoyance turning to anxiety.

"But she didn't think it was funny," Sam continued, oblivious to my discomfort. "She was mad at me for two whole days."

Was he making this shit up? I turned my attention to the cars rushing by.

"She didn't get that I was kidding," he said, looking bemused. "I mean, it *was* a joke."

My therapist would ask, How was I feeling right then? Afraid I'd be forced into committing murder, I would answer. *Use your tools.* Think positive was one, but I'd be damned if I could recall the rest. I was glad I had taken all the self-defense classes.

Wait. Stop. Didn't your instincts tell you Sam was a good person? Otherwise, you wouldn't have ridden with him.

My emotions shifted to tolerant, and I considered the handsome, physically fit man standing before me dressed in clothes too nice for a hike. *Was that a silk shirt?* Smooth brown skin and black hair made it difficult to judge, but the receding hairline suggested he might be in his sixties, close to my age.

"Why did you decide to come on this hike?" I asked.

Sam's expression was unreadable. "I only signed up yesterday. I saw your question about carpooling and responded."

Just yesterday? I shivered.

A vehicle signaled and pulled into the turn lane.

"Here's someone," I said.

But the car passed us by and headed up the hill.

My muscles had stiffened in the cold. I paced the length of the green gate. "I can't believe we picked the wrong spot," I said, waving my arms in frustration.

Sam held his phone to me, where he'd been checking the All Trails app. "The map shows we're at the trailhead." He pointed a brown, well-manicure finger. "See the blue dot?"

I looked at the map and interpreted it the same as Sam.

"How could two seemingly intelligent people make the same mistake? It doesn't make sense. We went to the right place, but everyone else went to the wrong place?"

Sam typed on his phone. "I sent a text to Martha, letting her know where we are."

We waited for a response, but none came.

"What time is it now?" I asked.

"Great." He held his phone to the sky. "No reception."

I groaned.

"You know what," he said, "I say we go ahead. It's a wonderful day, and I have good company." He gave me an engaging smile.

I peered into the dark woods where sunlight struggled to break through. I hesitated.

Sam adjusted his backpack and smiled again, with just a

hint of anticipation crinkling the lines around his eyes. "What do you say, Karen? Shall we go?"

We plunged into the darkness. I swung my arms and flung my legs, hoping exuberance would chase away the asps of angst writhing in my belly. Sam matched my pace.

Loosening our limbs loosened our tongues. I found out he was single with an adult son from the "not compatible" Karen. Recently retired from Intel, he had a nice annuity from his stock options. I felt comfortable in his presence, wondering if he could have been Mr. Right in another time. Fate was surely messing with me.

When Sam asked about my personal life, I gave him the abridged version. Gradually I felt more at ease and something close to happy. For the first time that morning, I gave Sam a genuine smile.

He smiled back. "So, what's your ex-fiancé's name?"

Was, I corrected silently, the smile skittering away. "Sam," I muttered.

He stopped, his eyes bulging. "No shit?" He smacked his forehead, incredulous. "What are the chances?"

My skin prickled. "Can we just keep walking? Please."

Sam shot me a strange look before he faced forward and continued along the trail. A breeze picked up, rustling the leaves. The woods were dark and ominous, the shadows full of secrets. I imagined the ghosts of my past hovering among the branches, watching. After a few minutes I felt foolish. I was being overly dramatic. I glanced at my companion, and he raised his eyebrows. I grinned in response. He returned the smile, then laughed, and the tension blew away in the wind.

Then a twig snapped.

I stopped in my tracks. "Did you hear that?"

Sam nodded. "Maybe a pinecone? They can weigh a lot."

As if on cue, a large pinecone rolled onto the path and rested at my feet.

I gasped.

Sam laughed and forged ahead.

You think I'm just a silly woman? I followed, staring at a bald spot on the back of his head. He wasn't so attractive after all. The snakes slithered back into my belly and coiled there, waiting.

Lost in thought, I finally noticed the trail had become steep. I stopped to take a drink of water, then took off my fleece jacket and wrapped it around my waist.

Sam gave me a concerned look. "You've been awfully quiet."

I shrugged. "I'm okay." I returned the canteen to my backpack. The knife clinked against the metal, and I thought about the future.

He was staring at me.

What was his problem?

"Let's go," I said, heading up the trail.

After some time, we reached a level area. We stood in the shade under a large oak, practically hidden under the drooping branches. We looked over the rim and down at the river. The effect made me dizzy. I thought about Fate. I thought about men. I was tired of them underestimating me.

Sam took pictures with his phone. "How about a selfie?" he asked.

"First, let me take one of you."

He handed me the phone and stepped closer to the rim.

Before I could change my mind, I lunged toward him with my arms extended and pushed. I enjoyed the surprise on his face as I watched him spin around, his feet kicking loose a few stones, then he disappeared from view. I heard him scream, heard a thud, then nothing. His phone lay on the ground, the screen cracked. I picked it up and called 911. I explained the situation to the dispatcher, doing my best to sound horrified and upset.

I pulled out my own phone and read the last autoforwarded message Sam had sent to "Martha." *I really like this Karen. Could she be the one?*

I heard sirens approaching as I wandered back toward the trailhead, absently checking my phone for the next hiking trip on the Join Up app.

* * *

KAREN A. PHILLIPS lives in Northern California and writes humorous and occasionally creepy mysteries. She has several short stories published in various anthologies. Her characters are engaging and fearless. "Killing Karen" is based on a real event when she went on a hike with a complete stranger. Visit her at www.KarenAPhillips.com

THE LAST MERMAID

RACHEL NUSSBAUM

The first time I went to see the Harbor Witch, I was only eleven, no older than you are now. We'd all grown up hearing the stories of her. Her two makeshift boat-homes were tied together with rope and knotted old sheets, and the lone pier where she docked was so rickety and rotted it was abandoned save for her.

Those of us who'd grown up on the island knew she had power. A lot of our parents feared her and stayed away, but the older fishermen would go to her when their wives were sick, or when they wanted a protective charm put on their vessels before they went out in choppy seas.

We were just children, Alyssa and I, naïve and unsupervised in the summertime but too young to take the ferry to the mainland on our own. So, we wandered the wharf, desperate for something to happen in a town where nothing ever did.

Not unless we made it.

When the Witch finally answered our hollering and climbed on deck, she actually looked surprised to see us. I can imagine we were a sight — two sunburnt little girls, soggy clothes drenched in sand.

But she was more of a sight. I'd seen her before, but only from a distance. Picking up her grocery delivery from the end of her pier. Gathering dried seaweed on the beach. Up close though, she was something else. Her gray hair covered her like a shroud, long enough that dead ends kissed at her ankles. Her skin was mottled by sun and age, and her beady eyes darted between Alyssa and me.

I remember I almost turned and ran, but Alyssa grabbed my arm and wrenched me back.

"Show her," Alyssa hissed.

With shaky hands, I reached into our towel bag and pulled out the Polaroids we had taken by the shore.

"We found something," I said, my voice trembling with excitement and terror. "We think it's from a shipwreck!"

The Harbor Witch stared at us for what felt like ages. Finally, she disappeared below deck. We looked at each other and didn't know what to do. We thought she'd left.

Suddenly, she reappeared with a plank and let it slam onto the rickety wood of the pier.

The Witch led us to the bigger boat, over a makeshift bridge made of plywood that was hammered in with rusty nails. She walked slowly with her driftwood cane, and nervous as I was, I filled the silence with the story. How Alyssa and I had been exploring the shores, looking for adventure. How we'd found the battered cargo crates wedged deep in a secret cove. The wood was weathered and smooth, but the edges were splintered on the rocks. They'd washed up recently, after being underwater for a very, very long time.

"At least, that's our theory," I finished, nearly out of breath.

The Witch said nothing as I spoke, just slowly led us

inside. I expected her home to look worse, as it did on the outside, with its stacks of garbage and a hoard of drying seaweed.

It was cluttered, but an organized clutter, furniture and decor packed together tight but purposefully. There was seaweed drying, but it was neatly hung from the ceiling to wilt in the windows, among dozens of other herbs. The floors were layered in faded ornate carpets, and the cupboards and shelves were packed tight with jars and books.

The Witch maneuvered behind a coffee table and lowered herself into a seat. She winced, breathing deeply before exhaling.

Finally, she looked at my bag and extended her arm. The tips of her fingers poked from the ragged sleeves of her shawl, beckoning. I yanked all the Polaroids out and passed them to her, my heart pounding as her sharp nails skimmed my palms.

Quietly, she studied the pictures of the crates, eyes narrowed, face unreadable.

"My grandma said a ship went down in a storm when she was little," I said, trying to prompt some kind of response. "Nobody died, but they were never able to find the wreck, no matter how hard they looked."

"The *Iapyx*."

Alyssa and I both jumped at the sound of her voice.

"That's right," Alyssa nodded.

The Witch let the Polaroids fall to the table, then with her cane, reached under the table and hooked a case forward. "And you come to me with this. Why?" she asked.

I looked nervously at Alyssa. It had been her idea.

"You've got magic, right?" Alyssa pressed. "Can you use it to tell us where the ship is?"

"I know where the ship is."

She said it nonchalantly, didn't even look at the two of us for a reaction. Just opened her case and started pulling out jars of powder and candles.

"How do you know?" I asked.

"Saw it go down. Been there a few times since," she continued, arranging the contents of the case on the table. "Storm took her off course, and the evacuating crew floated far in their rafts before rescue. Salvage teams couldn't find her because they didn't know where to look. But you—"

The Witch snapped her head at us then. I swallowed and took a step back.

"What would you do if I told you where the *Iapyx* is?" she asked. "Tell a salvage crew? Convince someone, somehow, you know where the wreck lies?"

She raised a brow at us, then opened a box full of coarse salt. She reached in and pulled out a knife, then poured a vial of liquid over it.

"That isn't what you came to me for, though, is it? Not what you truly hoped for," she continued.

Alyssa and I glanced at each other. We didn't want grownups to explore the depths of a wreck, to have all that adventure and glory. We wanted it for ourselves. We wanted adventure. Something unforgettable. I was too afraid to ask for it directly.

But I saw that look in Alyssa's eyes. She wasn't.

"We want it." Alyssa said, turning back to the Witch.

The Witch pulled a match from the case, and held it under her knife. White smoke snaked around it, and the smell of salt filled my nose.

"Say what you want, child."

Alyssa took a bold step forward.

"I want to find the ship," she said. "I want to be the one who gets to explore it and find its treasure."

And suddenly, the Witch darted forward and sunk the knife into Alyssa's throat.

Blood splattered across the table and the Witch's face. Alyssa screamed. She flailed as the Witch grabbed her by the back of the hair with one hand and brought the knife back into her neck, over and over.

"Stop!" I gasped, backing away on trembling legs. "Stop it!"

The Witch paid me no mind, but on the next slash, she did stop. She let go of Alyssa and let her sink to the floor. She gasped hard, blinking up at us.

"Alyssa!" I shouted, rushing to her side. I reached out, trying to stop her bleeding with my bare hands.

Except on Alyssa's next gasp, the gashes across her neck parted. They weren't bleeding anymore. Alyssa stared up at me, pulling herself up and wiping the blood away from her neck. She took a deep breath, and the four slits on each side of her neck parted. She looked to the Witch, then to me with wide eyes.

The Harbor Witch grinned at us then. Her teeth were short and sharp.

"The wreck is to the northeast of the island, a mile and a half from where you found the crates."

And she turned to me and raised her knife.

"You as well?" she asked.

My heart raced, fear and excitement and wonder swirled all at once. I lifted my hair and rushed forward.

It hurt at first, but once the cuts were placed, that pain fizzled into a dull sting, the kind you get when you get water up your nose. When the Witch led us to the water and we jumped in, the water filled my gills and that sting faded away. I took a few breaths in and out, marveling at the way the water rushed down my throat. It felt like a satisfying gulp of fresh air. Alyssa dove deep and swam in circles around me.

"They'll heal when the sun sets," the Harbor Witch called from her boat. "Don't linger in the depths when the light fades. You *will* drown."

"Thank you!" Alyssa called, surfacing and grabbing my arm. "Thank you so much! C'mon Dylan, let's go!"

Before I could look back, she pulled me underwater, and we swam off together to explore a shipwreck.

An adventure of a lifetime.

* * *

I WENT BACK to see the Harbor Witch alone, a few days after we explored the ship. I wasn't as afraid of her this time, so when she surfaced with a raised brow and lowered the plank, I climbed aboard.

"Back already?" she asked.

I reached into my bag and pulled out the Tupperware container of cookies I'd made.

"I know the sailors who see you usually pay you," I said. "I don't have any money, but I wanted to do something to say thank you."

The Witch stared at me for a moment before her face crinkled up and she erupted in laughter.

"Aren't you charming," she said, grinning at me with her little sharp teeth.

We sat together on deck. The Witch ate cookies, and I told her all about the unforgettable adventure Alyssa and I went on.

"It was just a cargo ship. Nothing fancy. Alyssa found a really pretty fountain pen and some old coins though! And I found this. I think it's a pin."

I pulled out the little silver trinket with the faded image of a lighthouse on it. The Witch reached over and took it.

Her sleeve slipped back a bit as she inspected it — her hands were wrapped in bandages.

"It's a cufflink," she said, passing it back. "What was the cargo?"

I took the cufflink and sighed.

"Just a bunch of old bottles. I couldn't read the labels, but I think they were alcohol. Nothing super exciting, so we didn't really mess with them."

The Witch laughed then, even harder than she did earlier.

"What's so funny?" I asked.

"You'll know when you're older," she said.

I frowned. My parents said that. Even Alyssa said that sometimes, and she was barely a year older than me. But I guessed if anyone would say something like that and mean it, it would be the Harbor Witch.

"I wanted to ask . . . why did you do it?"

The Witch raised her brows at me.

"Help us? I've heard you do magic before, but just little things. Not something like this. It was like a miracle."

The Witch gave me a toothy grin.

"Why not?" she said, looking out to the water. "Who will ever believe you?"

* * *

THE NEXT TIME I saw the Harbor Witch, many years had passed. We were teenagers, and our childlike wonder and innocence were long gone. Alyssa and I arrived on the dock, both sobbing. The Witch lowered her plank and wordlessly ushered us inside. I don't know if she even recognized us then.

I told her everything. The factory accident that killed my father and sent Alyssa's to the hospital. The unpaid bills that were stacking up, the factory that was dragging its feet on paying the families what they were owed. The greedy wretch of a landlord who, now with a street of families who couldn't make rent on their cottages, was considering selling it all off to the expanding housing development.

"My dad's not waking up. My mom and I don't have anywhere we can go," Alyssa heaved. "We don't have any money; we'd have to go to the homeless shelter on the mainland."

I grabbed Alyssa's hand.

"I don't want to lose anyone else. Please, help us," I sobbed.

The Witch's face was still. She was quiet for a long while. "What would you have me do?" she finally asked.

Alyssa gripped my hand tight and nodded.

"We need to go back to the *Iapyx*. Please," I said.

At that, the Harbor Witch looked up, into my eyes. She raised her brows.

"We learned about the wreck in class. The wine and spirits that went down would be worth a fortune," I went on. "We could save our houses. Pay our bills. Hire lawyers to get what the factory owes us, everything."

The Witch sighed.

"Magic so strong isn't to be used as a tool or toy. There are consequences."

"This is an emergency!" Aylssa gasped, lurching forward. "You let us use it when we were kids so we could play explorers, but you won't help us now?!"

"And I'll see those consequences myself, one day," the Witch said solemnly.

Alyssa collapsed to the floor, sobbing and shaking. I glanced nervously at the Witch. She stared at my friend with an unreadable face. There was something so ancient and frightening about her, but I knew she had a heart.

I reached out and grabbed her bandaged hands. "Please," I

whispered. "Please help us. We don't have anywhere else to turn."

The Witch's mouth twitched. She looked down at my hand and up at me. Slowly, she grabbed her cane and reached under her table for her case.

She cut us deeper this time, at least it felt like it. The blade was still hot with the fire she cleansed it with, and it stung in my throat as the cuts turned to gills.

"You have until the sun sets and rises once more this time. Get as much as you can; I won't do this for you again," the Witch said solemnly.

"Once is all we need," I said as we walked onto the deck.

"Thank you," Alyssa whimpered through her tears. "Thank you so much."

We jumped into the water together and watched the sun dim as we made our way to the shipwreck.

* * *

LIKE WHEN I WAS YOUNGER, I went back a few weeks later to see the Harbor Witch again. She was standing on her pier, like she'd been expecting me. This time, I had an envelope full of money to give her along with my silly cookies.

"Keep it, child," she said, pushing it back into my chest.

"I know you take money from the fishermen when you bless their boats. I have to give you something too," I insisted.

"You have more use for it. Keep it for you and your mother," she said with a wave of her hand.

"We have plenty, seriously. Thanks to you."

That won a toothy grin from her, and she turned to clamber across the plank to her boats. I followed after her, inch by inch. She clung to her cane and stepped slowly, and when she finally made it to the deck and eased herself into a nearby chair, she was nearly out of breath.

"Do you need anything?" I asked. "Water?"

"You know where I keep the knife? Fetch it for me," she asked.

I dropped my bag and darted across her bridge to her second boat. When I returned, she had helped herself to the Tupperware of cookies in my bag. I passed her wooden case to her, and she set it in her lap.

"You two got enough bottles then?" she asked.

"More than enough. We said we found them in crates that washed up on the other side of the island. Alyssa and her parents are buying a new house, and my mom's finally gotten a lawyer. He thinks we can get a big settlement."

"My condolences, by the way," the Witch said suddenly.

I blinked for a moment before I realized she was talking about my father. Things had been so busy since the accident. Between comforting Alyssa and helping Mom with her paperwork and the household, I'd barely had time to reflect. I didn't really want to. But with the money had come stillness. And in that stillness, the reflections were taking form whether I wanted them to or not.

"Thank you," I said gently.

"It doesn't stop aching," the Witch said, opening her case and drawing her blade, performing her cleansing ritual even with closed eyes. "But time washes it further and further away. Makes you colder, too."

I sat beside her. "Have you lost a lot of people?" I asked.

The Witch cracked her eyes and looked out to the sea. "Everyone I ever knew."

I frowned. "You know people here, though. All the fishermen and grannies know about you."

"Mmm." The Witch shrugged. "They don't *know* me, though. No one left alive does. Not even you, child."

"I know you're not human."

That made the Witch turn to me. Her mouth dropped a

little, the ends of her sharp teeth poked through her cracked lips.

"In all my elders' stories, you're like you are now. An old woman. My grandma told me about you. And *her* grandmother told *her* about you. In the time they were all born, grew old and died, you haven't aged a day. You've been like this for a hundred years and more."

The Harbor Witch stared at me, eyes wide, brows raised. The wrinkles in her forehead piled up to her gray, stringy hairline. Sharp teeth were on display as they curled into a grin.

She pulled her hair back, revealing deep, raised scars along her throat. When she brought the knife to them, they didn't even bleed as they opened.

The Witch cracked her neck and bent down, pulling the layers of her dress and shawl to the side. I nearly doubled back at the sight of her legs. They were dark and limp and shone dully, like a catfish that had been left to dry on the beach. She didn't even have toes, really. Her shriveled feet tapered off into boneless little frills.

I stared, a mix of awe and horror as the Harbor Witch brought her legs together and took her knife between what should have been her ankles. As she drew the blade upward, her flesh fused together. Just like she was zipping up a dress.

The Witch shrugged off the rest of her layers and bit the bandages away from her hands. Webbed fingers exposed, she pushed out of her chair and dove off the deck, into the water.

I ran to the edge. It felt like an eternity before she surfaced, and when she did, she looked younger. Not like a young woman, but her loose skin now hugged her face tighter, and her wrinkles weren't so deep. A million thoughts raced through my head, and I gaped like a fish. She grinned up at me, teeth brighter and sharper.

"I won't tell anybody," I said quickly.

She chuckled. "Who would ever believe you?" she asked.

"Walking hurts you, doesn't it? You don't have real legs. You cut them into you with that knife."

"All magic has a consequence," she said.

"I just . . . why?" I asked finally. "Why do you stay on land, pretending to be an old woman?"

The Witch flicked her tail out, fins now full and sparkling. "All the others are gone. Everyone I ever knew, everyone who ever knew me. The ocean is beautiful, but these waters are cold and empty. And even those who prefer to be alone get too lonely."

I didn't know what to say to that. I don't think she expected me to say anything at all. Instead, I reached my hand into the water, and she reached up and touched the tips of her fingers to mine.

* * *

I WISH that had been the last time I saw her.

Years passed. Alyssa and I drifted out of each other's lives as young adults — we both went to colleges on the mainland, but I got a two year degree at a community college before moving back home to help my mother run the inn she invested in. I'd see Alyssa when she came home from breaks from her big private school, usually with a flock of new friends she brought back with her.

And then one night, she showed up at my door alone, sobbing in the rain.

"I need your help," she said. "I think something terrible happened."

She told them. She told her friends how she got the money to pay for school. The *real* reason.

We found their car parked in front of the Harbor Witch's pier. The growing waves shook the ancient wood as we ran across it to the boats. I made it there first, jumping aboard and running below deck.

Her house was torn apart. Furniture thrown, meticulously stacked items scattered. I gasped when I saw the bodies.

I recognized the three bloody figures who littered the Witch's den. They had been with Alyssa whenever I saw her during this visit — a sorority sister of hers and two boys from their school. Their bodies were covered with bites and cuts. There had been a fight.

Even in her frail human form, the Witch had killed them.

There was a faint whistle — no, several faint whistles. I took another step and heard it again. It was breathing.

No. It was gasping.

I ran forward and finally, there the Witch was, half hidden behind a toppled chair, her eyes wide and still, practically lifeless. Her dress was stained in blood, and thick gashes lined her stomach. Her chest rose slowly, and I doubled back as the cuts parted.

Her knife. They tried to fight her off with her own knife. She was suffocating.

I ran to her and tried to lift her up. A pair of arms reached around my shoulders.

"We have to go!" Alyssa insisted, trying to pull me back.

"I can still save her!" I yelled.

"Dylan, the pier is breaking apart!" Alyssa yelled back. "We have to get out of here!"

"We just need to get her out to the water. Please, help me—"

Alyssa yanked me to my feet. "I'm sorry, Dylan, we don't have any time. We have to go now!"

I cried out, clawing at the air as Alyssa dragged me back up to the deck. She was right. The waves were overtaking the pier. The wood splintered under my feet as I half ran, half slipped across its surface.

We were soaked to the bone when we finally made it to land. Rotted planks washed out beneath us with the spray of the sea, and what was left of the pier had vanished beneath the tide.

The Harbor Witch's boats rode the waves through the storm, steady and strong. I cried out. I pleaded, prayed for them to capsize. Anything so she could get to the water, so she could live.

But in the morning, the news came through. The sheriff sent a boat out to check on her, and they found the bodies. All four of them.

I hadn't cried so hard since my dad died.

* * *

ALYSSA STAYED after what happened to her friends. Part of me was happy to have my best friend back, but part of me dreaded dealing with her grief over my own, being her anchor. They'd committed a horrific act, but they'd been her friends. Her good friends.

I was younger the last time I had faced death. I didn't realize how unfair it was that my father had died, but Alyssa was the one who broke down, who needed all the comfort. I didn't know if I could do it again.

To my surprise, though, she didn't need much comfort. After the police were done with the questioning, after she came back from the funerals on the mainland, she hardly shed any tears.

It didn't strike me as peculiar at the time. I was happy to have my own space to mourn the Witch, the mermaid only I had known.

I visited her grave, brought flowers and seaweed and even

cookies. The fishermen of the town had made sure she over-looked the ocean. Sometimes it rained too hard to go. I'd sit in my room, hold the cufflink I found on the *Iapyx*, and cry.

The sea and the sky seemed to be in mourning too, because it rained harder and longer than any summer before. It stormed into fall before the clouds dried up.

That was when Alyssa asked me to go out to the sea with her. It was bittersweet, walking through the sand and stones, to the old secret cove of our childhood.

When Alyssa turned to me, there was a nervous, giddy look on her face. She reached into her purse.

The knife. She pulled out the Witch's knife.

"What did you do?" I whispered.

"It was in Jeffrey's hand," she explained. "I grabbed it as we ran out."

Confusion and shock turned to anger, and that anger boiled over inside me as the gears clicked into place.

"You planned this. You sent your friends to steal the knife."

Alyssa said nothing.

"Why?" I whispered.

"I didn't mean for it to happen how it did. I didn't mean for anyone to get hurt. None of us did."

"Why?!" I shouted.

Alyssa's eyes widened. She pointed out into the sea.

"Do you know how many more cases of vintage wine and whiskey are just sitting there on the *Iapyx*?" She yelled back. "We could be wealthy. All that money from before didn't last forever, Dylan. I want to finish my schooling. I want to make something of myself! I'm not content to just live a boring life on this rock like you, no adventure or glory to speak of!"

"They all died because of this. Is that worth it to you?" I asked.

"Of course it isn't. But if I didn't grab the knife, it would have *all* been a waste."

She couldn't even meet my eyes as she said it.

"Go find your blood money and ill-gotten glory. I want no part in it," I spat.

I turned and left Alyssa there at the cove. She shouted after me, but I didn't hear what she said. I never wanted to hear her again.

But of course, you know that's not what happened.

* * *

I DIDN'T SEE Alyssa for days after that, not that I expected to. I never wanted to look at her again.

When her parents showed up at my mother's inn begging to know if I'd seen her, I knew something had gone wrong.

I don't think I've ever felt such dread, walking to the secret cove. I was hoping I'd be wrong. Hoping I wouldn't find what I thought I might.

Her skin was wrinkled and pale from the water. Her face was bloated, and her lips were blue. She swam to me desperately, calling my name.

"Dylan, they won't close," she gasped with a hoarse voice. "The gills won't heal."

She reached out to me, the knife clutched tightly in her hands.

There was webbing growing between her fingers.

"What did you do, Alyssa?" I whispered.

"I don't know!" she cried out. "I sanitized the blade before I used it — it should have been fine, right?"

Maybe she had indeed sanitized it. I didn't ask how. But it had been years since she last saw the intricate way the Harbor Witch cleansed and prepared her blade.

I remembered stories my grandmother told me about

mermaids once, when I was little. She told me if you eat the flesh of a mermaid, you'd be cursed to live forever.

I wondered what would happen if you caused one to die?

What would happen if you stabbed their own blood into you by accident?

The Witch had told us that all magic had a consequence. She said she'd see the consequences herself, one day.

I wondered if she could have foreseen all of this.

"Please help me, Dylan," Alyssa blubbered. Her teeth were already growing sharp. "You have to help me."

But there was nothing I could do, even if I wanted to.

* * *

THAT WAS NEARLY sixty years ago. I'm as old now as my grandmother was when she told me tales of the Harbor Witch herself.

The Witch had been right about the aches of loss. How time washes it further away, but never out to sea completely.

I told your mother the same thing.

And I tell you that now, as we walk to my secret cove.

It's a routine, whenever the two of you visit me at the inn. Usually, it's just your mother and I, and you stay with your grandfather. Your mother thought you might be too young to see this, to hear the story, but you're as old as I was the first time I learned of magic. I know it's time. I know you're ready. You like adventure, just like I did.

Alyssa doesn't look how she once did. Whatever she's grown into, she's not the same kind of mermaid as the Witch was. I don't think she's aged, but time has washed her further and further from the young woman she once was.

It hasn't made her any less monstrous. I think, now, the outside matches the inside.

Don't let her strange cries scare you — she can't speak

anymore at all. And don't let my bitter words lead you to mistreat her. My biases are my own, and if there's anything I learned from the Harbor Witch, it's that you must treat what little magic is left in the world with respect and gentleness. We'll bring her cookies and keep her company for a while.

It must be so lonely.

* * *

RACHEL NUSSBAUM IS *an author and artist from* The Big Island of Hawaii, *currently residing in California. Her horror and dark fantasy stories have been published in many anthologies and collections, such as "Adrift," featured in* Cosmic Horror Monthly #28, *and "Starved," published in* More Than a Monster *from Grendel Press. Her first novella,* We Rotted in the Bitterlands, *is available from Mannison Press. In the future, Rachel hopes to write full-length novels and illustrate her own stories and comics.*

LIGHT AS AIR

JL GEORGE

The Empress of the Four Corners is dead, and those who have failed her stand vigil beside her body.

Four white candles burn before effigies of four gods. The twisted, scarred face of the Lord of Fire gazes down upon the foot of her bier; the swirling, dove-gray robes of the Lady of Air whisper above her head. On her left, the Lord of Earth stands impassive as an oak, and on her right the Lady of Water breaks from the waves with seafoam on her brow.

Four guards – the Empress's most trusted generals – hold themselves upright as rods, each standing before his or her patron god. Each maintains a mask of impassivity as still as the dead woman's face, which is as serene in death as it was shrewd and sharp in life. They will remain there until first light, when the priests arrive to resume their rites.

As far as Elith of the Earth Corps is concerned, the whole thing's a fucking waste of time.

There wasn't a mark on the Empress's body. She wasn't old, but with two grown sons, nor was she young. But Elith knows – deep in the marrow of her bones *knows* – there was nothing natural about her death.

Yet here they all are, standing like statues, pretending everything is normal. The whole palace has ground to a standstill, even work on the great brassy globe of the Amplifier at a halt, when what they should be doing is hunting the culprit and serving up his head on a plate.

Elith grips the handle of her battle-axe and tries not to scowl. She dares a glance to her right, where Riana of the Air Corps stands at the Empress's head, a pale sylph in a habit the colour of summer clouds.

Riana, of course, has no trouble remaining impassive. From the day they met, she's been like the Lady of the Air made flesh.

ELITH IS seventeen years old and desperate. The Earth Corps is the only future she has allowed herself to imagine for the past six years. The others available to girls in her small town involve stone-picking and harvesting in the fields or marriage and squeezing out brats. Her elder sister has two already, a toddler of three and a squalling, red-faced baby whose wails only cement Elith's determination that that will never be her.

There are other boys and girls her age whose affinity for the earth is stronger, but Elith has trained hard. Proving herself here is the only way out she has.

She sizes up the other Earth Corps hopefuls first. To a one, they're sturdily muscled, feet rooted immovably to the ground. They wield their axes with brute strength and tear rocks from the ground as if they're scooping up handfuls of sand.

Elith takes down the first one she's pitted against easily – it requires only a little forward thinking and a little attention to the moves he signals louder than a battlefield trumpet to put him on his arse. The next is smarter, but Elith is faster. She works her way through them methodically. Halfway through the day, it's clear that she needn't have worried. She's in.

In fact, she's growing rather bored. So, she turns her attention to the other corps. Clear frontrunners are emerging there, too, as the chaff is winnowed away.

For the Fire Corps, the leaders are identical twins in red tunics, distinguishable only by the burned scar one bears down the length of his right arm. Individually, they are competent fighters; together, alternating patterns of distraction and attack, a perfect firestorm. But they rely on speed and on confusing their opponents. Elith suspects they'll tire themselves out fast.

For the Water Corps, it's a girl who moves with sinuous, swirling grace. Elith suspects she's doing something with water droplets in the air to move so easily – but if Elith could get a grip on her, she thinks she could take her down.

Then there is the Air Corps. Only one stands – or floats – head and shoulders above the rest, and it's not for lack of competent fighters. It's that this moon-pale slip of a girl does things with the air Elith has never imagined. She twirls her staff, and it lifts her like a dandelion seed on the breeze. She can make air hit with the force of a rock to the head or sweep her opponents aside like a tidal wave. And she does it all with an expression as immovable, as perfectly calm, as a graven image.

Elith can't wait to fight her.

PINK DAWN FILTERS above the horizon as they leave the temple. Outside, the sacred fires have burned to embers, and the air smells of ash and imminent rain.

Toran of the Fire Corps stomps off ahead of them, making a beeline for the barracks and his chambers without saying a word. That's to be expected. He wasn't the most talkative even before his brother died; since, he's been slightly less forthcoming than a granite slab.

Mesyl of the Water Corps murmurs, "You know where I'll be, if you need me," and follows the path down to the lake.

Some nights, she sleeps on a boat tethered by the jetty, claiming the stillness of land makes her uneasy.

Elith is about to head to the barracks when Riana stops her – with a hand on her wrist, not a word.

"What is it?" she asks, but Riana shakes her head.

"Not here."

She lets Riana lead her to the edge of the temple grounds, through the small gate in the stone wall to which only the priests have keys, but which Riana somehow manages to get open with a puff of breath and a frown of concentration. Elith watches with raised eyebrows. "That's a new trick."

"Just one you haven't seen before. Where would I be if I told you everything?"

They say no more until they're well away from the temple and among the trees, nothing but the smell of wet earth and the heavy hush of the forest on all sides. Even the dawn chorus is muted. Elith's feet ache from standing to attention all night; she practically groans with relief when Riana says, "We can talk now."

"So, are you going to tell me the big secret before I decide the undergrowth looks like a good place for a nap?"

"Elith." Riana's voice is reproachful. "You know why we're here. I think you figured it out almost as soon as I did." That's Riana's idea of a compliment. Annoyingly, her estimation of her own intelligence is as accurate as it is high. "The Empress."

Abruptly, Elith's exhaustion drains away. In its place comes relief that someone else shares her suspicions – someone as sharp as Riana. "She was killed."

"I agree." Riana steeples her fingers, presses her lips tightly together. "She was found in her chambers. That means the killer was someone who could walk in without drawing notice."

Elith is suddenly quite glad none of their comrades are around. "So, for now . . ."

"We carry out our own investigation. And we trust no-one."

THEY GET THEIR FIGHT, though not as soon as Elith would have liked. The first weeks of training are full of drills, most of which she picks up immediately. She suspects testing her ability to handle boredom is part of the point. But soon enough, they're allowed to pit themselves against the other Corps.

Elith can't help her grin when they finally face each other. Riana's face betrays no emotion. She doesn't even raise an eyebrow. Elith grips the handle of her training axe tightly, feeling the wood sing beneath her hands, echoing her own hunger for the fight.

The instructor nods.

The air hits her in the stomach like a giant's fist. She has not even raised her axe. By the time she regains her feet, Riana is in the air and bearing down on her, implacable and deadly. Elith surges up to meet her.

It's the first real challenge she's had beyond tedium. At first, Riana is too fast for her, and all she can do is back away, shielding herself and looking for tells in Riana's impassive mask.

It's useless. She can react instinctively to the shift of an opponent's weight the moment they commit to a punch, but one who manipulates the very air is another matter.

Riana's staff takes Elith's legs out from under her, and she hits the ground again, sprawling.

"Had enough?" Riana asks, her eyebrow arched. Her tone is dismissive, as though she were expecting this – but then, that's how she always sounds. She has the air of one who is above it all, looking down on the rest of them from some lofty perch.

It occurs to Elith that she's been thinking that way, too. Over the weeks of training, she has elevated Riana to the challenge of a lifetime: one to be defeated only with her own methods, her own cool, cerebral detachment. She should be thinking of her opponent like any other fighter.

Elith takes the proffered hand and is gratified by the tiny, surprised twitch of Riana's lips when she says, "Nah. Let's go again."

She settles into a fighting stance and stops thinking. This time, she lets herself feel.

This time, she holds her own. She knocks Riana back once, twice, letting instinct and not calculation tell her where each blow will fall, where the other girl will leave herself vulnerable. Like this, they are evenly matched; they spar until the instructor sighs and tells them to let somebody else have a go.

That evening, after curfew, Elith sneaks out of her dorm. Nobody stirs – the Earth Corps train hard and sleep heavily. Elith, though, is still burning with energy and the urge to get out, even if it's only to jump the wall and walk a few hundred yards into the forest. There are tales of wolves, but she's never believed them.

Still, the silence of the trees is a breathing, knowing kind of silence, and a part of Elith is always alert to it. When the crackle of a footstep sounds in the silence, she whirls to face it, stifling a hiss of pain when a hanging branch whips across her face.

There's no-one in sight.

Breathing slowly, blood pounding in her ears, she makes her way toward the sound. What she sees brings her to an abrupt halt.

In a moonlit clearing stands a figure in pale gray robes, white-blonde hair curling to her shoulders. Riana is clutching a length of wood, but it's not her staff, the standard weapon of the Air Corps. It's something shorter and thicker. Like an axe-handle.

Her eyes are closed, and she's murmuring something under her breath. Near her feet, Elith spots a disturbance in the earth – faint but present, as though some wild animal is about to emerge from its burrow.

Words escape before she can stop them: "What the . . . ?"

Riana's eyes snap open. She draws herself up to her full height, and while she doesn't hide the length of wood behind her back – Elith is sure she'd never do anything so childish – a touch of pink appears high on her cheeks. She's embarrassed.

A delighted grin spreads across Elith's face. This is the first time she's seen Riana anything but perfectly self-possessed, and being the one who got a reaction out of her is gratifying, even if it was by accident.

She presses her advantage home. "What are you doing out here?"

Riana sniffs. "Taking a walk."

"Strange walking stick." Elith narrows her eyes, studying the axe-handle more closely. The way Riana was holding it, and talking to herself, eyes closed in concentration – the disturbance in the ground – "Wait. Were you trying Earth-work?"

"It's good to know your opponents," Riana says, loftily. "Their techniques, the way they think."

"I think you're just sore because I put you on your arse in training."

"I promise you, it won't happen again," Riana tells her, cold and crisp as a January morning. "Anyway, I don't see what business it is of yours what I do. You shouldn't be out here either." She adds that last part like an afterthought, and it occurs to Elith that she isn't really upset at being caught breaking the rules, but at being seen practicing something she isn't good at yet.

Elith shrugs. "I suppose we'll have to keep each other's secrets."

Riana doesn't look happy about it, but she falls into step behind Elith as they make their way back to the barracks, tramping through undergrowth and over loamy dirt. Elith smiles to herself. The ice maiden can be provoked, after all. She's going to have fun with this.

.   .   .

THE LIST of suspects is extensive. There are the Empress's two sons, each with a small cadre of supporters convinced he has the better claim to the throne, though only Cavon, the younger of the two, really seems to want it. The elder brother, Ariol, is a meek and bookish type, and Elith thinks he would have abdicated his claim long ago if not for the threat of his mother's wrath. Investigating them is the biggest risk. They'll rule out other possibilities before taking it.

There are plenty of courtiers whose motives Elith has no hope of untangling. She's well aware she's a blunt instrument; those suspects who require subtlety are best left to Riana. That leaves Elith to look into their counterparts, Mesyl and Toran.

The next days are taken up with funeral preparations. They must drill their respective corps on ceremonial maneuvers, carry out their usual duties, and give reassurances about the safety of the realm they do not feel. It's only on the night of the funeral – after the pomp is over and the crowds dispersed, and a heavy blanket of exhaustion has descended over the palace – that Elith gets the chance to go snooping.

She saw Mesyl break away from the crowd and head down the lake path perhaps half an hour ago, so she heads for the boat first. There's no light burning in the cabin, but it seems too early for Mesyl to be asleep. After a moment's observation, her eyes getting used to the dark, Elith spots movement on the path that circles the lake, perhaps a third of the way around from where she's standing. She has to squint, but she's sure the willowy figure on its nighttime stroll is Mesyl.

She moves fast, hurrying to the end of the jetty and stepping onto the boat. There's a splash as it dips under her weight, and she glances sharply up the bank, but Mesyl continues walking.

A Water adept with Mesyl's power could certainly drown a person on land, but they found no water in the Empress's lungs. Elith looks for other weapons.

She finds a handful of books and scrolls, a sheaf of charcoal sketches – faces from the court rendered in flowing, stylized lines – and not much else. Frustrated, she crouches, prods the floorboards in case there's some secret compartment in the bottom of the boat, and feels foolish about it. She's not in a children's story, after all.

Then, something beneath the bunk catches her eye. A box, a fraction wider than Elith's handspan, carved from dark wood.

She takes it to the window to examine it in the moonlight. The box is locked – but it's made of wood and metal. She narrows her concentration to a point and runs her fingers over the lock, feeling for weaknesses in the iron.

A moment later, it pops open. Inside, glass jars gleam in the pale light. Elith holds one close to her face and finds it half-full of green powder. When she pulls out the stopper, its astringent herbal scent makes her wrinkle her nose.

No marks on the Empress's body – but there are poisons that leave no sign.

"Elith." Mesyl's voice behind her is calm and measured. "Now, what in the world are you doing here?"

RIANA DOESN'T LET herself get caught with her back turned again. Anytime Elith follows her into the woods, she's ready and waiting. Those nights, they spar playfully, delightedly, each revelling in the chance to stretch herself against a worthy opponent.

Elith never sees Riana trying Earth-work again.

One evening – at the tail end of a few days' leave, and after far too much wine – Elith stumbles from her dormitory bed in the small hours. The latrine outside the barracks is occupied, and her bladder is too insistent to wait, so she staggers around back of the building, planning to squat behind a bush.

Then she spots movement: a ghostly figure vaulting the outer wall.

She freezes where she stands, squinting. No, the pale silhouette is no ghost but a woman in dove-gray robes – Riana on the way home from one of her late-night strolls. Elith relaxes.

She stills again, pressing herself against the side of the building, when she realizes Riana isn't alone. Another figure clambers over the wall and jumps down to join her. The newcomer is taller than Riana and robed in the deep orange-red of the Fire Corps that always puts Elith in mind of old embers. A heartbeat later, a second, identical figure appears over the wall.

Toran and Solan, the twins who joined the same day Elith and Riana did. Elith finds herself frowning, keeping to the shadows, and watching the little group closely until the two boys break off toward the Fire Corps buildings. Riana stays where she is for a long moment before heading for her own dorm. Elith imagines the other girl is looking straight at her, pale gray eyes piercing through the gloom to find her hiding place in the shadows – but of course, that's impossible, and Riana turns away without acknowledging her.

Elith can't sleep that night. Somehow, she'd thought those nighttime rendezvous in the forest were something Riana only did with her.

It takes her an embarrassingly long time to realize she's jealous.

IF RIANA WERE HERE, she'd stay calm. She'd keep her voice measured, finding the words to keep the situation from descending into violence. Perhaps she'd even talk Mesyl into incriminating herself.

Elith is not Riana.

She's stronger on land than on the water, but Mesyl isn't expecting the attack. In a flash, Elith has her pressed against the cabin wall, one arm across her throat. With her other hand, she holds up the jar. "What the hell is this?"

She feels Mesyl swallow and gasp, her eyes going fearfully wide. "Don't drop that!" she croaks. "I need it."

Elith's eyes narrow. "Why? Planning on poisoning someone else?"

Despite her fear, Mesyl looks mystified. "Poison? Those are for me."

Elith studies her face closely and finds no trace of deception in it. Mesyl has never been much of a politician – she isn't a practiced liar. Then again, that's what a practiced liar would want her to think.

She steps back, leaving Mesyl to rub her bruised throat. "Prove it. Swallow some."

Mesyl puts out her hand for the jar, but Elith holds it away from her. There are poisons potent enough that a pinch of powder thrown in the face could fell her.

"Cup," Elith says.

Frowning, Mesyl does as she's told, fetching the earthenware cup that sits beside her bed and filling it with water. Elith tips in a teaspoon's worth of the bitter green powder and watches closely as Mesyl swirls the contents around, then swallows them down with a grimace. "Happy?"

"I suppose." Elith sets the jar down carefully. "So, what's it for?"

"You haven't answered my question yet."

"What. Is. It. For?"

Mesyl sighs, apparently too tired to get into a contest of wills with the most stubborn of her counterparts, and seems to wilt. Come to think of it, there are dark circles under her eyes, and her red-brown complexion looks faded, ashen. Gray has started to thread its way through her dark curls in recent years, but it seems to be spreading faster lately.

Elith has her answer before Mesyl even says, "I'm sick. I

was going to tell the Empress and resign my post. The healers say if I don't rest . . ."

There is no need for her to finish the sentence. With things in their current state, losing one of its most steadfast generals is the last thing the realm needs. Mesyl will have to hang on as long as she can.

"That's miserable." Elith's never been much good at sympathy. "Sorry."

Mesyl shrugs her off. "I think you owe me an explanation, now."

She hesitates. Riana said they should trust no one – but they've known Mesyl for years. Elith's not sure she ever truly suspected her. The worst that's likely to happen is she won't believe them.

She tells her everything.

"UGH. If I wanted to babysit, I'd have stayed home in my village," Elith grumbles, adjusting the formal robes that bunch up around her thighs and never seem to fit her right.

"Shh," hisses Aeryn, the other Earth adept who's been sent with her on this ditchwater-dull assignment. "If anyone hears us complaining about orders . . ."

Elith raises her eyes to the heavens. "Relax. We're not here because anyone cares what we think."

Aeryn joined two years after Elith did; guard duty for a minor official at a diplomatic function is the kind of thing she expects. Elith, on the other hand, is here as punishment.

She doesn't think she quite deserves it. In her book, any jumped-up Fire adept dumb enough to make a crude comment about the way she holds her axe handle fully deserves to get his nose broken.

But she's no longer sure it was worth it. Gods, she's bored senseless.

There are rumblings of unrest on the northern border. The neighboring country of Ia, a vast and chilly realm, has existed in uneasy truce with their own since Elith was a child. Their power is perhaps equal to the Empress's; each side claims it is the greater, but neither tests the theory.

But Ia has a new ruler – a distant cousin of the old king who never expected to inherit the throne. He is both inexperienced and ambitious, a dangerous combination. The Empress will be discussing options with the generals and a select few adepts from the lower ranks, invited to join the conversation because of their cunning. Riana is among them, of course.

The official Elith is supposed to be watching makes his excuses and moves from one group of chattering politicians to another. She trails after him at a distance and snags a wine glass on her way, already sure nothing of interest could possibly happen.

The group to which he attaches himself is the delegation from Ia. Despite the mild spring weather, they wear ridiculous, heavy robes trimmed in white fur.

"Of course," one of them is saying, "the King has the greatest magicians of the realm working on the Amplifier . . ."

Elith's ears prick up. A device to amplify the powers of adepts is the holy grail of warfare. Even the strongest Earth or Water worker has a range of only a few hundred yards. Air and Fire fare little better. An Amplifier could allow them to topple mountains, to burn cities. It would change the world completely.

The Empress has people working on one too, of course. The northern King is probably no closer, but the fact that his delegates mention it at all is telling. Is it saber rattling, or an attempt to draw out information about the Empress's efforts?

The official she's guarding at least has the sense not to be drawn out, but he does excuse himself hurriedly. He leaves as soon as is polite, though his hasty exit still draws raised eyebrows, and Elith and Aeryn follow him to the palace.

The Empress's council is still in session. The guards at the door

– both Air Corps, Elith notes – refuse to let the official in, but he keeps insisting, raising his voice until it echoes off the marble walls and the door cracks open from the inside. An advisor pops his head out to ask what all the fuss is about, and the official seizes his opportunity, insisting that he has information, and the Empress must be informed at once.

His embarrassment, once it becomes evident none of this is news to the Empress, would make a softer-hearted person cringe in sympathy. Elith is not a softer-hearted person. She bites back a laugh, grateful to be distracted from the evening's tedium, and Riana catches her eye across the room. It's impossible to know what the look in her eye means.

Later, after Elith has been relieved of duty, Riana catches her in the barracks courtyard. She detaches herself from the gloom behind the Air Corps block, a soft gray shadow like a cat. "You're a terrible babysitter."

Elith makes a face. "They shouldn't send a warrior to do a twelve-year-old's job."

"Are you? A warrior?"

She opens her mouth to retort but stops when she sees there's no malice on Riana's face, only a thoughtful frown.

"Are any of us?" Riana goes on, as though she's talking only to herself. "We train, we guard the Empress, we march and float in ceremonial formation, but we've never seen war."

"That could change soon," Elith says, remembering the diplomat from Ia and his smiling provocation.

"That's what I'm afraid of."

Elith raises an eyebrow. "What, the great Riana's scared she won't be able to handle herself?"

"It's not about handling anything. I don't doubt you could mow down half a battalion with that axe of yours. I could fling a dozen men across a battlefield. But compared to what's coming . . ." Riana sighs. "The Sun's crashing to Earth, and we're blowing out candles."

There's a heaviness in her voice Elith has never heard before.

The shadows that pool in her eye sockets and beneath her cheek-bones make her look hollowed-out and exhausted, a beautiful wraith.

Elith is accustomed to sparring with Riana, to testing her body and her skills against Riana's – even to the flashes of want she sometimes feels when she gets the upper hand and wrestles the other woman to the ground. Now, she finds herself wanting to cup Riana's cheek and breathe the warmth and life and arrogance back into her.

"It might not happen," she says. It sounds unconvincing even to her.

"Hmm," is all Riana says. She turns away, her expression shut-tering, and Elith finds, somewhere deep in the uneasy tangle of her emotions, that she cannot bear it.

She catches Riana's wrist and pulls her back. Their lips hesitate inches from one another for long seconds, and in the end, it is Riana who closes the gap.

They clash together hard, just like when they spar, leaving bruises in the shapes of mouths and fingertips. It's like Riana is trying to escape from something, to crawl out of the world and inside Elith's skin. Elith gives as good as she gets. She's done thinking for the evening, too.

She dozes afterward, and when she wakes in the early hours of the morning, Riana is already gone.

"I THOUGHT we agreed to tell no one else." Riana's lips press together in displeasure.

"C'mon. Even if Mesyl wanted to get in our way, she's not up to it."

Mesyl said as much, insisting she had no desire to get involved. Funnily enough, she, too, warned Elith before she left that anyone could be a suspect – even the other generals.

Riana sighs. "Next time you're planning on bringing somebody else in, give me a little warning, hmm?"

"Fine, fine." Elith flops down in Riana's preferred armchair near the fireplace. Even now, the fact that she's able to draw a snort of annoyance from her companion makes her smirk inside. Years of practice have made her pretty good at pushing Riana's buttons, even if she's still not quite sure how they work on the inside. "How did you get on with the politicians?"

"As you'd expect." Riana crosses to the side table where tea is brewing, its delicate, grassy scent perfuming the air. She pours a single cup and puts it to her lips, well aware there's no point offering Elith anything that can't get her drunk. "It was all very dull. Ariol's not responsible; I'm sure of that much."

"Tell me something I don't know."

A noncommittal sound. "How about Toran? Did you talk to him?"

Elith shakes her head. "He's locked away in his chambers. He has a couple of Fire Corps underlings telling everyone he's not to be disturbed. I didn't force my way in."

"Wise. We don't want anyone *else* noticing what we're doing." Elith ignores the barb and Riana sips her tea, frowning though the cloud of fragrant steam that rises from her cup. "But Toran refusing to come out like that . . ."

"Hard not to look like a man with something to hide if you, well, hide."

"Quite."

"I'll try again tomorrow," Elith promises.

"In the meantime, we should ensure he doesn't realize we suspect him." Elith sees something new in Riana's eyes now: a spark of promise. "He'll no doubt have his people keeping watch. If you're spotted running around the grounds late at night . . ."

Elith grins. "*Riana.* Are you asking me to stay?"

Riana shrugs one shoulder and her gray robe falls away, revealing creamy skin. "It's only prudent."

"Can't be too careful." Elith gets to her feet, and Riana crosses the room in three strides to meet her. Her mouth tastes of the tea, fresh and faintly bitter.

RIANA IS NEWLY PROMOTED to General, and though Elith knows the old leader of the Earth Corps will retire soon and the position will be hers for the taking, she chafes every time she has to call Riana Ma'am.

Mesyl has been in her position for two years.

They don't yet know who will be named Fire Corps General. The two brothers are equals in every respect, but only one can rise. Solan has been sent on assignment to the border with Ia, where there have been skirmishes between villages on either side, and Toran visibly resents that he was not allowed to prove himself, too.

The news of Solan's death comes with the dawn.

It's Elith to whom the messenger first comes. She carries the letter to her general, who invites his counterparts to look at it with him. Elith watches Riana's face as they read and guesses from the minute stiffening of her countenance that the news is bad. But it's only after an hour locked away in discussion with the Empress that they share the news with their adepts.

Toran blanches. "He should never have been sent alone," he bites out, an insolence that is only let slide because of his loss. "I should have been with him!"

Elith certainly isn't going to be the one to talk him down.

"Toran –" Mesyl starts, but he's striding out of the room before anyone can stop him.

Riana talks him down, in the end. She emerges from Toran's chambers deep in thought and only seems to notice Elith falling into step with her when she asks, "What did you say to him?"

"What he needed to hear." Riana shakes her head as though clearing cobwebs and meets Elith's gaze. "He'll be fine," she promises, but her smile does not reach her eyes.

ELITH HAS NO MORE luck the following morning. She heads to the Fire Corps barracks as soon as she slips out of Riana's chambers and finds a fresh bevy of guards stationed outside Toran's door.

"This is getting ridiculous," she tells them. "He can't hide in there forever." If she were Riana, she'd add something about his having duties, but she's Elith, so she glowers instead.

"The General isn't to be disturbed. He was very clear on that point." A faint wisp of flame flickers around the right-hand guard's fingertips. He controls the impulse almost immediately, but the implication is clear, and anger flares hot and bright in the center of Elith's chest.

"Get out of my way," she orders the guards. "*Now.*"

The one on the left looks as though she might be about to fold. "She *is* a general," she says to Flamey-Fingers. "We're supposed to obey orders."

"We're Fire Corps," Flamey-Fingers counters, "and Toran said trust no one."

Ugh. Elith's going to have to flatten them.

She doesn't have her axe, but there's ground beneath her feet. She reaches down with her senses, past roots and worms into damp black earth and rock, as Flamey-Fingers prepares to square up to her. He's brave; she has to give him that.

A shout from the direction of the Air barracks splits the air.

It could be a distraction, but Flamey-Fingers looks as confused as she feels. Elith spins in the direction of the noise.

A handful of gray-clad figures are running toward the barracks. Without a second thought, she joins them.

By the time she arrives, Riana is at the front door, leaning heavily on her staff, pale behind the soot that smudges her face. The edges of her robe are scorched.

"Whoever it was wore a mask," she says. "I couldn't see their face, but they were Fire Corps, I know that much." She holds up her blackened hem in evidence. "If I'd still been sleeping..."

Air Corps adepts cluster on the steps beneath her chambers. They gaze up at their general, battered and stained but unbroken, and seem to gain a fraction of her strength and determination. They stand taller and move quicker when she directs them where to go.

Soon, they are all sequestered in a room in the palace – Elith, Riana, Mesyl, and a handful of their most trusted advisors. Adepts guard every door and have been sent to fetch the princes. If Toran has noticed what's going on, he gives no indication; nobody has emerged from his chambers since the attack.

"You really think he was behind it?" Mesyl sounds dubious. "Toran's always been loyal."

Riana chews her lip. "I suppose it's possible another Fire adept acted alone."

"We shouldn't assume only Fire adepts are involved. The Empress wasn't burned, after all. Both princes have a claim to the throne, and there was a delegation from Ia here for the funeral. Any disaffected adept could be persuaded to work for them."

Mesyl is warming to her subject, but Riana's face is closed off. "I don't think so," she says. "We should be careful about throwing around accusations."

"Of course," Mesyl says. "But still. We have to consider all possibilities."

Riana frowns faintly. "I suppose so."

Mesyl nods, apparently satisfied. The conversation over, Elith sees her mask of calm slip a fraction as she finds a chair and sits heavily. "You alright?" she asks.

"My medicine." Mesyl's voice is strained. "All the excitement – I forgot about it."

"I'll take an adept and get it," Elith offers, seizing the chance to get out of the crowded room. The heat of packed-in bodies is making her nauseous.

"We need you here," Riana cuts in. "Tell me where the medicines are." She has waved an Air adept over before Elith can object, issuing instructions in a low voice. Elith sighs and sinks into a chair beside Mesyl.

THERE ARE *times when Riana says they shouldn't do this anymore. Elith doesn't think it's fear of getting caught – Riana has always known she's cleverer than the whole court put together. But the Empress knows that, too, and she involves Riana as much in politics as strategy. Riana is always busy. Their trysts grow fewer and further between, and it takes more and more effort for Elith to get a rise out of her. A little more of Riana becomes inaccessible to her every day.*

Elith tells herself it would be stupid to care. They've only ever been killing time together, distracting themselves from the day-to-day and the louring clouds of war.

The evening a messenger from Ia shows up at the palace, she goes to Riana's chambers after midnight. Riana has been locked away with the Empress and her advisors all day.

It's raining thin, needling drizzle, and by the time Elith makes it to Riana's door, the hems of her trousers are soaked and her hair drips water down her back. Once, Riana would have laughed; today, she only greets Elith with a tight smile and tells her to dry her clothes by the fire.

Elith holds her hands out to the fireplace, feeling her clammy skin tingle with its warmth. "What happened in there?"

Riana gives a drawn-out sigh. For a moment Elith doesn't think she's going to get an answer. "Our people have cracked it. The Amplifier. It works."

"But that's good, isn't it?"

There's a small furrow between Riana's brows. On somebody else, it might be endearing. "So does Ia's. If they strike first, we hit back. And if we do . . ."

"Better than not being able to protect ourselves." It's not that Elith is itching for a fight, exactly. It's more that she hates the idea of being helpless.

"Is it?" Riana looks out the window. The rain is pouring. "It will flatten cities. Kill civilians in their thousands. Now we have it, I'm afraid it's inevitable the Empress will use it." Her face is pinched and pale in the gloom.

"Stop thinking so hard. You'll strain something." Elith reaches for her, but Riana's fingers close around her wrist, cool and firm.

"Not tonight," she says. "I need quiet."

Elith hovers a moment longer. Then she snatches up her damp clothes and stomps into the rain.

An Air initiate returns with Mesyl's medicine, and she takes it gratefully, mixed with a cup of wine. Ariol arrives at the same time, complete with attendants, happy to be where it's safe. Cavon, on the other hand, is nowhere to be found.

"He's not one to be summoned by generals," Ariol points out. "You'll probably all be answering to him soon enough."

There's not even a hint that Ariol might be interested in the throne. Elith finds his lack of ambition impossible to grasp. She had to scrabble so hard to get here that to see an indolent son of the crown lolling about, reading books, sends hot sparks of irritation down her spine.

Riana takes charge. "One of us should fetch him. Elith, hold the fort here?"

She shrugs assent as Riana leaves and turns to Mesyl. "We could send a message to Toran," she suggests. "Offer him amnesty if he turns over the adept who went after Riana. Make him think we don't suspect him." She's not sure it would work – subterfuge is less her area than hitting things with rocks – but she knows Mesyl won't hesitate to tell her if she's being an idiot.

Mesyl doesn't say anything at all.

Elith leans across to look at her face, thinking perhaps the medicine has made her drowsy, but then she sees the ragdoll loll of Mesyl's head, the way her eyes are open and unseeing.

When Elith waves a hand in front of her face, she stirs faintly; the dull rattle of a sound that escapes her lips turns Elith's blood to ice. Then she is still.

Suspicion curdles in Elith's guts. She lifts the lid of the glass jar Riana's adept brought and finds that the smell is different: mouldy bitterness in place of leafy astringency.

"Help!" she yells. "Healers, *now!*"

It is too late.

And in the silence that follows, a Water adept turns accusing eyes on Elith. "*You* knew where she kept her medicines," he says, "and you've been in the middle of this the whole time."

"You'll have to teach me to do that sometime."

Riana alights beside her, staff spinning like a sycamore seed on the wind. "I thought you preferred to keep your head out of the clouds."

"I'm joking. Mostly." Elith grins. "I'll leave the above-it-all stuff to you." Though she's wondered, sometimes, how it would feel to swoop and soar as Riana does, to be as light as air.

Riana's answering smile fades faster than she'd like. "It's for the best. The view from up there isn't what you'd hope."

Elith snorts. "What are you on about?"

Riana's gaze is unreadable. After a moment, she tosses her pale hair and says, "Nothing. Come, we'll be late."

IT WAS an Air adept who brought the medicine. Elith didn't hear what Riana said to him before he left.

And it was only Riana who saw the Fire adept she claims attacked her. It never even occurred to Elith to question her word.

It would never occur to any of them to question her word.

Before Elith can open her mouth in self-defense, the door slams open. Riana is standing in the opening, her face a perfect picture of grief.

"Cavon should have listened to us," she says. "The killer found him before we did. Perhaps before we even came here – nobody had seen him since last night."

Her voice cracks. Elith has never heard it do so before. She realizes, with growing horror, it is practiced.

Riana's gaze searches the room and finds the tableau in the corner: Mesyl, slumped lifelessly in her chair; Elith, with the Water initiate's accusing finger pointed at her. The flicker of sorrow that crosses her face actually looks genuine. "Elith." Her voice is a wistful caress. "I had so hoped I wouldn't have to do this."

IT IS the night the Empress dies, and Riana has asked to meet her. Elith will realize later this is to ensure an alibi; tonight, all she thinks is that Riana finds herself in need of distraction. Things have been more fraught than usual of late, with barely veiled threats flying to and from Ia, and tests of the Amplifier blasting holes a mile wide in the forest.

There's something about the tension in the air that Elith thrives on, a crackling fire beneath her skin. She tries not to let it show, but it's there, lending a vicious edge to her laugh, an extra weight to her blows in training.

Riana, too, is alight with nervous energy, but she looks entirely unhappy about it. She keeps drifting from the moment, retreating to some place inside her head where Elith can't follow, and in the end, to get her attention, Elith sweeps her off her feet and onto the bed like they're teenagers sparring again.

Riana smiles tiredly up at her. Firelight glints in the opaque depths of her pupils. "I'm sorry," she murmurs, "I have a lot on my mind these days," and she curls her fingers into Elith's hair to pull her down into a kiss.

Elith sleeps dreamlessly that night. When Riana slips from the sheets in the small hours, she doesn't notice a thing.

"Why?" Elith asks, helplessly. They are alone at last, in the locked room at the very top of the palace where dangerous prisoners are kept. "To put Ariol on the throne? He doesn't even *want* it."

"Precisely." Riana speaks patiently, like a teacher leading a slow student to an obvious conclusion. "He's more open to being led. Cavon had the Empress's fire. He would've moved just as eagerly toward war."

Elith puts her head in her hands. A more proper general would talk about sacrilege, about treason, but all Elith can muster is, "Why didn't you tell me? We were supposed to be in this together."

The tilt of Riana's head conveys sympathy. "You wouldn't have understood. I was wrong about you before, Elith. You *are* a warrior. You were born for it – you would thrive on it. I'm fighting for peace."

"You're not fighting!" Elith tells her. "You're murdering people."

She thinks, perhaps, she is still hoping for a denial. None comes.

"I don't understand why you came to me. Why you confirmed my suspicions. You could've told me the Empress died from sudden illness or old age."

"You wouldn't have believed it. Better to keep you close, where you could be guided." Riana jerks to her feet. "Walk with me."

The Air Corps guards let them out of the room without question, and Riana strides along the corridor to the roof terrace, her hand on Elith's arm. The manacles on Elith's wrists clank with every step they take.

"I'd planned to blame it on Toran," Riana says, once they're out in the chill air. "He was the logical choice, but people will believe you paid off a Fire initiate just as easily. They'll say Ariol would have been next. That you planned a coup." She holds her staff in one hand, twirling it lazily. As Elith watches, she spins it faster, faster, and a cold wind begins to whip up.

"A coup? Me and *who*? Why? I'm a fighter, not a ruler."

"People don't need logic, Elith. They believe what *feels* true. And you're rude. Obnoxious. You roll your eyes at propriety, and people tolerate it because of your skills. You've never given the court much reason to like you."

"But *you* . . . you were supposed to–"

"I do." Riana grasps her wrist, her touch cool and unyielding. "I really wish it didn't have to be this way."

The wind she calls tugs at them, pulls them up, up above the palace roof and the grounds and the woods where they used to meet, all of it spread out like a toy town beneath them. The test areas in the woods are burned, black scars.

"I'll tell them you did the honorable thing," Riana says.

Elith spits up at her but misses her face and succeeds only in spattering the front of Riana's robe. "Fuck honor," she snarls. "Tell them you killed me."

Riana looks into her face, grave and steady. "That I can do," she says, at last. "They'll believe I had to." Her gaze, her attention, is entirely on Elith. For the first time, Elith sees the whole of her, so depthlessly sad and so terribly cold.

She's wanted to know Riana for so long. She guesses she's finally succeeded. All else seems to drop away – the Empress, the succession, the deaths, even the war. There is only this truth, pure and crystalline and icy.

Riana's grip on her wrist loosens. Elith drops through empty space, and, for one brief moment, she feels as light as air.

* * *

JL GEORGE WAS BORN in Cardiff and raised in Torfaen. Her fiction has won a New Welsh Writing Award, the International Rubery Book Award, and been shortlisted for the Rhys Davies Short Story Competition. In previous lives, she wrote a PhD on the classic weird tale and played in a glam rock band. She lives in Cardiff with her partner and a collection of long-suffering houseplants and enjoys baking, alternative music, and the company of cats.

MANIC PIXIE DEMON GIRL

LAURA RUTH LOOMIS

The man sprawled on his couch, listlessly scrolling on his phone. Every so often he checked his text messages, as if he could have somehow missed the chirp of a notification.

Across the room, invisible to the man, a handsome devil scrutinized him from a ratty recliner. Nick was a Devil Fourth Class, Thirteenth Division, in the standard uniform of dark suit and cape with the rank insignia in gold. His horns and fangs were sharp and polished, and his claws tapped the end table restlessly. Nick had risen (technically, fallen) rapidly through the ranks of the Nine Hells, and this human should have been an easy target.

Nick moved closer, murmuring in the human's ear in an otherworldly whisper. "Your girlfriend's going to stay mad at you, and it wasn't even your fault. Just look at all these hot women out there waiting to hear from you."

The man paused his scrolling to message a woman who sold her artwork online: *Hey, you're really hot.*

The answer came immediately: *Not interested. Married.*

Nick whispered at a frequency that only the man's

subconscious could detect. "What a bitch! Can't even take a compliment. You know she's lying about being married. You should tell her she's fat and ugly, and she'll die alone with her cats."

The man hesitated, his finger above the screen, then set the phone down.

Feminine laughter erupted across the room. Nick looked up, startled.

"Really? That's the best you've got?"

Nick's spot on the recliner was now occupied by a demon woman, her spiked tail poking from a whisper of a dress woven of spiderwebs. Her dark green face wore a scarlet smirk, and her hair was in a hundred tiny braids that were constantly moving, morphing into snakes and back into hair again.

She had no business here. It was an immutable law of the underworld: demons and devils did not mix. Devils obeyed their leaders and worked in unison to build a more evil order on Earth. Demons thrived on anarchy and launched their attacks at any target, including each other.

Nick scowled at the demon, baring his fangs. "This human is my assignment. Go find one of your own."

"You're not getting very far with him." She got up with an exaggerated yawn and stretch. "Want me to show you how it's done?"

"If I need advice from a demon on how to create chaos instead of getting the job done, I'll be sure to call you."

"Job?" The snake-braids writhed and shimmered as she laughed. "That's where you devils get it wrong. Evil is supposed to be fun." She strolled over to the oblivious human and purred in his ear. "See this woman? She rejected you, just like your girlfriend did after that fight yesterday. Like every breakup you've ever had. Like every woman that you tried to chat up at the bus stop, and they'd act interested until the bus came, and they'd blow you off without so much as a phone number. Women are always dangling it in front of you and then rejecting you." She was bent over, doing a bit of dangling herself, and Nick tried not to stare.

The human's jaw tightened. Her voice was getting through.

The demon ran a hand through the human's hair, like a breeze ruffling it. "They're laughing at you. All of them, they're always laughing at you. You should tell that woman she's a whore. Treat her like the worthless bitch she is."

The human's face reddened with anger. He glared at the woman's face onscreen, cursing out loud.

Inspiration struck. Nick whispered in his other ear, "Send her a dick pic."

The human undid his pants, aimed his phone and snapped a picture, then messaged it to the woman online, cackling.

"See? That was fun." The demon reached her fist toward Nick. After an awkward few moments, she said, "You're supposed to bump it with your fist."

Nick did the best approximation he could, considering he couldn't make a fist without his claws piercing the palm of his hand. Devils were all about sharp edges.

She returned to the chair, her long green legs sprawled across the arm. "Do you have a name, or is it just Class Z, Subclass 666, Level 3 under-devil?"

"Level 4. And you can call me Nick."

"I'm Monica. Short for Demonica. And you're taking all this much too seriously, Nick. So you move up to Level 4—"

"I told you, I'm already Level 4."

"Whatever. I don't even know what all those devil levels are." Her scent was a heady mix of jasmine and brimstone. "Why bother, if you're not having some fun along the way?"

"And you demons have it so much better? No one in

charge, total chaos all the time, tearing each other apart every chance you get? This is your idea of fun?" If only her legs weren't so distracting.

"Don't knock it until you've tried tearing someone apart. But really, the stories are exaggerated. We all do our own thing, and most of the time we don't bother each other. There are plenty of humans to go around, more than enough to corrupt."

"But once you corrupt one, what do you get? At least I get a promotion."

"I told you. It's fun."

"Yeah? That and ten skulls will get you a cup of hot brimstone at the Hellcup Café." He stood over her, arms folded. "Monica, do you always barge in on devils when they're trying to work?"

"Not always." She grabbed his collar, pulled his face close, and kissed him. Nick was too startled to respond, even as her forked tongue slid into his mouth. The scorching tingle in his lips spread all the way to his clawed feet.

Monica pushed him back and rose from the chair. "Today was your lucky day." She stepped through the wall and disappeared.

* * *

NICK's PROJECT hummed along in the days that followed. The man started telling his girlfriend little lies and finding excuses to be alone with other women. He downloaded a dating app and scrolled through women's profiles.

And then . . . nothing. Nick was used to following a few straightforward steps and having the soul fall into his hands. This man had gotten stuck on something, maybe just his own stubbornness.

Arriving at the fiery halls of the Fourth Hell, Nick strode

through the flames to the office of his superior. Usually, Nick enjoyed making his weekly progress report, but this time there was almost no progress to report. And Old Scratch, the ranking devil in his unit, wasn't fond of excuses.

Scratch motioned Nick in but didn't look up from his desk, where he was cleaning a nasty-looking curved knife. The room smelled like blood. Scratch was larger than most devils, with ruby eyes and a scar on his cheek from a long-ago battle with a demon. He kept Nick waiting just long enough to wonder if Scratch already knew of his failure and was preparing the knife for him.

Finally Scratch looked up. "Nick. What have you got?"

Nick had rehearsed the conversation in his head. He planned to fill the air with half-truths and promises as thick as the smoke in this room. "A little progress. He's harassing women online, sending out dick pics, that sort of thing."

Scratch waited, as if expecting more.

"That's pretty much it." The smoke cleared in Nick's head as Scratch's blazing red eyes cut through any obfuscation.

"He's not cheating on the girlfriend?"

"No."

"How many women is he harassing?"

"Uh, one."

"Really? Because I'm sure I heard you say *women*, plural." Scratch stood up slowly, towering above Nick. "You know better than to lie to devils who outrank you, right?"

"Of course. I meant to say one woman."

"I had high hopes for you, Nick. You were supposed to be the star of this division of Hell." Scratch plunged the knife into the desk. "Either you show me some progress, or I send you to the acid lake to set an example for the new recruits." He pulled the knife back out. "Dismissed."

Nick felt Scratch's eyes on him as he walked away. He

needed to turn things around, fast. He could only think of one place to go for help.

And he'd like some more of that forked tongue.

* * *

NICK KNEW where the entrance to the Pit was located — all the devils knew. Seeing it up close for the first time, he was awed by the size of the volcano. Nick landed on the lip of the crater, gazing down at the bubbling cauldron of lava. How would he find her if he got inside?

Nick pulled his cloak tightly around him, pushed the hood over his face, and jumped.

The volcano's heat pressed all around him. Ordinary fire was no problem for a devil, but this was too much. Even with his eyes closed, the red heat seared at his vison. The foul vapor forced its way into his lungs.

Gasping for breath, Nick felt his feet land on solid stone. While the heat was still oppressive, it no longer threatened to burn through his clothes. He pulled his hood back and looked around. The air in the Pit reeked of sulfur, but he filled his lungs with relief.

The cavern was gigantic, with dim light provided by lava lamps along the walls. Some unseen force held back the lava overhead. Holes in the floor led to pools of magma or to darkness. There were openings along the wall, leading to shadowy passages.

The cavern was filled with demons: flying around, talking and laughing in groups, playing darts, dancing. They flitted in and out of the passages. Some were grotesque, and some were weirdly beautiful, but each was unique. Over-head, a demon with bat wings and a giant vulture were locked in a ferocious battle while those on the ground watched in amusement. A creature made of thousands of hands crept along the wall. A golden-haired child bared horrendous bloody fangs. Where should he start looking for Monica?

A man with a bull's head thundered his way across the room to glare in Nick's face. "You don't look like you belong here."

"I'm in disguise to look like a devil," Nick said smoothly. Some of the other demons nearby looked over, then went back to watching the winged creatures tearing each other apart.

The bull-headed demon moved closer. "You smell like a devil."

Nick considered escape routes. He could run for one of the portals in the wall, but he had no idea where they led. There was a hole in the floor behind him, leading only to darkness. He was used to being able to talk his way out of awkward situations. "I'm looking for someone. Green, snakes in her hair, goes by Monica. Maybe you've seen her?"

The demon lowered its horned head, preparing to charge. Nick braced himself.

A golden dragon flew from one of the portals and aimed itself straight at the bull-headed demon, roaring. The other demon stumbled back into the dark hole, its cry abruptly swallowed by silence.

The dragon disappeared, and in its place, Monica hovered in a black leather dress and winged shoes. A series of squeaking noises filled the air as she fluttered to the ground next to Nick and grinned. "Fancy meeting you here."

Nick looked around, but the dragon didn't reappear. "What just happened?"

"An illusion. I'm pretty good with those." The squeaking continued, and Nick realized they weren't winged shoes after all. The noise came from a pair of bats strapped to her feet.

"Interesting place you demons have here. It's so . . ." Chaotic? Confusing? Disturbing? "Different."

"What brings you here? Thinking of switching teams?"

Nick nearly spontaneously combusted. "That's not even possible. No one does that."

"You'd be the first."

"I believe in the devil way. Order. Logic. Purpose. But I was curious."

Monica ran her tongue along her teeth. "That's not a sin." Her amber eyes burned into him, incinerating his tissue-thin excuses for being here.

"You were pretty good with my human project. Is there someplace we can go and talk?"

The winged creatures battling overhead thumped to the floor, not moving. A demon poked at them with its foot, then shrugged and wandered off.

"Follow me," Monica said. She led Nick through a series of doors, and he found himself outside the volcano. Monica stepped onto a passing cloud, pulling Nick after her.

"I haven't been doing well with my project," Nick admitted. "Usually I'm really good at luring humans into sin, but this one, it's like he doesn't even hear me."

"You're too focused on work." She smoothed the snakes away from her face. "They're already talking about you like you're competition to knock Old Scratch out of the way."

He was *what?* "Who told you that?"

"I have my sources." She leaned in close. "You need to relax, Nick. Loosen up. Have some fun."

Nick wanted to argue with her. Devils didn't have fun; they were devoted to their job. But his only recent success had come with her help. "What kind of fun?"

"Let's go someplace with a lot of sinning going on."

"Congress?"

She wrinkled her nose. She was adorable when she wrinkled her nose. "Too much like working."

"I know!" Nick's face brightened. "Let's hit a casino."

* * *

Twenty minutes later, the bats having been freed and sent on their way, Nick and Monica strolled invisibly onto the casino floor. The smoke made him feel immediately at home. Slot machines mimicked the sound of cascading coins, although they only dispensed electronic receipts these days. The invigorating energy of sin buzzed all around them. Gambling addicts and alcoholics promised themselves they'd stop soon. A bachelor party trolled for hookers while the men sent loving texts to their wives and girlfriends. Drunk businessmen groped at cocktail waitresses, who had to smile and wish them a pleasant stay. Amateur poker players unsuccessfully tried to cheat the house. The house very successfully cheated the players. Nick eagerly drank it all in, nudging Monica to point out a pickpocket swiping chips at the craps table.

It was one glorious swamp of human misery.

"It's so easy here," Nick said. "We could pick any business traveler and get them to charge a pound of cocaine to the company card. Even Scratch would have to be impressed."

"Stop thinking about making points with your boss." Monica disappeared a bottle of champagne from a nearby table, slipping it into her impossibly small purse. "Start enjoying."

There was a rhythm to it, the lies and rationalizations, the swirl of intoxication, the greed and arrogance leading to empty pockets and despair. They watched a couple furiously break up after the girlfriend gambled away the down payment for their house. "But I had a system!" the woman screamed through her tears. "It wasn't supposed to lose!"

By the elevator, Monica saw a sign advertising the top-floor wedding chapel. "Ooh, let's go see who's been dragged to the altar drunk out of their minds and probably half naked."

Nick laughed and followed her into the elevator. He enjoyed visiting churches; they were among the easiest places to find sin. Gossip and backbiting, vanity, hypocrisy, and outright malice — a buffet for his diabolical tastes. The bride and groom would probably wake up tomorrow with killer hangovers, wondering when they got the tattoos and why they'd misspelled each other's names.

But inside the chapel, Nick found the couple sweetly serene, her in a simple white dress, him in a gray suit. They were in their thirties and disgustingly sober, with the feel of a longtime couple. Their handwritten vows mentioned the things they loved most about each other: his remembering her favorite flower and food and coffee, her willingness to try crazy new things like parasailing and a last-minute wedding. Friends and family crowded the small chapel, watching with tears and smiles.

Monica strolled up to the bride and whispered in her ear. "You're not really sure about this guy. What about your ex? You can still back out and admit this is a horrible mistake."

Nick tried the groom. "She has all those annoying habits. And that last little argument you had, maybe it wasn't so little after all. You shouldn't have to give up other women."

The couple continued to gaze lovingly into each other's lives, their smiles shining like halos.

"You may kiss the bride."

Nick looked over at Monica, and an emotion washed over him that he couldn't name. He couldn't keep his eyes off her beautiful, juicy lips. He wanted . . . what? To hear her say sweet nothings to him? Ridiculous. And yet here she was, getting him to try crazy new things. He ducked as the bouquet sailed over his head and landed in the hands of an elderly woman who laughed uproariously.

Monica ran a forked tongue across her lips. "Let's go see that human project of yours."

* * *

THEY RETURNED to the man's home, and were about to float through the wall when Monica put an arm in front of Nick. "Do you hear that? That's not his voice."

Nick listened at the door. He couldn't make out the words, but the voice was familiar.

He took Monica's hand and switched to full invisibility — not just to mortals, but to everyone. After a moment, Monica followed suit. They passed through the wall.

The man was sitting in his usual spot, scrolling on his phone. Perched on the arm of the couch was the unmistakable shape of Scratch.

Scratch's voice came in a hypnotic whisper: "You don't want to cheat on your girlfriend. She makes you happy. You want to make her happy. Looking on dating apps was just a childish fantasy. You can let that go now, because you're man enough to be faithful to her."

Monica yanked Nick's arm, pulling him back outside. Their images blinked into visibility.

"What the heaven is going on?" Nick sputtered. "That's Scratch. My boss."

"He's sabotaging you."

"But . . . devils don't do that."

"This one does." Her snake braids twisted themselves into an elaborate coronet around her head. "Obviously he knows

183

you're competition. He wants to make you fail; then he can swoop in and succeed, and take all the credit."

"Or maybe he's trying to get out of hell and escape to the other place?" Unthinkable. And yet Nick had seen it with his own eyes.

"We need to figure out a way to stop him." The way she said *we* sent a buzz through Nick's body. "What about your human project's girlfriend? Where does she live?"

In the twitch of a tail, they were at the woman's apartment. She was red-faced, dressed in sweatpants and a t-shirt with her hair pulled back, doing a furious aerobic routine in time with a video. The music was some old disco tune. When her phone buzzed, she stopped mid-kick to grab the phone. She read her boyfriend's text, frowning.

"Oh, no he doesn't." Monica's voice in the woman's ear was as smooth as sweet cream liqueur. "Why is he being so attentive all of a sudden? It doesn't feel like love; it feels like guilt. He's hiding something." She put a hand on the woman's face. Nick wanted her to touch him like that. He wanted her snakes twined in his hair. He wanted to kiss her on the—

"You gonna help me with this, Nick, or you just gonna stand there looking cute?"

Nick snapped back to the present and moved to the woman's other side, whispering. "You've seen him check out other women when he thinks you're not looking. What do you think he does all day when you're not there?"

The woman stared at the phone and pursed her lips, undecided.

"Remember that dating site where you met?" Monica purred. "I'll bet he's reactivated his account."

The woman hesitated, then looked up the website. A moment later, she hurled the phone across the room. She yanked open the hall closet, pulled out a baseball bat, and bent to retrieve the phone before storming out.

Nick and Monica spent the next two hours on a cloud above the man's neighborhood, munching popcorn laced with ghost peppers and gleefully watching the show. It started with a smashed windshield and escalated into a screaming argument that had the neighbors physically holding them apart until the police led them both away in handcuffs.

"Not bad." Monica tossed a ghost pepper in the air and caught it with her tongue. "When he gets back, he'll be all over that dating website, screaming about crazy bitches and sending dick pics all over the place."

Nick chuckled. "Let's see Scratch try to mess with that."

"He'll try again." Monica gave him an inscrutable look. "We need to find a way to neutralize Scratch."

Nick was struck with an idea. At least, afterward he was almost sure it had been his own idea. "Let's go visit Scratch's human project."

* * *

THEY TOOK a side trip to the gate of the Nine Hells. "You'll have to wait outside." Nick peered through the bars. "You'd stand out a little too much."

Nick turned and nearly impaled himself on his own fangs. Standing next to him was a devil, with uniform and rank insignia matching Nick's.

"You were saying?" The devil spoke with Monica's voice. "I told you, I'm really good at illusions." With a wave of her hand, she conjured a swarm of fanged butterflies and birds that flew around Nick's head. Their eerie song reverberated in the air for a moment after they disappeared.

Nick looked her over. He couldn't find a single flaw in the disguise, from her polished horns to her clawed hands. "Okay. Remember to walk in step with me."

The descent was quick, and Nick's nerves calmed enough to stop checking that her disguise was working. As they passed through the Second Hell to the barren ice of the Third, Nick saw with new eyes, trying to imagine how it looked to Monica. The blank, barren walls had a soul-sucking monotony that had never bothered him before. Even the tortured souls trapped inside the ice panes all looked alike after a while, their agonized expressions and soundless pleading all running together. Nick was tempted to smash a hole in the wall just to let their screams out.

A regiment of first-level devils marched by with their commanders. Even the new recruits marched in perfect step together. The nearest ones eyed his rank insignia as they passed, wistful envy on their faces. If they were relentless in their evil, they'd achieve that rank someday. For the first time, Nick wondered if any of this was worth having.

What if Monica was right, and the only thing worth having was fun? He wasn't even sure what fun was, but he knew he'd never had any in this place, and he never would.

In the Fourth Hell, they found the board where the devils' assignments were posted. His own most recent one was marked as a success, with the next assignment pending. Sweet.

Then they saw it: Scratch's assignment. While his under-lings spread ordinary evils, Scratch took the powerful sinners, the ones who could harm or destroy huge swaths of humanity at once. His target was a billionaire executive who routinely subjected his workers to dangerous conditions and lined his pockets through embezzlement. Now he needed to be persuaded to risk bribing public officials to let him dump chemical waste in a public waterway. Almost too easy a job for a prominent devil like Scratch.

* * *

Nick brought Monica with him to the executive's mansion. It was gigantic, with cathedral ceilings, velvet curtains, and an indoor pool. The man sat in front of his computer in a dimly lit room, bearded chin in his hand. He kept looking from the landline phone to the clock, as if expecting a call.

Nick glanced at Monica. The desire to impress her was as sharp as the burning in his mouth. "So, I'll get him to do something . . . good." The idea was terrifying, and yet, somehow, intoxicating. He would do an act of good that was secretly an act of evil because it would undermine Scratch. It was reckless, chaotic, almost unthinkable. He was thinking very hard about the unthinkable.

"I know you can do it." Monica melted into invisibility beside the window.

Nick bent next to the man. "You don't want this. Stealing a few dollars here and there, that's one thing. But poisoning the water will kill people. You won't know their names, you won't know which cancers were your fault, but you'll always know that you took people away from their families."

The man shifted restlessly. Nick wasn't sure if he was getting through or not. The man checked the clock again.

Nick kept pushing. "And for what? An extra zero in your bank book? You already have more than you'll ever spend. More than anyone could. Sit back and enjoy what you've got, instead of risking prison for the momentary thrill of feeling like you've scored a win."

The phone rang. The old man reached for it, stopped, and let it ring. The sound died away.

Nick put a hand on the man's shoulder, causing the slightest twitch. "You did the right thing." Nick wanted to laugh, hearing those words coming from his own fanged mouth. "You're not a bad man."

Several things happened at once. Hands seized Nick's arms and held them tight against his body. The human got up and wandered out of the room. Devils appeared all around Nick, popping into visibility and snarling at him. Directly in front of Nick, Scratch towered over him, his face blazing with fury.

"What do you think you're doing?" Scratch didn't give Nick a chance to answer. "You're going to the Ninth Hell, traitor. Let's see how you like a few centuries of torture in the acid lake. What is *wrong* with you?"

Scratch wasn't just furious — he seemed genuinely stunned, as if he couldn't imagine one devil betraying another like this.

The curtain twitched, and for a moment Monica came into view. She ran a forked tongue along her grinning lips before fading away again.

I'm really good with illusions.

The truth hit him like a thousand pitchforks. She'd set up the whole thing. And she'd done it for *fun.*

He was about to spend years being tortured at the bottom of the Nine Hells. He'd spend all that time plotting his revenge on her — something showy and cruel that would get her attention.

Anything that would get her to kiss him like that one more time.

* * *

Laura Ruth Loomis is the author of the science fiction comedy The Cosmic Turkey *and its forthcoming sequel* The Star-Crossed Pelican, *as well as a short story collection,* Lost in Translation. *Her fiction and nonfiction have appeared in* The Saturday Evening Post, Writer's Digest, On the Premises, Women on Writing, *and elsewhere. By day, she's a social worker. She can be found at LauraRuthLoomis.com, on Twitter at @Laura-Ruthless, and on Threads at @lauraruthless.author.*

A MOTHER'S PRIDE

MICHELE STUART

"Shut the muffin! All the taste is getting out!"

"How do you ask?" I said.

"Please shut the muffin!"

Cory giggled and squirmed in her seat. I tipped the muffin top onto the bottom, so the butter-soaked surfaces met, and slid the plate across the table to her. Cory loved my quarterly trips to the nearest town because I always came back stocked up with as many treats for her as I did staples for the pantry. Mama said I spoiled her. I said Mama was one to talk.

"You know, most people eat them cut open," I said.

"That's silly," Cory declared, with the absolute certainty of childhood, and disengaged the hinges of her lower jaw. She popped the muffin into her maw, letting her eyes close as she savored. I never tired of watching her eat.

Mama thinks she'll always be a dainty eater, probably never able to take in more than a rabbit. But not me. I see her daddy's strength in her. For about the thousandth time that morning, like every morning, I wished he were here to see it too. And, as always, I set that thought aside. Even the strong die. Nothing to be done about it. She might never be able to take in a wolf like he could, but she'd be a hunter to strike terror into the hearts of mama bears when she came for their cubs. I was sure of that, no matter what Mama said.

I was outside taking in the laundry, ahead of the coming storm, when Cory emerged from the woods leading the human child by the hand. Maybe the smell of the blood that covered them masked his scent, or maybe I was just lost in my memories again, because they took me by surprise. The boy was traumatized, bloody and scraped, dehydrated. Really, it would have been best to put him out of his misery, and would save us a truckload of trouble. I'd just come to that conclusion when Cory, her face lit up like a sunflower reaching for the summer sun, said, "Can I keep him, Mommy?"

The child followed her meekly, saying nothing, though the tear tracks on his filthy face said he'd cried at some point. Mama came out of the house, and she and I exchanged a look. Hers said, *This won't end well.* I tried to make mine say, *It could,* but I suppose I knew better, even then. I just couldn't bear to break my baby's heart.

I took the boy into the house while Mama started following his trail back the way he'd come, making sure nobody could follow him here. She'd tell me later about the car wreck, miles and miles away. It was a miracle the boy had wandered so far through the woods without becoming the victim of a wildcat or a nasty fall. He wouldn't have made it through the night, the way the weather was looking.

I cleaned the boy's wounds and got some water into him and a blanket around him. He wasn't as badly hurt as it had first appeared — cut and bruised all over, but nothing broken so far as I could tell. He didn't talk, though I didn't know if that was natural to him or if it was the trauma. Cory made efforts to help, offering him her toys to play with, but I could see that his lack of response frustrated her.

Mama was just coming through the door when I picked up the first whiff of Cory's rising hunger and caught her watching the boy. Mama followed my gaze and shook her head.

"She's not ready."

"She smells ready."

"There's a difference between wanting a thing and being able to take it. That's more than she can chew."

"David took a doe at her age."

"David was male and half again as big as most."

I just nodded, watching my precious baby, the scent of her hunger making me salivate.

"Let's leave it to her," I said. "See what she does."

Just when I was sure Cory was going to take him, he picked up her rag doll and curled up in front of the fireplace, hugging it close to his chest. Her look softened, and I guess mine probably did too. Who doesn't love baby animals?

I set about making dinner. I cooked the meat just enough so it wouldn't sicken the child, then added some potatoes and carrots. When he still hadn't moved after I'd put all the food on the table, I picked him up and plopped him into a chair. He was entirely unresistant. I wondered if he was locked in some dark place and would burst free someday in a torrent of words or screams.

Mama put a steak on each plate, and I watched to see if the boy needed help cutting his. Cory cut hers in half with a swift, decisive stroke. Then she unhinged her jaw, popped one of the slabs of meat into her mouth, and started to chew. The boy dropped his fork, his blue eyes wide. *Here it comes*, I thought. But he remained silent, though I could smell the fear wafting off him, both sharp and sweet. I had to press my palms into the table to keep from reaching across it and snatching him to me. I exchanged a glance with Mama. She didn't seem as affected as I was, and I wasn't quite sure how I felt about that. She looked tired. She reached over to the boy and started cutting his meat up into bites he could eat.

"Cory," I said, "Eat the rest of your meat with your knife and fork."

"Why?" she pouted.

"It's one of those skills you have to learn."

"A hiding skill?"

"Exactly. A hiding skill. Think of it as a game."

That brightened her up. She looked at the boy and tried imitating the delicate way he ate his small bites of food. That only lasted a few minutes.

"This takes forever!" she said.

I couldn't help but laugh. Even Mama chuckled. I noticed that Mama had also cut her meat and was taking it in bites that wouldn't call attention to herself among humans. I wondered if her jaw was sore, or if she just had no appetite. She caught me looking and maybe caught my train of thought, because she made a show of chewing up the last quarter of her steak and then growling at Cory. The boy shrunk back in his chair. Cory giggled.

"It's okay," Cory said to him. "I'll protect you!" She growled back at her grandmother. It made me proud to see how fierce and fearless she was. Just like her daddy.

That night I slipped out of the house and into the woods, making double sure the boy's trail was obscured. The heavy rain was a blessing. Cory stirred when I left, but Mama didn't move. She'd been sleeping the sleep of the old and tired, the sleep that a predator would prevent her ever waking from. She was awake when I got back, though, or else the sound of my sluicing the dirt off my face and hands at the pump had wakened her. When I went inside, she was stoking the fire in the iron stove and putting a pot of coffee on. The kids were asleep on a bearskin, not too close to the hearth. I thought a little color had returned to the boy's face.

"They're miles away," I said, taking the mug of coffee she offered me.

She looked at me with a question in her eyes, and I shook my head. "No signs of his trail. Even I couldn't pick it up."

I felt the tension drain from her. She'd been worried. She turned away from me and went on with cooking.

We started calling him Blue, for his brilliant blue eyes. I knew he could make noise, because I'd sometimes hear him whimpering in the night like an orphaned puppy, which I suppose he was. Sometimes I'd pick him up and rock him until he quieted, then put him back down next to Cory. He'd snuggle up to her warmth, like he felt safe there. It must have been pure, dumb luck that guided him over those many miles through the woods that day. It was like the child had no survival instincts at all.

A few days later, Cory and Blue were off in the woods behind the house when the sheriff's department SUV drove up and stopped out front. Two men got out, and the one with the hat on took it off as I walked out of the house to meet them.

"Ma'am," he said. "I'm Deputy Miller, and this is Deputy Crawford. We're wondering if you've seen this boy."

He held out a picture of Blue. It had been taken at a birthday party, probably his last one, as he didn't look much older now. There were five candles on the cake.

I shook my head. "No. Is he missing?"

I noticed the other deputy looking around, taking in the lay of the land, I supposed.

"Can I get you some coffee? Water?"

The polite one said, "I would love a cup of coffee. Thank you, Ma'am."

He wanted to get into the house. That was fine. Nothing

for him to see there. I led them inside and saw that Mama was already starting a pot.

"This is my mother, Agnes. Mama, these men are looking for this child."

Deputy Miller held out the picture. Mama examined it, then shook her head. "I don't know him. He's missing?"

"He is, Ma'am," Deputy Miller said.

The other one still hadn't spoken.

"That's a shame," Mama said, as she poured out coffee. They both declined sugar and non-dairy creamer but accepted seats at the kitchen table.

"How long?" I asked.

"Five days now," Miller said. "There was a car accident. His parents were killed."

"Oh, no," Mama and I said, at the same time.

I continued, "An accident near here, five days ago? I had no idea."

Crawford was still more or less examining every part of the house he could see, but Miller seemed to be relaxing a little.

"No," Miller said, "not all that near here. But we're — well, we're not quite ready to give up the search just yet. It's unlikely he'd have gotten this far through the woods on his own, but I guess anything's possible, right?"

I frowned. "I suppose . . ." I said. "This wood around us is thin and more or less tame. But it gets wilder, deeper in. There are bears. Wildcats . . ."

I let my voice trail off and sipped my coffee. Miller nodded in somber agreement.

Crawford said, "Could I use your facilities, Ma'am?" As if he could be more obvious.

"We have an outhouse around back. I'll show you."

"No need. I can find it."

I thought his face scrunched up a little at the word "outhouse," though he tried hard not to show it. Soft.

I nodded. "Okay."

Let him look around. I didn't want to have to kill them. I liked this homestead. It had been well-kept by its previous owners. But if it came down to it, I would, and we'd be gone before they were missed. I suspected, though, that Cory had taken Blue to her favorite spot down by the creek, well out of sight of the house.

Crawford came back after a good long while, smelling significantly less wary than he had previously.

"Well, thank you, ladies," Miller said, standing up. "If you do hear or see him, please call." He put a business card on the table.

"No phone, but we'll find a way," I assured him.

"You live all the way out here," Miller said, as Mama and I walked outside with them, "with no indoor plumbing? No phone or electricity?"

I nodded. "Yeah. They don't run cables out this far. But we have the truck. We go to town for supplies. Even take in a movie on occasion. It suits us."

He didn't say any more, just tipped his hat before putting it back on, climbed in the SUV, and turned it toward the road.

"Deputy!" I called, and he stopped and looked at me. "What's the boy's name?"

"Oh, sorry. Ashton. Ashton Carlisle."

"Thank you."

I'd been right about Cory. She had taken Blue to the creek. When they got back, they were both damp, their wet hair stuck to their heads.

"Who was here, Mommy?" Cory asked, sniffing the air. A pang of pride shot through me. Already she had a hunter's senses and instincts.

"Men looking for Blue."

Mama glanced at me, and I silently shook my head. Best if he forgot his real name and Cory never knew it. Wouldn't want her blurting it out at the wrong time, in front of the wrong person.

"You take him inside and get some dry clothes on him. Give him some of yours."

"Yes, Ma'am," she said. She took Blue by the hand, and he followed her obediently into the house.

"She thinks he's a pet," Mama said.

"Seems so."

"He's not a pet, Joanna. He's food."

I looked at her, and any anger that I might have felt was washed away in the sorrow of seeing how drawn her face was.

"It will be okay," I said. "She'll figure that out on her own."

"What makes you so sure?"

"She's her father's daughter. She's a predator. But predators can be children too, for a while. Besides, it's not a bad thing for her to be exposed to humans. She might not want to live wild when she grows up. She might want to pass."

"That boy's five. Maybe six. What's he going to teach her?"

"How frail they are," I said, then walked into the house.

Police came again, a few weeks later, then no more. When I made a trip into town to stock up on supplies, I used the computer at the library to read up on Ashton Carlisle. The case was still open, but his relatives had had a memorial service for him. There was no mention that he had been mute. I picked up a few books on that trip as well. I had to admit that I'd sadly neglected Cory's book-learning, but it was something she'd have to know if she did choose to pass. And I expected she would.

Sure, some of us live completely wild, out in the few

untamed places that are left on this earth. Some can't pass for human, even if they'd like to. They'd look a little too "off," like when the really slick animated movies come so close to looking real it discomforts people. A little too big, too heavily built, jaw protruding just a bit too much. But some of us look more or less like large, big-boned humans. Not too pretty, by their standards, but we could get by okay as long as nobody cut us open and took a look at the thickness of our bones and muscles, the way some of our joints were formed. Some have taken to city life, living among their prey, looking at the urban streets as just a different kind of wilderness. That always seemed like asking for trouble to me. I wondered what they did if they ended up in an emergency room or someplace else inconvenient. Mama had raised me in a middle that I was content with. I liked being mostly self-sufficient, but I didn't mind buying some of our clothes off the rack or even having a restaurant meal every once in a while.

Blue still didn't speak, but he got stronger as we passed from summer into fall, and sometimes he laughed. Some of the shadows faded from those startling blue eyes. I would watch him and Cory play and wonder what was going to come of this. One day I caught Mama teaching him how to tell which way the wind was coming from, and he managed to sneak up on Cory and pounce on her back. When Mama saw me looking, she shrugged.

"May as well give the child a fighting chance," she said.

Cory had to learn to check her strength when playing with him. It was a valuable lesson. Of course, I'd never say *I told you so* to my mother, but I caught her smirking at me once or twice in a way that said she knew. Sometimes he did get hurt, though. Cory would pull his arm too hard, or push him, and he'd cry. A couple of times, during their hunting game, I felt her hunger come upon her, saw the fierce light in her eyes, and I thought the moment had come at last. That this would be it. Then Blue would whimper and throw himself at her, wrapping his arms around her waist in a hug that might have harmed another human child, and her hunger immediately ebbed. She'd wrap her arms around him and hug him back, much more gently, then ruffle his hair, and they'd resume their play.

Blue often trailed along when Mama or I took Cory out hunting, though after a time we were comfortable enough to leave him at the house, if he wanted. But he liked to come along. I'd have thought the woods might traumatize the poor thing, given what he'd been through, but he seemed to love the wilderness nearly as much as Cory did. He learned to be still and quiet, neither of which seemed too hard for him. He was such a quiet child anyway. He showed a particular interest in the creek. Much as I hate to admit it, he got a little more adept than Cory at catching fish and frogs. She wanted to brute force everything. She was all speed and savagery, but Blue would settle into the water and just wait until the fish got used to him being there, and then, inevitably, one would swim too close to his hand, and he'd slowly close his fingers around it and toss it up onto the bank, beaming with pride. Soon he could catch the ones that took both his little hands to hold. He seemed to like it when the fish he caught were served for dinner.

He wasn't as good with larger prey, like squirrels or rabbits, which was good, I suppose. I didn't want this human child to excel in Cory's domain. She was a whiz at snagging squirrels. She was so fast. It warmed my heart to watch her. Mama and I decided to move her up to rabbits. I was going to demonstrate, but Mama said she'd do it.

I stayed home with Blue, reading to him from a story book, while Mama and Cory went out, so I didn't actually see it happen. But I knew, as soon as they got home. I knew as soon as I saw the look of confusion on Cory's face and of resignation on Mama's. I swallowed hard, set Blue down, and went to make coffee.

Blue was picking up on the fact that something was wrong too, but he didn't know what. He and Cory climbed into my old rocking chair together, not sure what to do. I heard Cory whispering to him how Grandma hadn't been able to catch the rabbit, but how she herself had come this close and was sure she'd get the next one. I was sure too. It hurt me that her moment of glory had been darkened by this mood that had fallen over the house, that she would not crow with pride over her hunting prowess at the dinner table.

At least five times, over dinner, I swallowed back the word that was on the tip of my tongue. *Stay*, I wanted to say to my mother. *I'll take care of you. I can do it easily. We can move to a town, if you want.* But I knew she would not. She was too proud to let me care for her until the end, and it would break her heart to have to deny me. It wasn't as if she were pregnant, or wounded, or anything she'd get over with time and care. There was no healing from age.

I heard Mama leave in the middle of the night. I was still awake when dawn came, barely fading the darkness. It would be a gray, rainy day. I hadn't felt so tired, so weary to my bones, since David died. I knew I'd have to have the talk with Cory that day. I would explain how those of us who live to old age, which wasn't a lot of us, would go off alone when we could no longer provide for ourselves. I would explain how each of us knew when that time had come, or so I'd been told. It's not as if a single failed hunt was a death sentence. Of course not. It was an accumulation, just as I imagine it was for aging humans and other animals.

What would we do, out there on our own, in our final days? I don't know. It's not like our elders came back to tell us. Maybe Mama would find a way to keep herself going for years. Maybe she'd pick a fight with a bear and go out gloriously. But what she would not do is be a burden to her family. This might not be everyone's way. It's not as if we have strict laws and rituals. Like humans, our customs grow over generations from the practices that help us survive. And things change with time. Maybe I would not go off this way, when my time came. But my mother did.

I knew Cory missed her grandmother, but youth has a resilience about it that seemed to be fading from my memory. Or maybe that was just my grief talking. I had plenty of good, strong years left. Plenty of years to watch my daughter grow into the hunter I knew she would be. In these spring days, it seemed as if she were blossoming as fast as the pansies and daffodils. It was a little shocking. Some days I felt like I could see her growing. She'd started wearing her grandmother's clothes over the winter, and I took her with me on my supply run and bought her some jeans and new shoes, and some for Blue as well. I got bolts of fabric and sewing supplies so I could sew for the kids on Mama's old treadle machine. I figured they'd both soon be outgrowing clothes as fast as I could make them. I didn't expect Cory to ever achieve her daddy's size, but she probably weighed as much as me now. I've always been small.

Blue wasn't going through quite the growth spurt Cory was, but we'd always figured him for a few years younger. I didn't think he'd ever match even my size, though many human men do. Of course, I had no idea what kind of stock he came from. Maybe he'd suddenly become a bruiser later in life. I thought he was average-sized, for a human child, but he got tougher with each passing day. Most humans would be surprised by his strength and agility. He had a few scars that probably would have given a teacher or police officer pause, but he'd healed up fine. And truth is, sometimes if Cory got too rough, he gave back as good as he got.

I loved to watch them play, and my mood lightened as the summer days stretched on. I learned to carry the weight of Mama's absence, just as I had David's. By the end of summer, both the youngsters were actively contributing to the household, Cory with her hunting and Blue with occasional fishing, but mostly with the gardening I taught him. By the end of summer, I could leave most of the weeding and watering to him while I sewed or cooked or laundered. Oh, the sewing. He might not have been growing quite as fast as Cory, but a shirt didn't last too long on either of them before it was pulling across their shoulders and leaving their wrists bare.

I was sewing the day I heard Blue scream. It was a gorgeous late summer day, the heat making everything lazy. I'd thought the kids were down by the creek, but Blue's screams came from just at the edge of the woods. They'd been climbing trees — or more accurately, falling from them — and he'd landed badly. One foot was at the wrong angle to his leg, and blood gushed from his other calf. I could see the shape of the jagged ends of broken bones under his pant leg. Cory was off to one side, frozen. I thought she was in shock for a moment, then I caught the scent of her hunger and knew she was reacting to the blood and the helplessness of her prey. *I should have let this play out,* I thought, even as I was scooping him into my arms, a mother's instinct overruling a hunter's in the moment. Cory broke from her reverie and came running after me as I strode to the house.

I settled him onto the couch. His screams subsided to a series of gasps and whimpers. I got some aspirin into him, for all the good that did.

"Sit by him, Baby," I said to Cory. "I'm going to make him something for the pain."

As I waited for the water to come to a boil, I started to think again. What was I going to do about this? I was not equipped to deal with an injury of this type. He wasn't like us. He wouldn't heal like we do. If the bones didn't get set right, at best he'd be crippled. At worst, he'd die an agonizing death from infection. I supposed I could cut them off. A good, clean cauterizing cut. And then what? What would he do without legs?

"Can you fix him, Mama?" Cory asked, as if reading my thoughts.

I decided I had best take this bull by the horns. Dancing around it wouldn't make it any easier. "No," I said, turning from the stove toward her. "No, Baby, I can't fix him."

She blinked at me, her mouth hanging open. That was the moment, I knew, when she realized that her mother, in fact, could not always make everything okay. I wanted to crawl into a hole and die.

"We have two choices, as I see it," I went on, forcing my voice to steadiness. "We can take him to the doctor in town —" she nodded in enthusiastic agreement, until I added, "— and leave him there. We'll drop him on our way out of town."

"W-what? Leave him?"

"Yes, Honey. If we do that, we'll have to leave this place. We'll have to leave him. They'll figure out who he is quick enough, even without him talking. They'll start looking for who's been keeping him all this time. And we'll have to be gone when that happens."

"But . . ." She looked around at her home, and then down at Blue, at a loss for words, then blurted, "But we can't just leave him!"

"There is another choice."

She looked up at me with such hope on her face. "What?"

"The kind thing to do would be to put him out of his misery."

"What . . . what does that mean?"

I finished the brew that Mama had taught me. It would take the edge off the hurt, but certainly wouldn't dull it entirely. I blew on the tea to cool it some, then took it over to Blue, hoping he was too delirious with pain to understand us. I raised his head just enough to get him to sip the tea, slowly.

"What does that mean?" Cory asked again, her tone more insistent.

"When an animal is in great pain," I said. "When you know you can't do anything for it, it's cruel to let it suffer. I've taught you that, haven't I?"

She nodded, then said, "But Blue's not an animal."

I ignored that.

"He doesn't heal like we do, Cory. He's in agony and that's not going to end any time soon. Do you want to see him like this for weeks and weeks? Even if he does heal, he'll be a cripple. And if he doesn't, his death will be terrible."

She swallowed and looked down at him. I could still see the spark of her initial reaction, behind her concern for her beloved pet. I could see it in the way her nostrils flared, and the way she licked her lips without, I was sure, realizing it.

"You wouldn't have to do it," I whispered to her. There I went, being too soft on her again. Mama would certainly have wanted her to do it. Maybe David, too. But maybe not. She'd been his special girl. "I'd be fast," I said.

I could see her resolve weakening. I set the mug aside, my whole attention focused on Cory, and hers on me. She swallowed, and I chose to think I saw her nod, just barely. I turned back to Blue. He was staring at me. He was still whimpering nearly continuously. Tears streamed from his amazing blue eyes and his lips trembled. He knew. Maybe he wasn't really hearing our words, through his fog of pain and tea, but he knew. I hesitated for just a moment, considering the most merciful death I could give him, when he uttered the first real word we'd ever heard him say.

"Cory!" he wailed.

I saw, in that instant, how wrong I had been about Blue. I saw that his survival instincts were strong. I looked up and met my daughter's eyes as she lunged over the couch at me, her weight sending me sprawling, her jaw unhinging as she dove for my throat. I'd never been so proud.

* * *

MICHELE STUART LIVES with her husband in the southeastern United States. Aside from the husband, she loves writing, reading, art, languages, listening to podcasts, working out, eating, and lying around. Find her on Mastodon (@crystalbrier@wandering.shop), BlueSky (@crystalbrier.bsky.social), or at her website, https:// michelestuart.me

A MURDER IN BEL HAMMOND

KAREEM MISKEL

It was the final round. I'd bought my way up to a twenty-sided die. One blow for luck, and I let it fly. It hit the table rolling and landed on fourteen. Across from me the house player scowled and studied my cards. "Priest of shields," he called.

I stared at the cards in front of me. That was a defensive call. Desperate. Now he couldn't win anything even if I lost. I flipped over the Priest and found a red eye staring up at me. He begrudgingly dropped fourteen silver chips on the table. "Better luck next time," I said, sliding the chips into my purse.

A tap on my shoulder turned me around. It was one of the guards, a plain-looking fellow in scale armor. "Mr. Stang invites you to join him for dinner."

I glanced at the window that loomed above the gaming floor. "I'd be honored." Stang was new in town, and he'd wasted no time turning an old warehouse into an upscale gambling hall. I counted thirty-five tables and forty guards. One of those numbers was off. My guide led me up a flight of stairs and into a lavish dining room. The window to my right ran almost the full length of the wall. To my left were a pair of smaller windows with wooden shutters. Outside was the alley.

A well-stocked table greeted me from the center of the room. Fruits, cheeses, a pitcher, and two glasses. I was flattered. My host shuffled around from the opposite end to introduce himself.

Anto Stang was tall for one of his people, standing as high as my chest and sporting a chubby body. His skin was the color of tanned leather, his hair short and brown. A pair of slim, pointy horns sprouted from the top of his forehead and curved backward. His tail danced behind him, shuffling the blue and silver finery he wore. He smiled graciously, but he had the eyes of a man who thought himself clever.

I'm easy to underestimate. I'm no taller than the average woman, and my slim body looks frail under loose clothes. I've got a practiced smile set into a sweet, bronze face complete with dimples. I giggled vacantly and ran my fingers through my short, brown hair. A lot of humans find korrigans attractive. It couldn't hurt to let him think I was one of them.

"Good evening," he said folding his thick hands around mine. "My name is—"

"Oh, I know who you are," I blurted out and faked a blush. "Sorry. My name is Vinara Tavey."

"A pleasure to meet you, Miss Tavey." He pulled a chair out for me. "Please. Make yourself comfortable."

I sat down and pretended not to pay attention to the pair of armored guards posted at the other side of the room. Or the one behind me.

"I've taken the liberty of preparing some refreshments," he said filling the glasses. "Stolish honey wine. I think you'll like it."

"Thank you." I lifted my cup. "To new friendships."

He raised his glass and took a sip. I pretended to drink.

"I understand you've had a pretty good night in my gambling hall."

"I have. This is a lovely place you've put together."

"A few of my house players think you're cheating. I'm sure it's just a misunderstanding, but I hope you don't mind helping me clear it up."

"No misunderstanding," I confessed. "I was cheating."

A stunned flinch. A disappointed frown. "My dear, you've no idea how much it pains me to hear that. Why would you do such a thing?"

"To meet you, of course."

He wagged his finger at me and said, "You're trying to flatter me."

"Not at all. How else was I supposed to win an audience with Anto Stang?"

"Why would you want to?"

"Curiosity. Contact-building. And to fulfill my contract with Gaspar Vartares."

Anto recoiled.

The guard behind me took a step forward. A slender dart whipped from my sleeve, sinking into his neck. He dropped to the floor. I pulled a hidden knife and pressed it against the korrigan's throat as his remaining guards drew their swords. "Let me go," Stang commanded, "or they'll kill you."

"We both know they won't," I argued. Then I put a dart in his neck too. He wouldn't be unconscious for long — his people were pretty hardy — but he was out for the moment. The two guards shimmered and returned to their posts. Downstairs, there were still forty guards watching over the hall. Impressive work.

I threw Anto over my shoulder and climbed out the window. My accomplice was waiting at the end of the alley in a black carriage. We were gone before anyone knew something was amiss.

The driver and I said nothing. There was no need. Everything was running smoothly.

As the carriage made its way along the cobblestone streets, I stared vacantly into the city. Bel Hammond is called the City of Second Chances for good reason. There are dozens of cities throughout the Garvan Commonwealth, but Bel Hammond is where you go when no one else will have you. We don't much care about your past mistakes or former shortcomings. You get a clean slate and more than enough space to get lost in.

The infamous evening fog crept in. The moon might have been full, and the stars might have been out, but no one could see them through the night mists. Fortunately, the magical lampposts would burn away the fog in short order.

In a city of more than a hundred thousand, the korrigans are outnumbered by humans eight to one, but it's still their city. They built it and they run it. If you need to be reminded of that, you can just look at the magic lamps. Or the lift chambers in tall buildings. Or the stores that sell enchanted items. Throughout the rest of the world, magic is rare. You could live your entire life without ever meeting a single wizard. But the korrigans can all do some sort of magic or another. Most can't do much, but they can all do some.

Anto stirred awake mid-travel. "Where am I?" he croaked. "What happened?"

"It'll come to you," I promised.

A few seconds later he exclaimed, "Wait. You kidnapped me!"

"There it is."

"Why?"

"I'm taking you to see Gaspar."

He sputtered. "I'll double whatever he's paying you!"

"And will you uncut my throat when he finds out? Relax. Gaspar can still make money off you. He probably won't want you dead."

"'Probably'? Is that the best you can do?"

"You rudely declined his offer of protection. I'd say 'probably' is rather generous."

We came to a stop in front of Gaspar's house. It was no great mansion, but with twenty rooms, it was larger than most. The carriage driver, an ugly bald ogre of a man, yanked Anto from the car.

The house interior was carpeted, draped, gilded, and decorated in a dozen ways rich people decorate their homes. The doorman took my cloak and led us to the sitting room.

Gaspar was slim with a handsome narrow face, short black hair, and a thin mustache. He was fond of brown and gold, as evidenced by his silk robe. The golden hue of his skin and his peppery accent made me guess that he was from some southern nation. Maybe Alumayne or Mulhara. Frankly, I could never tell the difference and didn't care enough to ask. He stood up to greet me much as Anto did. "Vinara, you treasure. You came through again!"

"Have I ever let you down?"

"Not yet. You'll have to tell me how you got past all those guards."

"Not as many as you think," I said. "Stang here's an illusionist. He only has about fifteen real guards at his little gambling den."

"Really?" Gaspar chuckled.

"Most of his business is covered in illusion as well. It's how he managed to make a warehouse look so reputable so quickly. The enchantments are impressive, strong enough to sustain themselves if he's gone or unconscious, but pliable enough that he can control them on command."

Gaspar's face lit up. "You're a charlatan?" he said to Anto.

"I have the greatest respect for charlatans! I can make us both very rich, my friend. You'll see. Thench!" The ogre stepped forward. "Make our friend comfortable in one of the guest rooms. We have much to discuss!"

Thench nodded and carried Anto out of the room. Gaspar grinned at the korrigan's protests. "I don't know how you do it, but you always come through, especially with the little folk."

Gaspar never said it out loud, but he'd guessed some time ago that I had the ability to sense magic. With some training and practice, I probably could have been a talented spell-worker, but there was a deep distrust of human wizards in the Commonwealth. It wasn't just among the korrigans; other humans didn't like them either. It was one of those social taboos that was *almost* illegal. "Now, about my payment," I said, knowing that Gaspar was wanting something else.

"Of course, of course." He tossed me a small bag.

I counted the fifteen gold chips inside. "So, is that it?"

"No. Are you free to help me with something else?"

I took a seat across from him. "It depends on the 'something else.'"

"I'm afraid one of my people ran into some grave misfortune tonight."

"You need me to clean up the scene?"

"On the contrary. I want you to catch the murderer."

As a bounty hunter I'd had to solve crimes before. Over the years I had done it for nobles, merchants, and other honest business folk, but never for the notorious Captain of the Qarama Syndicate; he usually handled this sort of thing himself. "Okay. I'll follow. Who's the corpse?"

"He went by the name Kalan Durel, but his real name was Sylvas Grey."

I didn't like the sound of that.

"It's every bit as bad as you think," Gaspar said, reading my face. "He was an undercover sentinel."

I leaned back in my chair and murmured, "I need a drink."

Before I could stop him, Gaspar rang the tiny silver bell next to his chair, hailing a portly maid. "Bring Ms. Tavey a glass of wine, will you? Something sweet and red."

The maid gave a tiny bow and turned to me. "Would you like a drop of pique, Milady?"

Pique was a drug made from some root in the wildlands. One drop would add several intoxicating effects to even the weakest wine or spirit. It was illegal almost everywhere, but as much fun as it was, it was the last thing I needed. I shook my head and turned back to Gaspar. "You want me to work through the murder of a sentinel?"

"I'll pay handsomely, of course."

"Damn right, you will."

"Sylvas is from Caradon. He moved to Bel Hammond a year ago. He's been undercover as Kalan ever since."

"How long have you known he was a guard?"

"Since before he got here."

The maid came back with my wine. I drained the glass and continued. "Okay. Why didn't you just kill him yourself?"

"For the same reason I want you to investigate his murder."

"You don't want trouble with the sentinels."

He nodded. "It was easier to hide things from him until his commanding officer got bored."

"Who is his commanding officer?"

"A constable named Banion Burkos. He transferred from Caradon as well. That was few years ago, but my spies say he's been around."

"I know who he is."

"There's more," he said. "Sylvas was found dead in his

home. He lived in one of the Esterville apartments on the south side of Old Gran."

"In Constable Hayne's ward," I finished. "So, we're looking at a jurisdictional issue."

"But I have the utmost faith," he said. "If anyone can solve this, it's you."

"Yes," I said. "And for five plat, I'll do it."

"Five platinum chips?" he exclaimed.

"Due before I leave."

"Nonsense! I'll pay two plat."

"Five plat or I walk," I insisted. "That's the price of putting me on a murder case between two constables." I thought for a moment. "And a vial of pique. The good stuff, not that swamp water you peddle to the cankers in back alleys."

Gaspar capitulated with a sigh. "You drive a hard bargain, Vinara. For that price, I want it done before sunset tomorrow."

"You'll get your results," I told him. "Like you said, I always come through."

* * *

IN SOME WAYS, criminals are actually more honest than official folk. When a councilman hires you, they don't really care if you solve the crime; they just want you to get their son's name taken off the suspect list. When a constable asks you to investigate the murder of the magistrate's nephew, he's just looking for a name good enough to get the magistrate off his back. All the better if the man's guilty, but no one really cares.

Gaspar cared. The person who murdered Sylvas Grey had interfered with his business. The way he saw it either the murderer knew Sylvas was a guard and bought Gaspar trouble, or they didn't know and attacked one of his people.

Either way, it had to be answered. That complicated matters a bit.

Old Gran was the river that cut Bel Hammond in two. It poured down from the Vandian Mountains and emptied into the Bay of Ventures. Esterville was, as the name suggested, on the east end of town. There were apartments of varying quality. Sylvas's was a three-story brick place in fair condition. I arrived in a carriage cab and found a dozen sentinels standing around idly while two constables argued over which of them had the bigger sword.

Warrick Hayne and I went back a long way. He was a tall, stocky man with no hair on his head and no humor on his square face. We weren't friends, but we worked well together even though he was born stuffed from both ends: a silver spoon in his mouth and a stick up his backside.

I had never actually met Banion Burkos. At forty-some years old, he was a decade Warrick's junior. Brown stubble peppered his sharp chin and chiseled jaw. He wasn't much bigger than me, but his strict posture made him seem larger.

Both were dressed in the blue and black uniform of a sentinel constable with Warrick's slightly more decorated for valor, vigilance, bravery, and other such nonsense. As for their swords, they were the same length.

Their debate slowed to a halt as I approached. Warrick was particularly stunned. "What the devil are you doing here?" he demanded.

"Good to see you too, Constable Hayne."

"Yes, yes. It's a pleasure. Now, what are you doing here?"

"The same thing you are, I'd wager. I'm here to investigate a murder."

Banion cut in. "I'm sorry. I don't believe we've met. Are you a constable?"

"She's a bounty hunter," Warrick answered. "Her name is Vinara Tavey. The constabulary sometimes hires her as a consultant. But I didn't ask her here, and it's obvious that you didn't either."

"I was hired by Gaspar Vartares."

"Vartares," Banion spat. "No doubt, he wants to angle suspicion away from himself."

"That's exactly what he wants," I answered.

"Well, you can return to your employer and tell him that he'll not escape justice this time!"

"Gaspar knew about your plant from the outset," I said. "If he was stupid enough to kill a sentinel, the constabulary would have nailed him by now."

Banion regarded me closely, trying to learn every detail of my history and character with a glare. "Hear me, Miss. I will not allow you to take part in this investigation. Should I find you pursuing this, I'll have you chambered. Is that clear?"

Warrick spoke up again. "This is not Caradon, Constable Burkos. So long as she doesn't tamper with evidence or influence witnesses, she is free to investigate as she likes."

"This is not your investigation, Constable Hayne. I'll thank you to stay out of my affairs."

"Until we hear from the magistrate, we don't know whose investigation it is. But it doesn't matter. Her rights are a matter of law."

They argued for a few minutes more before the magistrate arrived. Havrol Lind didn't look happy as he stepped out of his carriage. And why would he? The hour was late, and the air was damp. He was a korrigan whose brown skin was turning gray with old age. His horns spiraled like a ram's, and his tail dragged behind him languidly. He wore a professional, black tunic and walked with a cane. His keen eyes fell on each of the constables and then on me. "Glory, Woman! What are you doing here?"

"Pleasure to see you again, Your Honor."

"Damn your pleasantries, Tavey. Answer the question!"

"I was hired by Gaspar Vartares to look into the murder of one of his employees."

He glowered at me. "And what do we have here that's causing such a to-do between the city's constables?" he demanded.

"A murder has taken place in my ward," Warrick answered.

Banion stepped forward. "But it was one of my guardsmen."

The magistrate frowned. "Sylvas?"

"Yes, sir."

The old korrigan scowled. "I warned you that this could happen."

"Sylvas was a dedicated guardsman, Sir. He knew the risks."

"Because he was smarter than you, Burkos!" he said, stabbing his cane upward toward the constable's chest. "You've played this stupid from the beginning! Why should I give you another chance to muck it up?"

"Because I'm the person most devoted to learning the truth. Let me be the one to follow this through, Sir. I'll bring Gaspar in once and for all."

Havrol's eyes became narrow. "Sounds to me like you've already decided the truth."

"It seems obvious."

"With indisputable logic like that, why investigate crimes at all?" Warrick argued.

Burkos sneered. "If he's innocent, then the examination will reveal it to be so."

"More likely, your personal feelings will cause you to make a mistake," Warrick said. "Who knows what oversights could be caused by your anger? It's better for everyone if this is dispassionately investigated."

"Probably," Lind remarked, "but if it were one of yours, I'd wager you would want to be at the fore of the probe." He looked up at them. "Don't suppose I could trust the two of you to play nice?" The constables exchanged cold glances. "I thought not. Burkos, it's your lucky day. I'm inclined to let you investigate, but I don't trust your objectivity. Fortunately, there's an experienced investigator here who can take you to task. Right, Miss Tavey?"

I raised an eyebrow. "You're hiring me?"

"Not at all," he chuckled derisively. "You won't see a single rusty chip from the city on this. You're already working for Gaspar. I'm partnering you with Burkos so you can keep each other out of trouble."

Burkos protested. "With all due respect, Your Honor, I would rather—"

"I didn't ask what you would rather. It's either this or Hayne takes charge. Your choice."

The constable gave a resigned nod. "Yes, Sir."

Hayne left without argument.

The magistrate spent a few more minutes bullying us into good behavior before he followed.

Burkos posted his men around the premises and secured the scene. Who knows how long Sylvas had lain dead on the floor of his home while two professional peacekeepers circled each other in the street? His body had already begun to stiffen, the contraction of his muscles contorting him into an agonized pose on the floor. His skin was pale and waxy. His eyes were staring blankly into whatever secret awaits us in the afterlife.

The victim's apartment was small and sparsely furnished. There was a front room, a small bedroom, and a tiny larder. The front room had a few chairs and a dinner table large enough for two. The bedroom had a hay-stuffed mattress laid on the floor and a side table with a flower sitting in a clay vase. The flower was a star-shaped explosion of black petals that became dark red toward the edges.

Banion kneeled next to the body and began his examination. "Poison," he remarked. "The oru-gull, if I'm not mistaken." He looked up at me. "It's an Azhari name. It translates to—"

"The Final Night. I'm familiar with it." This constable knew his stuff. Oru-gull was rare this far north. "You're right. The thick, red streaks in his eyes give it away."

"The rigidness of the body suggests he's been here for a few hours."

"How'd you find out what happened?" I asked. "Who told you he died?"

"I found out," he snapped. "That's all you need to know!"

Apparently, Banion was the clever sort who secretly kept spies around the city. "Very well."

He started moving the body and searching the victim's bare skin.

"What are you looking for?" I asked.

"An injection point. This poison creates a distinct, red mark when it touches the skin."

"Which is why assassins don't use it like that," I said. "The entire point of using the Final Night is to make the death look natural. It doesn't work immediately, so the killer can make a clean getaway before the victim dies of what appears to be a sudden illness."

"Did your criminal employer teach you that?"

I ignored him. "We should backtrack his movements. The poison was probably put into his food or drink."

"Well, if you can guess where he might have eaten or drunk, feel free to let me know."

A few minutes into our partnership, and already his attitude was getting on my nerves. I went into the bedroom and came out with the flower. "Do you know what this is?" I asked him.

"Should I?"

"Yes, actually. It's called a candied coral. It's an edible flower that only naturally grows in your home country."

He scowled at me.

"Unless I'm mistaking your accent."

"I left Theign many years ago," he answered.

"My point is, they're hard to grow outside the Theignish meadowlands. I only know one person here who raises them."

* * *

I WAS NEVER one to frequent Lady Arende's Spring and Spa. I've little use for the sort of comfort offered there, and I have always been confused by the name. Why not just call it "Lady Arende's Brothel"? No one looks down on such things in the Commonwealth. Maybe it was just to make it seem like a classier establishment. If that were the case, it didn't really need the help. The "Spring and Spa" was in an old mansion on the other side of the river. It was a huge place made of smooth whitestone with a lot of columns.

Arende herself had soft, honey-colored skin and gorgeous amber eyes. Her hair was a curtain of black velvet that draped past her shoulders. That night she was wearing a dark purple dress that looked like it had been carefully poured over her. It splashed onto her elegant shoulders and down her ample bosom. From there it flowed to her flat abdomen and onto her shapely thighs. It rained down from her thighs as dresses do in a ruffling cloak that kept the mystery of her legs from those unwilling to pay.

I have never bedded a woman before, but if I did, this is where I would start.

We sat in Arende's personal dining area. It was much nicer than Anto's. Her servers poured us each a glass of wine, and to my surprise, Banion accepted. "Why, yes, I did know Kalan. He was here earlier tonight, in fact." Her lips sank into a frown. "So sad that he has passed on. How did it happen?"

"We're not sure," Banion answered quickly. "We believe that his heart simply failed him, but we would like more information. You say he was here earlier tonight. Did he exhibit any signs of illness?"

"No more than usual."

"He was usually ill?" I wondered.

"Not with any physical malady. I tended to Kalan myself per Mr. Vartares's request."

Constable Burkos grumbled. "Gaspar requested that you service Kalan personally?"

"It would be more accurate to say he insisted upon it."

I tilted my head. "Why would he do that?"

She shrugged. "He didn't say, and I didn't ask. I do know the poor man couldn't have been less interested in what I had to offer."

"I find that hard to believe," I blurted.

"It's true. Kalan had an affliction. He preferred the touch of men."

The constable stiffened noticeably. His sneer was brief, but you could feel it in the air.

I spoke before he could respond. "Forgive me, Lady Arende, but I find it odd that you would view an attraction between two men as an affliction."

"You misunderstand me, Dear. Attraction to men is an affliction regardless of who you are; it matters not what apparatus one is born with. To love a man is to invite heartbreak and pain. Most men avoid this by having the good sense to love women. But some men don't have this option, poor dears. All we can do is accommodate their tastes as best we can."

"If you wanted to accommodate his tastes so much, why didn't you assign him to one of your men?" I asked. "Why did you tend to him yourself?"

"I told you. Gaspar insisted it be me."

My curiosity got the better of my professionalism. "Was he able to . . . ?"

"Oh, yes. Don't let them fool you, Darling. Any man can perform with any warm body if he needs to. Or if he's lonely enough. And Kalan was incredibly determined."

I continued. "You say that Gaspar insisted that you service him personally. But you don't work for Gaspar, do you?"

"No. But we have an arrangement."

"Did he ever speak to you before you serviced him?" Banion asked.

"Of course. Before and after. He was very eager for good conversation. Always so charming and polite."

"What did you talk about?" he pressed.

"Constable Burkos, my clients expect a certain level of confidentiality. I see no reason to ignore it when they leave this world."

"This is a possible murder investigation, *Milady*. You will answer any and all questions asked of you."

As smooth as silk, Lady Arende leaned back in her chair and swirled the crystal wine glass in her hand. She met the constable's gaze with iron resolve. "I'm afraid I can't remember."

Burkos fumed. I took over the conversation before he could explode. "Did Kalan have anything to eat or drink while he was here?"

Her expression softened as she looked at me. "Oh, no. He never ate or drank anything during his visits."

"But he had a candied coral," I said. "Surely he could only have gotten it from you."

"A gift. He had developed a taste for them as a young man and agonized over the ones in my garden. I could endure it no more. I insisted he take one with my regards. Tell me the dear man got to enjoy it before he died."

I frowned. "I'm afraid not."

* * *

We climbed into Burkos's personal carriage and waited in silence for several uncomfortable seconds. "So where are we off to now?" I asked him.

He stared into the night for a few seconds before saying, "I knew about Sylvas's preferences."

"Of course, you did. You were lovers in Theign."

He looked at me with a stunned expression.

I shrugged, "Anybody listening to that conversation could tell."

"Lady Arende?"

"Anybody," I repeated.

"So very clever," he sneered.

"Is that why you sent him?"

Banion took a moment before answering. "Sylvas was incredibly principled. But so are many of the sentinels on Vartares's payroll. Women are one of his most common tools to win them over. Sylvas was under orders to infiltrate Gaspar's organization and to keep his sexuality a secret so as to avoid such temptations. The conversations between him and Arende were likely part of his investigation, but I never told him to bed the women."

"You had to know it might come to that. An unmarried criminal who doesn't bed free flesh would arouse suspicion."

"Obviously, it didn't help. I wish to interrogate Gaspar

Vartares. Perhaps I can get him to reveal when he learned Sylvas's identity."

"I told you. He always knew. He decided it was less expensive to lead him in circles until you got bored."

"You'll forgive me if I don't take your word on that."

"Fair enough. But questioning my client is a waste of my time."

"Do you have another idea?"

"You're assuming that whoever killed Kalan knew that he was Sylvas. It's possible he was killed for some other reason."

He considered that for a moment. "You suspect Ingrid Noname?"

"Kalan worked for Gaspar. Ingrid is his chief rival."

He nodded. "Very well." He opened the carriage door. "You question Ingrid. I'll question Gaspar. We'll meet in two hours."

"At the sentinel barracks?"

"No. At my house." He gave me his home address and rode away.

I hailed a carriage and travelled as far as he was willing to take me. The cabs tended to avoid Sammath Borough, and with good reason. The law had all but surrendered the neighborhood. Some years back when it was a slum that no one gave a damn about, Ingrid Noname bought all the land and claimed it in the name of the Vargos Coalition.

People didn't like the Qarama Syndicate, but most would take them over the Vargos if they had any choice. The Qarama made their living in extralegal dealings like any career criminals, but they preferred to keep their felonious behavior bloodless. Don't get me wrong, the Qarama would skin a man alive if it protected their business, but they'd rather find non-violent paths to conflict resolution. With the Vargos, a misstep meant an ugly death. If Anto Stang had refused an offer from Ingrid, he would already be buried in different corners of the city.

To Ingrid's credit, she took care of her own. The Borough grew and thrived as crime replaced the standard economy, and it was all well-kept. There were taverns, whorehouses, smoke dens, and peddlers of all sorts, but none of it was decrepit. Even the apartments were well-maintained. No one was living in luxury, but if you were careful to watch your purse, your back, and your mouth, you could live comfortably.

Comfortably, but probably not long.

The cab dropped me off just outside Sammath Borough. A ten-foot stone wall surrounded the neighborhood with an archway welcoming anyone stupid or brave enough to enter. Not sure which one I was. The wall wasn't to keep people in or out; it was simply Ingrid's way of marking her territory.

The atmosphere was immediately different as one left behind the relative safety of decent society. The tavern parties were raucous. Women and men dolled up in gross parodies of formality paraded the streets selling their flesh to whoever was buying. Urchins of all ages scurried the streets for easy marks to pick clean. One man was openly selling rat and racoon meat. There was a deal on every street and a dagger in every shadow. This was the sort of place I was willing to go to get Gaspar a name, and he didn't think my work would be worth five plat!

It probably doesn't speak well of me that I was so comfortable in the Borough, but it had a certain homey feel to it. Something about the openness of the corruption put me at ease.

I approached The Bastard's Tap and got the stink-eye from the guard. The big, ugly woman gripped the hilt of her sword. "Vinara," she sneered.

"Kari. Is the boss in?"

"Upstairs," she nodded me in.

The Bastard's Tap was a good place. Or, rather, a fun bad place. There were dice games, card games, knife-throwing, and a bar that served drinks other than wine and ale. What wasn't to like? However, too many hateful eyes followed me to the back of the tavern, up the stairs, and over to Ingrid's private table.

Ingrid stood when she saw me. Her roundish korrigan face lit into a smile. She was only slightly over half my height with a pair of thick horns that jutted upward from the side of her forehead. She was starting to show her age, with patches of gray in her reddish-brown skin, but she was as sharp as ever. The four guards surrounding her gave me a look much like the one I got from Kari, but unlike Stang's men, these guards were all real. "Please — sit," she said.

"Thank you," I replied.

"I hear you doing Gaspar's bidding tonight."

"It pays the bills."

"I could pay your bills," she purred. "Ingrid take real good care of you!"

"You know me, Ingrid. I like to run around too much to give you the kind of service you deserve."

"And what kinda service Gaspar deserve tonight? What he got you doing?"

"Investigating a murder, of all things."

"Ha! Got you playing sentinel now! Never thought I'd see the day! This about his man killed over in Esterville?"

"Yep."

"You not thinking I had something to do with that, are you?"

"You're not one to waste a good murder. When you kill someone, you want people to know it."

Ingrid giggled and waved her finger at me. "I not waste a

good murder, she say. I like that! So why you come all this way to my borough?"

"I know you've got eyes on Gaspar's operation. I was wondering if you might have heard anything."

The Vargos captain stroked her chin and stared at me. "All right. Dagger for dagger. I give you, then you give me, all right?"

"Sure."

Ingrid leaned in. "Don't know a thing about this murder, but I know other stuff. Maybe they connected. Maybe not. I hear Gaspar just buy off a man in the sentinels. A big one. A constable!"

"Have you heard which one?"

"No. But only a matter of time. Don't nothing get past Ingrid for long. Now you!"

I nodded and looked around. No use in keeping it secret now. "The victim went by the name Kalan Durel. But his real name was Sylvas Grey. He was an undercover sentinel working for a constable named Burkos."

Ingrid gasped. "The Hell you say!"

"This fellow is the ambitious sort. He's got spies around the city and he's smarter than most. Might have some eyes and ears in your organization as well."

A long, somber silence. She didn't like the sound of that. "You always do right by me, Tavey. You always welcome here. But right now, I got some thinking to do."

"Of course." I stood.

"And Tavey. You find a way to take care of this Burkos fellow, I maybe float some gold chips your way. Hell, maybe a whole plat!"

"I'll keep that in mind, Ingrid."

* * *

I WAS surprised when Banion gave me a Westown address. I guess I shouldn't have been. It was in the heart of his ward, but it never occurred to me that he could afford to live there. Westown wasn't full of opulent mansions, but it was more expensive than the average constable could manage.

Banion Burkos lived in a house not much smaller than Gaspar's. It was black brick, two stories with a basement, and real glass windows. This was a man who was used to the good life, but probably living at the edge of his means.

I knocked on the door and waited for an answer. When I got one, it was about what I had expected. Constable Burkos looked angry and a bit disheveled. "Oh. It's you. Come in."

If the outside was impressive, the inside was immaculate: luxury furniture, Theignish carpeting, and expensive art. One could be forgiven for wondering how he afforded it all, but I didn't wonder. The answer tickled the hairs on the back of my arm like a summer storm. It gave me butterflies in my stomach.

"What are you grinning at?" he asked.

"Nothing. I just didn't realize you were nobility in Theign, that's all."

A deep breath punctuated his irritation. "Lesser nobility," he said. "But we were ostracized when my mother died, and my father dared to try to manage the affairs of our house without a woman present."

"You seem to have done pretty well for yourself."

"We didn't have much when we arrived in the Commonwealth, but my father made sound investments and left me a little . . ." He shook his head as if snapping out of some spell. "Never mind. Can I get you something to drink? Tea? Or wine perhaps?"

"Constable Burkos!" I gasped. "Are you intending to drink while you're on duty? Again?"

He grinned at me, a strange expression on his face. "I

think both of us are done with our duties tonight." He walked me to his dining room and offered me a seat at his table. "Wait here. I have something special in my cellar."

He returned a few minutes later with a bottle and two glasses.

I was so amazed by the strange liquid that I didn't notice the careful, flourished way he poured it until he poured the second glass. "You're a wine-lover, aren't you?"

"Absolutely," he said, sitting down.

"What is it?"

"People call it thella berry wine. Tell me what you think."

I lifted the glass and studied it for a moment. The wine was cloudy and bright, more lavender than red or purple. I took a drink. It was fragrant and sweet, but "It doesn't taste like wine," I told him.

"It isn't. People call it that, but there's no such thing as a thella berry. Thella is a reed that grows along the rivers in the Azhari Dominion."

"I see."

"Just a reminder that the Azhari can make things other than poison." Banion's expression sank. "When Sylvas and I were young, we used to talk about buying our own vineyard, but life happened. And now . . ." He let the thought finish itself.

I raised my glass. "To Sylvas Grey. As great a sentinel as there ever was."

Banion smiled and took a drink. "I spoke to Gaspar," he said before a bitter sigh. "I think you're right. He didn't kill Sylvas. Did you get anything from Ingrid?"

"Nothing useful. I'm sure she's hiding something, but I can't say what. I thought we could go to her doorstep together. Maybe you can unsettle her enough to reveal something."

"I would be willing to do that. Tomorrow."

"Perfect. I've had a long day." I drained my glass. "Tomorrow, then."

"First thing in the morning?"

"Closer to noon," I told him. "Ingrid will not be able to speak to us first thing in the morning. Trust me."

"Very well. Would you like to meet back here?"

"Absolutely."

We said our goodbyes, and I left him to his night. Tomorrow morning, Constable Burkos would wake up and get ready for a trip to Sammath Borough to question a suspect in the murder of his friend and lover. But it didn't matter. I already knew who killed Sylvas Grey.

* * *

NEVER LET it be said that I'm not punctual. I arrived at Banion's house an hour before noon. But I wasn't alone. I was accompanied by six sentinels, Magistrate Lind, and a gray-skinned korrigan wearing blue robes. When Burkos answered the door, he wore only basic brown trousers and a look of confusion. "Magistrate, Miss Tavey. What is it? Has there been progress in the investigation?"

"That remains to be seen, Banion," the Magistrate replied somberly. "Let us in. We need to talk."

"Of course." Burkos did as he was told.

The nine of us marched in.

Banion's confusion struck him dumb for several seconds until finally his eyes settled on the robed korrigan. Then his expression changed from one of bemusement to dread. "Magistrate," he said. "I don't consent to—"

"The contract you signed when you took the position of constable allows me to search your house whenever I damn well please," Havrol interjected. He turned to the other korrigan. "Well?"

"The woman speaks true," she answered.

"Get rid of it."

She waved her stubby hands in an arcane pattern. Bands of shimmering light slowly streaked across the home of Banion Burkos. It was still a nice place, but much of the grandeur disappeared. Sofas of mahogany and silk became couches of ash and cotton. Theignish carpeting became dull rugs. The luster and polish abandoned the house and turned the home of a former Theignish noble into . . . just a place, really.

Lind shot him a look of disappointment and disgust.

Banion's only defense was to say, "Being a sorcerer isn't illegal. I've done nothing wrong."

"Then why did you try to hide it?" Lind accused. "See what else he's hiding."

Four of the sentinels walked away while Banion tried to wake up from the nightmare he'd fallen into. But the nightmare was just beginning.

"How'd you figure it out?" the Magistrate asked me.

"It's not a very strong illusion," I lied with a shrug. "A part of it shimmered away for a second when he was out of the room."

"You lying bitch!" Burkos roared forward, held back only by the remaining guardsmen.

Moments later, one of the sentinels returned. "I found this in his office, Your Honor." He handed the Magistrate five platinum chips.

"This is an awful lot of money for an honest constable to have lying around. Where'd you get it?"

Every word in Banion's vocabulary struggled to fight its way free.

Then it got worse. Another one of the sentinels came in holding a vial of white liquid. "I found this in his wine cellar."

"Pique," the Magistrate spat. "I've seen enough. Banion

Burkos, you are stripped of your rank, position, and privileges effective immediately, and you are to be held pending trial for possession of a forbidden material, corruption, and suspicion of murder."

Banion was too stunned to defend himself as he was dragged away.

Once he disappeared, I looked down at Havrol. "I figured Sylvas would have known he was a sorcerer. Maybe he tried to blackmail him?"

"It's worse than that," Havrol said. "We've been investigating the possibility of a corrupt constable. It looks like we found him."

"He brought him in because he wanted to make it look like he was working relentlessly to bring a crime captain to justice," I put together. "Figured he could trust his friend."

"Poor bastard was more honest than Banion thought."

"For what it's worth, Magistrate, I hoped I was wrong."

"It's not worth much, I'm afraid." He sighed. "It's so hard to find honest folk nowadays." His eyes landed on me. "I've half a mind to conscript you. You may be a coldhearted canker, but at least you're honest."

* * *

AND THAT WAS THAT. Gaspar had his name, and the job was done. There was only one thing left to do.

When night came and most of the world fell asleep, I made my way to the woods east of Bel Hammond to meet an old friend. "Constable Hayne. Funny meeting you here."

"Shut up!" he hissed. "We can't be seen together."

"No one's going to see us. Now, my money?"

"Yes." He pulled out his purse. "Two platinum chips, as we agreed."

"Two platinum chips, plus expenses," I corrected. "So, seven."

"Seven platinum? Are you insane? I'll pay you four. Not a single—"

Warrick grunted as he found my knife at his throat. "Listen, you son of a bitch. I killed a sentinel for you. I framed a good man for you. And because I did, the Magistrate's office is no longer looking for a corrupt constable. My services are easily worth twelve plat. You're getting off cheap at eight."

"Eight?"

"The price went up when you got mouthy. Now, are you going to pay me? Or am I going to have to take it off your corpse?"

"Of course, of course!"

As soon as I released him, his trembling fingers fished eight platinum chips from his purse and dropped them into my hand. I gave him a couple gentle slaps to the cheek. "Don't look so glum. You're bound to get control of Burkos's ward until they find his replacement. Between the extra pay and the bribes you're getting from Gaspar, you'll be fine." I walked away with a surge of happiness that only a heavy purse can bring. I tell you, there's no feeling greater than the satisfaction of a job well done.

* * *

KAREEM MISKEL WAS BORN in Chicago and raised in Mattoon, a small Illinois town where he graduated high school and lives today. He loves to write fantasy, science-fiction, and horror of all kinds. He prefers constructing smaller narratives, tending toward flash fiction, short stories, and novellas. Kareem has self-published two books: Curiosities *and* Rising Conflict.

THE NIGHTINGALE'S CURSE

PATRICK DUGAN

hy do Mondays always suck? It was two in the morning, and I had just picked up news of a powered attack at the Waterfront in Jersey City on the police scanner. Probably a drug bust gone bad or one of the street gangs enforcing their territory.

After parking two streets over from the fight, I ran toward the sounds of automatic weapons fire. From the light show I saw over the buildings, somebody was laying down heavy ordinance. I pulled my costume's mask over my face and sealed it in place. Anvil was on the scene. The noise increased as I closed in on the disturbance. Panicked dock-workers escaped past me as they fled the battle.

I cut across a football field, not bothering to stop for the chain-link fence that I hurdled like I was a track star. I exited on the far side of the field and came up short. A full-blown war had erupted at the marina.

Police cars had surrounded the marina's parking lot. New Jersey's finest fired their weapons at a monster. The thing stood fifteen feet high and was made of glowing gray-green sludge. Tendrils of slime hung from its arms as it roared its defiance. As bullets struck the creature, spurts of goo erupted, but the bullets didn't yield any effect.

I arrived behind the police barricade, stopping next to the officer yelling orders to the others. "Anvil here. Can I be of assistance?"

The salt and pepper haired officer looked me up and down, taking in the gray and red costume I wore. His name badge read Sergeant Andy Mays. "Seriously, another of you freaks. We need the A-Team, and I get F Troop."

A loud scream interrupted the discussion as Bull Horn unleashed his sonic attack on the creature. Other independent Gifted fought the monster, hoping their heroics would earn them notice by an established team.

A tendril of goo lashed past us, ensnaring an officer before throwing him the length of the marina. Another struck a cruiser and flipped it over as the creature advanced on the row of police cars.

"Well, quit yer gaping and fight if that's what yer here for," the officer said before calling in for more backup. Without hesitation, I threw the officer out of the way as a massive piece of concrete sped at us. I charged the projectile and smashed it with my fist. A shower of pebbles and dust was all that was left of the rock.

I nodded to the officer as he climbed to his feet, then charged into battle. Or at least that had been the plan. A blob of goo struck me in the chest, propelling me back past the police cars. I landed hard on the pavement, cracking it in the process. Air whooshed out of me from the impact. I shook my head and pushed myself to my feet. Or at least I tried to. The viscous goo had cemented me to the ground like super glue. Everyone else was too busy to notice me stuck to the ground. I'd never live this down if it were caught on camera.

I triggered the blades on my arm guards with a twist of my wrist. The scalpel-sharp blades sliced cleanly through the goo, but not enough to release me. After a minute of futile attempts to cut myself free, I retracted them, disgusted that I'd been trapped so easily.

It was from this vantage point I first saw The League of Patriots arrive. They were one of the strongest Gifted teams and on our side. Slipstream, his neon red and yellow suit bright against the darkened sky, flashed past, a stream of ice shards firing from his outstretched hands. Titan leapt thirty feet over me, landing out of sight but causing the ground to buckle from his weight. With Titan here, the police were as likely casualties as the villains he fought. Good guys were supposed to protect people, but the Patriots were reckless and wanted the limelight, whatever the cost. Usually that cost was innocent victims.

This was my big break, and I was stuck flat on my back. I resumed my struggles to free myself. The creature roared as the battle progressed. A body crashed to the parking lot. They must have been hit during the fighting. Police officers ran by, eager to be away from the wholesale devastation that Titan was leaving in his wake.

As I thrashed back and forth, I spied a small figure hobbling across the parking lot. "Help me!" I shouted over the sounds of the battle. At this point any assistance would be more than I could do. As the form resolved itself, my heart sank. An elderly woman, hair disheveled and clothes hanging off her gaunt frame, stumbled over. When I needed a hero, I got a homeless woman.

She assessed my predicament and knelt beside my head. "If I help you, will you assist me? A man's life hangs in the balance."

"After the fight, I will do whatever you ask."

She pushed herself up and turned her back on me. Before she crept away, I shouted, "Wait! I will help you."

Slowly, she returned to her previous position. "I have

your word you will help me first? Time is short, and a hero will die if we don't act quickly. Only I can heal him."

"I will."

A hand emerged from an overlong sleeve and touched the sticky goo. A warm sensation rolled over me as the substance liquefied and peeled away from my body. "What should I call you?" she asked as I stood up. I offered my hand to help her up.

"I go by Anvil."

The fight had spread. Titan smashed at the monster with a battered police cruiser as others attempted to stop the rampaging creature. A black bolt of energy announced Dark-star was fighting with the monster. The Exiles were here, and that spelled major trouble. They had destroyed Fort Knox and almost defeated Omega Squad. I had no business being here.

An armored boat rose from the water behind the fight. Master M lifted it using invisible bands of telekinetic power, setting it on the bed of a waiting tractor trailer. "They are stealing that ship."

A firm grip on my arm stopped me from chasing it. I experienced lightheadedness for an instant before it passed. "You must help me. Are you a man of honor or just a false idol?"

I tore my gaze from the spectacle and returned to the old woman. I had given my word and I intended to keep it. "You're right. Let's go."

She maintained her grip as she led me across the parking lot toward a whitewashed concrete building that had seen better days. All of us who grew up in the surrounding neigh-borhoods were from poor, working class families. It housed the repair bay and storage for ships over the winter. A flash of neon yellow caught my eye. I hadn't known it was Slip-stream when I saw the body impact the ground. What had once been a signpost pierced him through the abdomen, blood seeping around his fingers as he held onto the metal.

Having a power, or a Gift, as they called it in the media, gave you many advantages. Most Gifted were stronger, faster, and less prone to damage than a normal person. We also healed much quicker than normal people, but no amount of healing would fix a piece of metal shoved through your gut.

"Pick him up gently and follow me." I stood gaping as she walked away.

"He's already dead, or close enough to it," I said to the woman. I couldn't believe that Slipstream was dying in front of me.

"Get him or he will be dead, you idiot. I can fix this if we hurry."

This might be my chance to earn a spot with the League of Patriots. I could be the one known for saving the injured Slipstream. "We should call an ambulance. There is—"

Her voice hit me like a whip. "Now."

Without thinking, I ran over and broke the post off before hoisting the downed man. Given my strength, he weighed next to nothing. Slipstream groaned as I followed the woman who walked much faster than she had before. We crossed the railroad tracks and climbed a short flight of steps leading to a faded blue door. She rapped her bony hand on it. After a moment the door creaked open to reveal a small boy, probably eight or nine years of age. He had long dark hair and wore robot pajamas. His eyes widened as he saw me carrying the injured man.

"Oh my god, that's Slipstream!"

"Adam, run ahead and ready the room." The boy dashed off with the energy reserved for the young, down stairs that must lead to the basement.

I stepped inside as she closed the door behind me. The

room held a large, overstuffed red couch, La-Z-Boy recliner, and a table holding a Sony TV set. The news was broadcasting from down the street, covering the massive battle as other Gifted joined the scene. I watched as more teams arrived, and I wasn't there to show what I could do.

"Take him downstairs."

I hesitated. *Why was I doing this?* Slipstream needed an ER, not a vagabond, elderly woman. Her hand settled on my arm again, and the dizziness hit much stronger this time. I gasped at the sensation of icy water flowing through my veins, numbing me. Slipstream moaned loudly as I placed him on the floor. I wanted to break free from her icy grip, but to my surprise, I'd had a better chance of escaping the goo that had trapped me earlier.

As my vision dimmed, I swore I saw a young woman standing there. Maybe she would help me.

* * *

MY HEAD THROBBED. No, more like my head was being used as an anvil by a giant blacksmith hammering a red-hot poker into my brain. As I lifted my arm to rub at my battered temples, I realized my arms weren't moving. I struggled to force my eyes open. I felt so weak that my breathing came in fits as the muscles fought to do their job.

"The weakness will pass."

I twisted my head until I saw the young woman perched on a stool a few feet away. She had long, dark hair that fell past her shoulders and porcelain skin as though she'd never seen the sun. She wore a white jumper decorated with beige arm guards and gloves that nearly matched her skin tone. "Who are you?" I croaked through cracked lips.

She brought over a squeeze bottle and squirted cold

water into my swollen mouth. It tasted like heaven. "You may call me Nightingale. I am a healer . . . of sorts."

Thoughts bubbled up from earlier. The fight, Slipstream, and the old woman. "Slipstream?"

She smiled. "He survived. I healed him enough that his own body will do the rest. His team found him a few hours ago — unconscious, but alive, I assure you."

"The old woman . . ." I struggled to keep my thoughts focused as I drifted in and out of consciousness.

The bottle touched my lips again, dispensing more water. I pushed it around my mouth the best I could, trying to soothe the dryness of my tongue. My head cleared enough to allow me to think. "I followed an old woman here."

"You did, and bringing Slipstream here saved him."

I tried to move my arms, but they wouldn't budge. Glancing down I realized thick straps bound me to an examination table. I pushed again, trying to bring all my strength to bear. "Don't struggle, you'll just hurt yourself. The bands inhibit your power."

I thrashed as hard as my weakened state would allow. Nothing. Panic set in as I realized how powerless I was. "Help!" I shouted. "Help me!"

She *tsked* at me before putting the water bottle to my lips. I spit the water at her. She shrugged and returned to her seat. "You can scream all you'd like. No one will hear you."

I took stock of the situation. The walls were heavy stone block, without windows. The ceiling was covered by sheets of riveted metal. A stout metal door was the only exit from the room. I slammed my head on the table. Staring at the ceiling I asked, "Why are you doing this?"

She didn't answer for a long moment. When I turned my head toward her, our eyes locked. She pursed her lips in thought before she said, "I haven't told this story for a long time, but maybe it will help you understand, and you'll agree to help me."

I bit my tongue before I told her what she could do with the idea of helping her. She'd imprisoned me and wanted my help? Forget it.

She sat back on the stool, placing her fingers on her chin. "I guess I'll start at the beginning. I was born in 1678 just outside Salem. My given name was Susanna, and I was a stupid girl who learned things the hard way."

* * *

SUSANNA RETURNED from the chicken coop, a basket of fresh eggs held carefully as she walked. It wouldn't do for the eggs to break on the way back to the house. Smoke trickled out of the chimney before being caught by the breeze and whisked away. Her pa had built the stone walls of the house before she'd been born. The steep slope of the roof kept the snow from piling up during the hard winters that would be here "fore ya knew it." She slowed her pace to enjoy the warmth of the sun on her face. Who knew how many more nice days they'd have before the season changed?

"Susanna," her ma called, "we've chores to do an' you wastin' the morn. Step it up, Girl."

Her cheeks flushed as she hurried her pace. She stopped as her pa and two other gents approached the house. They didn't get many visitors at the farm and only traveled to Salem Village occasionally. Her ma would strap her, but curiosity won out over good sense.

She recognized Master Bradbury by his collarless black coat and white linen shirt. He carried a book under one arm and gestured with the other. "They pressed Corey and arrested more, William. It's not safe for our kind here. You should take your family and go before they come for you and yours."

The other man, tall and broad of chest, wore a fine black coat with an ascot ruffled over it. He barked a harsh laugh. "They are secluded out here and if they are careful, this will pass."

"No, Cotton Mather is whippin' things up. More people indicted, and hangin's will be next, mark my words. I'm makin' a run for it," Bradbury said as he brushed the hair from his eyes.

"Bah, you'll bring the eyes of the church, if ya run. They'll think you're guilty. Will you stand idle as they hang your kin to protect your secrets?" The big man gestured back toward Salem village. "They be watchin' the roads for witches, and you'll just announce yourself to 'em and likely expose the rest of us."

"William, are ye not worried about your girls—?" Bradbury stopped talking as he saw Susanna standing in front of them.

Her pa shook his head. "Mary's taught the girl the arts, but she knows to keep 'em to herself. I've a bit of worry, but the lass has a good head on her shoulders, even if she's listenin' in on conversations not meant fer her ears."

With a squawk, Susanna ran for the house, mindless of the eggs bouncing in the basket. She entered the kitchen and set the basket down, noticing two of them had broken in her flight.

"You look like Satan's chasin' ya," her mother said as she stepped up behind the shaking girl. "What's ailin' ya?"

Her pa strode into the house. "She was listenin' to Master Bradbury. He's gonna take his mother and his family and run fer New York. Talk is the old woman has been accused. Can't say I blame him much. Wouldn't do at all if she burnt the judges to a crisp in front of the courts."

Her mother gasped. "Should we be doin' the same, William? I've birthed a few babies and had Susanna help a few recover from their wounds. We might be next."

He scratched his head as he slumped into a chair at the table. "If we run, we put the rest in danger. I thought we'd escaped all this after leavin' Europe, but it follows us like bad news." He held out his hands to his daughter. "Susanna, ya know ya can't be healin' no one, no matter how bad it is, even if they'll die without God's touch. Promise me you'll not use the arts while they're huntin' witches."

Her stomach clenched and her palms went clammy, but she nodded solemnly to her father. "I promise, Pa. I won't use my touch. Not even on the chicks."

He ruffled her hair. "That's my good girl. Now help your ma with the chores. I've gotta getta mess o' stuff done 'fore dark."

The cold wind had blown in, signaling the end of summer and the time to prepare for the winter to come. All the meat was salted and stored for the coming months; the produce had been dried or canned to get the family through the winter. They had a surplus of corn and beans, so Susanna and her pa loaded up the wagon to trade for the sugar and flour that her ma wanted.

Susanna watched as her father hitched their horse, Bluebell, to the wagon. Pa always spoke in whispers to the horse as he worked. He patted her on the muzzle and climbed into the driver's seat. Susanna pulled her shawl around her, trying to keep herself warm as they rode into the village.

They passed a small pond as they traveled; on the bank sat the dunking chair they'd used on a few of the accused witches. Ma and Pa had stayed away, but she'd heard them talkin' about what happened. Why would they hurt people like that? They could heal with a touch, the touch that God had blessed her with, but the church thought such things witchcraft and the sign of the devil. Why would the devil want her to heal people?

She leaned against her father as they rolled on. The forest muffled the sounds of the wheels creaking, lulling her with the rocking motion of the cart. When loud voices reached her ears, she sprang to alertness. Men stood around two women, pushing and shoving them forward. A small crowd of followers yelled awful things as they made their way along the rutted path. Her father pulled the reigns, stopping the horse.

"What's goin' on here?" her pa asked, his voice so loud that it cut through the shouts of the ten people who followed the leader and two of his men.

The Magistrate held up a hand, halting his procession. "I'm Thomas Hart, the Magistrate of Salem Town, and these two are witches. We mean to make sure they aren't putting spells on any more folk. Now good sir, allow us to pass on with our business."

Her father stepped down to face the man. He peered at the two girls who huddled between the two men. Blood and filth caked their ragged, torn clothes. "They can't be mor'n eleven or twelve. These two aren't old enough to be in league with Satan. Send 'em back to their parents and let their daddies deal with whatever they've done."

One girl sobbed on the verge of hysteria. "They killed my parents. Said they were witches. Now they gonna kill us."

William folded his arms across his chest. "This true?"

The Magistrate's face reddened. He stood straighter to face down her father. "They hexed us. We fought back."

One of the guards interjected. "Felt like my skin was being eaten by ants. I swear. I struck that dirty witch down."

"Goodman, get back on your cart and leave us be. Thou shalt not suffer a witch to live; 'tis written in the book."

With a start, the smaller of the two girls pulled free with a scream and ran into the woods. Bluebell bucked and bolted, striking William, who spun around and fell to the ground. Susanna grabbed for the reigns, pulling with all her might.

The Magistrate and the guard chased after the frightened girl. Susanna leapt off the cart only to find her father lying broken on the ground. Blood sprayed from her father's legs where the wagon wheel had run over them. She realized that he would die if she didn't heal him.

The second guard came around the cart, saw the carnage, and began to vomit.

Conscious thought fled as she ran to him. She dropped next to her father, placing her hands on his face. His eyes widened in fear. "Let me go. Don't."

Susanna ignored his pleas. The power of God surged through her hands and into her father. The bleeding stopped, and bones knitted together as if never broken, the raw meat of his legs becoming pink as new skin grew over the massive gashes.

The power flowed through her. While her father's body mended and became whole again, hers showed the wear the power of God took from her. Wrinkles formed on the backs of her hands. Her skin lost the pinkness of youth; spots appeared as the skin took on a leathery appearance. Her back began to ache as she healed her pa's wounds.

"She's a witch!" cried a follower as they advanced on her. "She's used unholy power to save one of Satan's own."

"No—" she began, but a rock struck her in the cheek. Warm blood flowed from the gash. More stones and shouts of hatred bombarded her. She cast herself over her father to protect him. A hand grabbed her shoulder.

Her mind lashed out, and the man screamed. Life flowed into her. The power sang as she stood. She rounded on the group and lashed out. "Kneel," she ordered, and they did. She touched the larger girl's forehead and she fell over, asleep. As she strolled among them, a lingering touch pulled the essence from the hateful people, leaving a corpse in each of their places.

"Susanna, stop!" she heard her father command from behind. The last of her tormentors lay dead on the ground at her feet. Her hands were no longer painted with age spots nor marred with wrinkled skin.

"You would have died, Pa. I couldn't let that happen." She knelt next to him. Guilt surged threw her like a flood. "They would kill me for using God's power to save you."

Tears flowed down his face. "I know. You did God's will. Help me to the cart. We need to be away from here."

With an effort she lifted him up. Bluebell had stopped a short distance off. Susanna patted her snout and whispered to her as she turned the wagon around and returned to her father's side. Her father pulled himself up while she pushed him from behind.

The Magistrate returned. The remaining guard hauled the terrified smaller girl behind him. His face blanched when he saw the corpses that littered the ground like the leaves of the fall trees.

Susanna fell at his feet. "Magistrate, it was terrible!" She grasped his leg and unleashed her power. The man grunted and fell face first. The guard pulled a knife and raised it to strike her.

"Stop!" she yelled at the guard.

The knife froze in mid swing. Another touch, and he dropped to the ground. The girl whimpered as Susanna looked at her. "Are you hurt?" Susanna asked gently.

"You're a demon. You murdered those people."

I just saved her life from these people. How could she fear me? "What do you think they would do to you?"

The girl's eyes darted everywhere as panic set in. Susanna reached out to calm her, but the girl backed away in terror, crawling backward across the ground to get away. Susanna let her go, knowing God would determine her fate.

* * *

"My parents and I ran that day. I don't tell this story very often. Too many painful memories . . ." Nightingale's voice trailed off.

"So, you've been alive for over three hundred years? That's impossible."

She smirked at me. "You believe me a liar?"

I shook my head a bit more vigorously than I should have. Stars swam before my eyes, causing me to blink them away. "No, you look so young. Wouldn't you be an old—"

Her smile widened as the pieces came together. "I can use my power to stay young and healthy as well as heal others. If I extend myself, as I did in saving Slipstream, I age rapidly."

"Then how are you back to being young? You said you healed him after we came here?" A headache hammered at the back of my skull, dulling my thoughts.

"You, my dear Anvil." She stepped over and placed her hand on my forehead. Dark circles grew under her eyes as I felt the warmth of her touch soothe my aching brain. "I have to absorb life energy from others to fuel my Gift, unlike yours which is self-sustaining. From what I've been able to find out, only a few have such requirements."

"So, you're like a psychic vampire?"

She pulled back as if I'd slapped her, but her tired smile returned. "In a manner of speaking. My Gift heals, and I offer it freely to those in need. Were I not to replenish my energy, I would die, and the healing would go with it. Is it so bad I take life from the evil to protect the good? Slipstream has saved many lives, unlike Titan who kills indiscriminately.

Without Slipstream, the Patriots would kill many more innocents. Is what I do wrong?"

I paused. Did the ends justify the means? If she took the life of a criminal to save an honest man, was it wrong? But who determined what was evil and what was good? "Were the people you killed as a child also evil?"

She regarded me for a moment after returning to her seat. "They would have murdered those two girls to cover their crimes. I would say so."

"They thought the girls were witches. Is self-defense evil? Is protecting your family a sin?"

"The Magistrate and his men raped those girls and were getting rid of the witnesses. They were evil and deserved to die." If flames had leapt from her eyes, it wouldn't have surprised me.

"But the townspeople hadn't. You could have put them to sleep instead."

"Anvil, you of all people should understand the heat of battle. Do you always make the correct decision mid-fight?" Her tone reminded me of the way a teacher speaks to a dull child. The condescension in her voice made me want to lash out at her.

"Of course not. Regardless of that, why am I here? You've saved Slipstream and are young again, yet I'm still strapped to the table." I tried to keep my attitude in check. I don't think it worked.

She studied me for a minute. "I have a proposal for you. A normal person dies when I take their essence, but Gifted can sustain me without dying. I would like you to stay with me and allow me to absorb your energy as needed so that killing others won't be necessary. God has granted you his greatest gift. He sent you to me so that we could do his work together."

My jaw dropped. Be her slave? "So, you expect me to

agree to stay strapped to a table as your personal battery? Forget it, lady. Unhook me, and I'm outta here."

"There are benefits for you as well." She rested her chin on her hand, eyes boring into me. "I can enhance your power. You will be stronger than Titan. No more collateral damage after we remove him and you take his place. You'll be famous. People will worship you. In return, you allow me to maintain myself and heal those in need. I think it a fair trade."

I stared at her in disbelief. I had no words to answer her.

"I'll leave you to think about my offer. Sleep well, and we'll discuss it in the morning." She strode out of the room, leaving me alone with my thoughts.

Could she really do that? I had been living in a dump in Jersey City for three years, stopping petty criminals, waiting for my break. If she could enhance my strength, I would be unstoppable. No more working at the gas station. I could drive a nice car, have an uptown apartment. If she healed the good guys and used my power to stop killing people, didn't it make it acceptable?

For hours I wrestled with the decision, but in the end, I heeded my dad's advice — if it seems too good to be true, it probably is.

I needed to free myself so that I could call in one of the teams like Omega Squad or the League of Patriots to take her in. That might be enough to get me on a real team.

The straps still held me in place, and I couldn't use my strength to break free. That's when I realized I still wore my wrist gauntlets. With a slight twist, I felt the click as the locks disengaged. I rocked my hands back and forth, hoping the edge of the blades would wear down the straps.

I worked at it for a couple of hours and wasn't any closer to freeing myself. A small noise from the door alerted me I wasn't alone. I closed my eyes, pretending to sleep.

"I know you're awake."

The boy stood next to me. He gave the look all kids give stupid adults. I deserved it on many levels. "You got me. Are you supposed to be up?"

He shook his head. "Mom would kill me, but I don't like it when she does this. I don't want you to end up like the last one. You being a hero, and all."

I swallowed hard. "The last one?"

"Yeah, he got old and died a while ago. He was really nice to me, but I don't want that to happen to you." He stepped around to the top of the table. A series of pops and the straps came loose. I slid off the table, my joints aching after a night of being stuck in the same position.

I knew that I really had to get out of there and expose Nightingale for what she was, At least I hadn't fallen for it like the last poor schlub. "Thanks, Adam. How do I get outta here?"

He gestured for me to follow him, and I did. He crept up the basement stairs, quiet as a mouse. Unfortunately, people don't call you Anvil for being quiet. The stairs thudded under the heavy soles of my boots as I tried to tiptoe. We reached the top, and Adam pointed at the front door. "Go."

"Thanks, Buddy." I took two more steps before I heard her.

"Stop." Nightingale's voice came from the hallway. She wore a long, white linen nightgown that covered her from neck to toes. Her hair had been pulled into a ponytail. "I see I have my answer."

My heart raced. I couldn't fight her when her mere touch was deadly. The door stood too far away. I did the only thing I could think of. I grabbed Adam and held him between us. "I'm leaving, and you won't stop me."

Her eyes widened in shock. "How hypocritical of you,

Anvil. You cast me aside for killing evil men, then take a child as a hostage. I thought you were a hero?"

"I don't want to hurt Adam, but I won't stay here as your slave." I took a step toward the door. She took a step as well. "Stop! I don't want to hurt him, but I will if it means getting free of you."

She ignored me. "Adam, do you see now? See how vile these heroes are? They don't care for commoners, only for themselves. Baby, you need to do what I told you."

I tightened my grip. Adam cried out in pain. I took another step. A few more steps and I'd reach the door. Nightingale swooped in closer. "I'm sorry, Adam. I don't want to die."

"Adam, you must save yourself. You know what to do."

The door. Get to the door. That's when I felt the flow of power as Adam's hands closed on my arm. "I'm sorry, Anvil," he said around his sobs. I gasped as the breath escaped me. My limbs twisted in pain, causing me to crumple to the floor.

Nightingale stood over me as I fell, Adam still holding my arm that withered into a weak, wrinkled piece of flesh. "Adam, you see how evil they are. We do God's work in punishing these false idols."

Tears streamed down his cheeks. "Yes, Mama. You were right. They are evil."

The last thing I saw was Nightingale embracing her son as my vision faded to black.

* * *

PATRICK DUGAN IS *the author of the award-winning* Darkest Storm *series published by Falstaff Books. Other titles include* Stone Cold Witch, Never Steal From Dragons, The Shadow Blade Chronicles, *and the* Watchers of Astaria *series from Distracted Dragon Press. Other publications include* Fairy Films:

Wee Folk on the Big Screen, *a collection of fairy essays from Educated Dragon Publishing. Patrick is a member of SFWA.*

Patrick resides in Charlotte, North Carolina with his wife, two children, and their spunky Cavalier King Charles, Blaze. In his spare time, he's a PC gamer, homebrewer, 3D printer enthusiast, and DIYer. You can usually find him in the Hearthstone Tavern or wandering Azeroth as a Blood Elf Warlock in the evenings. You can learn more about him at https://linktr.ee/patrickdugan

SPLITTING IMAGE

SARA JORDAN-HEINTZ

eatrix Bissette dipped the end of her quill in the inkwell on her overcrowded desk. As she began crafting the second paragraph of a letter home to her sister Antoinette, she debated the merits of mentioning the sudden decline in her health — the bouts of dizziness, headaches, and fatigue greeting her with added frequency, like an undesired suitor.

I don't want her to fret any more than she already does, Bea thought to herself as she changed course, instead mentioning the recent acquisition of new blackboards for each of her students and the success of the ladies' luncheon for a local charity. Young Lillian Anderson had even convinced her to participate in a horseshoe-throwing contest. That day in particular had tired Bea, who despite having only twenty-two years to her name, at times felt like an old lady.

After finishing her correspondence, Bea sealed the letter and placed it on a stack of papers she'd yet to find time to organize. There is always much to master when one takes a position at a new school — no two institutions ever seem to live by quite the same set of rules or philosophies, she mused. But Bea was determined to impress the crotchety headmistress, Agnes Chambers, who always wore a dour expression on her heavily lined, pasty white face. The woman couldn't even be bothered to make eye contact with Bea whenever the two passed through the same hallway.

Nevertheless, Bea had to admit, despite her youth and greenness on the job, her pupils adored her. After all, she taught English courses not just to improve their conversation skills and letter-writing abilities, but also to inspire their creativity. It was 1885, after all, not 1685. These young ladies had potential outside the private sphere of domesticity.

She'd always dreamed of visiting the Scottish Highlands, never having been farther north than Glasgow until recently, and now, she was more than 680 kilometers from her home in Dumfries.

To her delight, a teaching position had opened up at the elite all-girls Henderson Academy of Inverness, a boarding school for girls ages ten to seventeen. The opportunity had been made possible by a letter from her former employer, Mrs. Caswell, of the self-titled school for young ladies in south London, ebullient with praise. The gesture had been slightly stunning, due to the nature of Bea's sudden discharge from her post after less than two months on the job.

She had taught elocution, pleased with the children's noticeable improvement in grammar and diction. To earn extra coin to send to Toni, Bea even helped serve the evening meal. It was a small, homey environment that she loved.

One late afternoon, Bea made a quick dash to the corner sundry to purchase additional flour needed to make biscuits for dinner. Upon returning from her errand, she rang the doorbell at the back of the dining hall. The door was opened at once, and there she was met by Mrs. Caswell who just as quickly closed it. Bea politely knocked again, shifting the heavy flour sack from under one elbow to the other.

When no one responded, she went around to the front and let herself in the main entrance. She found Mrs. Caswell seated at the head dining room table, quickly making out a check. Upon noticing Bea standing over her, Mrs. Caswell handed her the payment and asked her to leave at once.

"Thank you, Dear, but that will be all," she said, thrusting the check in Bea's direction, her eyes averted to the window as the sun cast its orangey glow about the space.

Bea reached out her flour-dusted fingers and accepted the funds. She then packed her bags and caught a train for home, uncertain how she'd explain her sudden dismissal to her family.

But then, references arrived in the post. Glowing, in fact, of her abilities. Once the new job was secured, she made haste in her move. It pained Bea to be so far away from her younger sister, but the money she sent for Toni's living expenses was essential to the girl's survival. Not much work beyond taking in mending came her way due to her condition.

When Antoinette was two and Bea was six, their parents perished in a fever that had swept through their small town, killing a fourth of the population. The girls had gone to live with their mother's sister Louise and her husband Hugh. Although not a nurturing couple, the affluent Dankworths exposed the girls to fine literature, horse racing, and trips to London for the theater. They even paid for Bea's college education. A girl could have it worse.

When Toni entered her fourth year, doctors ascertained she was profoundly deaf and likely would never speak. After Hugh agreed to send Bea to school to become an English teacher, she knew she'd be supporting both herself and Toni for the rest of their lives.

Bea looked at the clock on the wall. Nearly seven p.m. The late summer afternoon had played tricks on her sense of time. She gathered the papers she had yet to grade, stuffing them, her needlepoint, and a grimy half-eaten apple in her attaché case. As she looked up to her open doorway, she saw a rumpled man with white hair doubled over trying to catch his breath.

"Good heavens, Miss Bissette, how in the blazes did you get back to your classroom so quickly? Not ten minutes ago I saw you exit the library and slowly make your way across the green. I briefly lost sight of you, and now, here you are."

Bea glanced at her colleague, science professor Dalton Hewitt, whose classroom was just across the hall from hers. His normally playful chocolate brown eyes were imbued with worry and his heavy beard and thick mustache concealed a tight jaw.

When she didn't immediately reply, he furthered, "I made an impromptu jaunt to the library to search for a copy of a book I've misplaced. I spotted you rummaging in a box of poetry volumes, digging furiously for something. I called out in greeting, but it was as though you had not heard me. My, you must be the fastest stroller I've ever met."

"Mr. Hewitt, I've been chained to my desk for hours. I haven't left the building since seven this morning. It must have been Mrs. Grey you saw. I'd loaned her my woolen shawl this morning. Perhaps, from the back, we bear a slight resemblance."

She didn't wait for a response. Clutching her attaché case, she made her way for the doorway, and as if to assuage the professor's bemusement, gave a small curtsey and bid him "bye the nou."

Back in her living quarters, Bea ate a slice of turkey with mashed potatoes and peas from a tray Cook had brought to her room half an hour ago. With the woozy way she felt on her feet, she hadn't cared to venture clear across campus to the dining hall, and instead had sent a student with a message to the kitchen.

Bea found her work challenging yet fulfilling. The youngest of her students were at that curious age when the mundane held much intrigue. Why this, and why that? When was this first invented? How do the lyrics to this song begin? Did Miss Bissette have a beau back home? The older girls, who neared the age when some would drop out next semester to accept marriage proposals, quietly, yet efficiently, completed their coursework without much fuss.

As she dumped out the contents of her attaché case, a book thudded to the floor, its binding spliced open and its pages facing up. Bea bent to retrieve the errant tome, placing it right side up on her end table. She gasped when she read its title: *Maud, and Other Poems*, the first collection of works Alfred Tennyson had published following his becoming poet laureate in 1850. It was the book Toni had requested Bea obtain and send to her through the post, at her earliest convenience.

Hmm. I must have made mention of seeking out this work to a group of girls and one of them so graciously located it and dropped it off at my desk when I stepped out briefly for a glass of water, she reasoned to herself.

Her letter to Toni and the book, now ensconced in brown paper wrapping, sat in the outgoing mailbox in the main office. One last thing on her to-do list, she sighed with relief. It was Friday morning, and other than prepping for the coming week's lessons, she found herself without any commitments until after the lunch hour. Bea walked the short distance to the shed and collected a trowel and other implements. The groundskeeper had been away for several days visiting an ailing relative, and weeds were sprouting between the rows of violets planted around the fountain.

She pulled out a pair of worn gloves and got to work prying the green menaces from the ground. She glanced up at an open window to see a gaggle of girls parade around the second floor gymnasium, laughing raucously, clearly improvising their calisthenics while their instructor was collecting their exercise canes — most likely held up due to them deliberately being misplaced.

How I wish I could run up there and give those young ladies a firm scolding, Bea thought to herself as she yanked on a weed firmly rooted in the soil. Giving Mr. Ashbluff such trouble. We all know what has delayed him. Perhaps the ringleader of the gang might care to go help him "discover" where those canes may have danced off?

* * *

"Ash Butt is such a bore. I hate all these silly exercises we must do," groused a girl called Lilly.

"And how are we supposed to work off our 'nervous energy' doing these delicate little routines, wearing dresses to our ankles and bloomers to boot," shouted the rather brassy Bridget McSweeney.

Standing in the hallway was Miss Bissette; the glare spreading across her pretty face like a fast approaching storm stopped the youngsters mid-word. Hands on hips, she slowly walked into the gym, never taking her eyes off the merrymakers. Some of the girls promptly sat on the floor and folded their hands in their lap. A few of the younger ones just stood, mouths agape at getting caught messing about.

Shannon, the most fidgety of the students, walked to the window to view the passers-by until their instructor returned. Glancing at the students and teachers walking about the grounds, her deep blue eyes landed squarely on the woman kneeling before a bed of violets, carefully, yet determinedly, pulling out weeds.

It was Miss Bissette.

For once in her young life, Shannon didn't boisterously call out to her pals. She slowly walked to the group of girls, tapping two of them on the shoulder. She motioned for them to follow her to the window, and then she pointed.

In unison, the three girls' heads jolted to the left, then right toward the outside, and again at the English teacher standing before them — in two places at the same time.

Just then, Mr. Ashbluff returned to the gym along with the student who had helped him "locate" the equipment. Miss Bissette was suddenly gone.

"The window. Look out to the garden, and you'll see her," Shannon announced, finding her boisterous charm once again.

The fifteen girls assembled in the class took turns sticking their heads out the window, where they saw Bea pruning the flowers, refuse neatly piled next to her, awaiting its journey to the burn pit.

* * *

AFTER CHANGING her clothes and grabbing a cucumber sandwich, Bea made her way to her classroom to greet her eldest pupils who would be discussing *Uncle Tom's Cabin*, a widely popular book in the States that had been sweeping through Europe since it was first published in 1852.

As her third class for the day came to a close, she bid her students farewell while they excitedly discussed their weekend plans and which of them would be going home for a brief visit with their families. Bea contemplated going for a walk in the Highlands; feeling the fresh mountain air might reinvigorate her senses and help ease the throbbing in her forehead.

"I'm glad I caught you before the day concluded." Professor Hewitt stood in the hallway between their classrooms, his hand reached out as if to prevent her from leaving.

"I request a moment of your time to talk. Privately."

"What's this about, Professor?"

"Please, call me Dalton. I'd rather this conversation remain on friendly terms. Several girls in my fourth period chemistry class expressed great concern about your wellbeing. Even your soul. Something about an incident during gym class."

She stepped away from him, her petticoat brushing the side of his pant leg. He made a grab for her left arm, clasping it in his sweaty palm. He locked his door, and then explained he preferred speaking with her in his fourth floor office.

"That's just as well. I can't stand the smell of those chemicals in your classroom." Bea secured her own classroom door and followed Dalton up the steep, narrow steps that led to the faculty offices, reserved for men. With pursed lips, she waited while he withdrew a key from his jacket pocket and lit the lamp.

She was surprised that despite the cramped quarters — the room was more akin to a large closet than an office — it was warmly decorated with throw pillows and lace accents.

"The pupils said you went to the gym and watched them with an eagle's eye until their instructor returned."

"Poppycock! Such imaginations they have. I saw them messing about in the gym. A window was open. I knew they were up to mischief-making with Mr. Ashbluff detained, but I never left the flowerbeds."

"As you stood in the gym, keeping them in line, a few girls

peered out the window, and to their utter amazement, viewed you tending to the flora."

When she didn't respond, he continued. "Tell me, Beatrix, if I may be so bold as to call you by your Christian name, at the teachers' institute you attended in Cardiff, did they teach you the latest in efficiency? Being in two places at once. I mean, I've heard of it being done. The ancient Greek philosopher Pythagoras could do it. And the Virgin Mary has been known to appear to her devotees. Take the story of Our Lady of the Pillar. While Mary was living in Jerusalem, she supernaturally appeared to the Apostle James the Greater in AD 40 while he was preaching in modern-day Spain."

"A philosopher and the Holy Mother. Yes, that is the company I keep, Dalton — I mean, Professor. I'm sorry to be off in such a flurry, but I really must clear my head. I haven't felt well all week. Please excuse me." She rose, opened the door, and entered the hallway. As she was about to place one satin shoe-encased foot on the top stair, his voice halted her.

"The first documented occurrence of multiple personality disorder was that of Mary Reynolds in 1815. Except in your case, it's not merely alter egos taking up space in your mind. I think they, or it, has the ability to travel."

"I see. And this information comes from . . . ?"

"Are you familiar with the Society for Psychical Research?"

"I am not."

"It was started a few years ago by a group of prominent men. Their areas of study include thought transference, mesmerism, mediumship, Reichenbach Phenomena, apparitions and haunted places, and séances."

"Junk science."

"To some."

"Professor, I realize that sometimes when the girls get excited about something, really passionate, their imaginations take over their brains. Whatever they've convinced you of, it's pure fancy."

"I'm a member of that society," was his response.

"But surely you regard yourself as a man of science. Of facts."

"What if these phenomena are someday proven to be just as real as gravity?"

"When the world's leading scientists believe in mind reading and spirit communication, then drop me a postcard to let me know, aye?

Bea continued down the staircase nervously pushing a strand of hair behind her right ear. She wanted to be alone. Perhaps she'd even arrange a meeting with Headmistress Chambers, expressing her concerns about the academy having such a man as Dalton Hewitt in its employ.

"Bilocation."

"I beg your pardon?" she said, glancing at the man who stood a mere two steps behind her on the staircase.

"Double walker. The Germans call it doppelgänger, but I don't think the other you comes from another world or plane. What I think is happening to you is a split of mind and body. Your spirit wanders while your physical self remains behind."

"Preposterous."

"Is it? Lately you've complained of various maladies. Tell me, do they worsen and then suddenly improve?"

"Hard to say."

"I don't think it is. When one part of your personality splits, it drains you of your energy, or life force. Then when the other 'you' returns to its captivity, you become whole again."

"If what you say is true, then why me? What has occurred to bring on this most unusual condition?" Bea questioned.

"Intense emotions. Traumas. Neglect. You lost your parents at a young age, did you not?"

"Yes, but Toni and I had a perfectly fine upbringing. I have no complaints."

"Your kind wouldn't. You have an accommodating personality. I'm sure you always have."

Bea lowered her line of vision, fixating on what appeared to be a splotch of coffee staining the stair runner.

"I had these nightmares one summer when I was sixteen. Every night for several weeks, I'd wake up so out of sorts, on edge. Aunt Louise attributed my demeanor to girlish flights of fancy. Budding womanhood. That type of thing."

"But you didn't believe that."

"I didn't know what to think. I'd dream of running through the mud in a treacherous thunderstorm, or of falling and skinning my knee. Sure enough, when I'd awake I'd have a visible wound. Sometimes mud about my ankles."

"Did anyone ever appear in these dreams?"

"Yes. Many people. Some I knew, others were strangers. There was often a burly man, quite obese. He spoke with a Russian accent. He would ask me questions."

"What kind of questions?"

"I don't know. It was so long ago."

"Could your sister have known this person? Met him before?"

"Oh, I don't think so. She doesn't know anyone I don't. You think he's real?"

"I want you to send Toni a letter. Give her as many details as you can about the Russian and anything you may recall of those dreams."

"His face."

"What about it?"

"My sister has a vivid memory. If I could draw what he looked like, that may prove helpful."

"Let's make inquiries with Madame Grecé. You describe the man to her, and she can do a sketch we can send to your sister."

"I'm willing to give it a go."

* * *

"How about this, ma chérie?"

"A longer forehead, and more of a point to the chin. I think the eyes need to be set farther apart, too," Bea instructed Madame.

"Un moment, s'il te plaît. Now, will this do?"

She rotated the canvas so Bea could better see the charcoal portrait.

Yes, the image looked like the man from her dreams.

"Is it lacking any details that may be useful to Toni?" the professor asked.

"No, I think this will do. I could send it out with the mail tomorrow."

"If this person exists, do you think Toni would remember meeting him?" Dalton inquired.

It seemed unlikely Toni would know anyone Bea didn't, but it seemed lately that anything was possible. Antoinette, being deaf and mute, often went unnoticed by those around her, drifting in and out of a room or hanging back from a crowd, able to understand the conversation by reading lips. When thick mustaches obscured the words, she instead relied on body language and eye contact.

Bea knew the reply from her sister would take a week. In the interim, Bea threw all her concentration into lesson planning, marking papers, and tutoring students. While her malaise hadn't gone away completely, it had eased, with no reported sightings of her "other self."

Bea was growing restless, fearing daily that her double,

the split of her spirit — whatever it was — would again reveal itself. It was one thing for students or staff to claim having an encounter with the other Bea, but what if the headmistress saw it, too? Was that why she'd been dismissed from her prior employment? Had she simply been paid to leave immediately and take her double with her? Obviously, Mrs. Caswell, proud woman that she is, would never bring her lips to utter that she'd seen a spirit or whatever this being was.

Were people afraid of her?

Maybe she had nothing to worry about. Perhaps there was a simple explanation for what people had been seeing. She found any excuse she could to avoid Dalton. She had no time for the theories he read from his alternative science tomes. Once she heard back from Toni, she'd know what to do.

Then, on Friday afternoon, a letter was delivered to her personal quarters. Bea could tell by the tiny, neat script where the letter had originated. She tore open the envelope and quickly read its contents:

Dearest Bea,

I believe I do know the man whose likeness you sent to me. His name is Dr. Alexander Volkov, according to Aunt Louise's memory. He was a tenant at Mrs. Campbell's boarding house some summers ago. I think you were about sixteen at the time. I recall running into him on occasion at the pharmacy, and I know he came to dinner a few times. About what, may I ask, do you care to get in touch with the gentleman?

I will also ask Uncle Hugh if he has any recollections upon his return home from Epsom Downs in Surrey. I do hope he hasn't gone and wagered a month's household allowance again. (I am sighing quite loudly as I finish writing this note to you on the secretary in my bedroom).

Your loving sister,

Toni

Bea felt it only polite to let Dalton know Toni had identified the mystery man. But how could he have figured so prominently into those bizarre dreams when Bea didn't recall ever meeting him?

"Beatrix. What I'm about to ask is a very sensitive question. You don't have to answer it."

"All right. Go ahead."

"Do you think this doctor could have touched you in a way that was inappropriate? That those weren't dreams at all?"

"At my home? Come to my bedroom in the middle of the night and had his way with me?" The pitch of her voice noticeably climbed. "How would he have gotten in the house? A 250-pound man climbing the trellis?"

"Do you remember any other details about him?"

"Not necessarily. I told you earlier he was a larger man — he probably had trouble slipping into a crowd unnoticed."

"You said Toni was also going to make inquiries with your Uncle Hugh?"

"Yes, she said she'd ask him if he knew anything that may help us."

"Do you trust your uncle?"

"Whatever do you mean?"

"I thought you told me once he had a gambling problem. Gone a lot. No children of his own and completely inept when it came to rearing two nieces he probably resented having to care for."

Bea sat across from Dalton, her eyes averting his intense gaze.

"I don't know of any association my uncle could have had with this man beyond casual acquaintance. Let's drop this topic for now. I have a lesson to prepare."

* * *

THE NEXT MORNING, Bea and her fellow teachers were summoned to Headmistress Chambers's office for a meeting before the school day began. She noticed the school's seamstress was absent.

"All, I plan to discharge Sally McIntyre, effective immediately. Upon suspicion of misconduct, I had two of my assistants search her room last night. I found some very expensive silk hidden under her bed, plus a fine silver carving knife. When confronted, she confessed to taking them."

Bea could see the fabric piled on the edge of Agnes's desk while the woman fingered the carving knife, moving it about for dramatic effect before setting it down with a thud.

Bea tried to maintain a neutral expression, all the while seething inside. No one in this school worked harder than young Sally. Why, barely older than the pupils herself, she put in fourteen-hour days to send her wages home to Wicklow for her widowed mother and seven siblings.

This wasn't right. Just because she possessed the items didn't mean she'd intended to keep them.

"I am making inquiries this afternoon for her replacement. In the meantime, Bea, I will need your assistance for some minor mending, as the need arises. You're all dismissed."

With that pronouncement, Mrs. Chambers turned her back to her staff and gazed out her floor-length window.

What a heartless old crone. Bea allowed that thought to enter her mind where it resided for the better part of the day. She crawled beneath her blankets a full hour earlier than was her norm, so overcome with disgust and the beginnings of a tension headache.

Activity in the hallway woke her early. She could hear

doors opening and closing, like people were running to and from their rooms. She put on her robe and slippers and slowly made her way to the door, cracking it ajar to peer out.

"Whoever threatened her is going to get it. The Ag Hag won't stand for this kind of disrespect."

It was Bridget McSweeney standing with a group of girls and a few kitchen servers. What were they doing in the teachers' living quarters?

"Girls, what's going on?" Bea asked.

"It's old Headmistress Chambers. Got quite a fright this morning, she did. Did serve her right."

"That's enough out of you, Bridget. I said you could come with me if you helped me carry the extra tablecloths to the dining hall," replied Carla, who was usually on breakfast duty.

"Carla, what is it? What's happened?"

"Go see for yourself."

Following the woman's outstretched hand, which pointed left, Bea made her way down the hallway. She knew Agnes's lavish living quarters took up nearly the entire west wing of the building. Bea inched her way along, walking as gracefully as she could.

As she entered the headmistress' parlor room, she caught sight of police inspectors examining the space. She stepped inside and found her feet carrying her to Agnes's bedroom, a place she'd never visited before.

A table and chairs had been overturned and pages ripped from books. There were claw marks on the curtains. Personal belongings had been strewn about the space. A ransacking, Bea wondered?

Several feet above the bed, Bea saw a long dress affixed to the wall by a carving knife, its blade positioned in the bodice of the garment, as if intended to symbolize being stabbed in the heart.

Oh Sally, I hope this wasn't—

But if this happened last night or in the wee hours, Sally would have been long gone. Why, Bea had seen the carriage pull up for the disgraced girl about half past noon. Unless Sally had returned . . .

Heartless.

"Quite a development, isn't it Beatrix?" Dalton stood in the doorway, a self-assured expression on his face. "Threatening the headmistress and desecrating her property. I knew you were fond of Sally, but this may have been a bit of an overstep, Bea. Don't you think?"

"What are you talking about? I know nothing of this. I heard movement in the hall. Voices. Girls milling about. I ran into Carla. And Bridget. They said—"

"Where were you last night? Or perhaps the question is, how were you feeling?"

"Dalton, I couldn't have done this."

"Your room is a three minute walk from here. In the cover of darkness, knowing Agnes was likely still at her desk across campus, you could have entered, maybe with a key you'd swiped earlier in the day, along with the knife you pocketed after we were dismissed yesterday."

For once in her life, Bea had no rebuttal. She honestly couldn't be certain she hadn't committed this act of rage.

She bid the professor good day, side stepped him, and went back to her room.

* * *

WAS it too early to consider putting in her notice? Was it better to leave now, before any more incidents occurred? Bea wasn't sure what else her double was capable of doing, freely roaming the grounds while Bea was otherwise occupied.

A shudder ran down her spine. But it was only a breeze

from her open window, which ruffled the loose papers on her desk.

"I ought to write to Toni again." Bea glanced at the basket at the foot of her bed. It contained a few petticoats, stockings and three hats — the latest mending work, courtesy of Head-mistress Chambers.

Now everywhere she went, girls whispered as she passed by, and her students always seemed a bit distracted. Her colleagues kept their contact with her to a minimum.

Except Dalton.

Were they becoming friends? She had to admit there was no one else at the school she felt she could confide in — or even wanted to, for the record.

Bea collected her sewing supplies and was reaching for the basket of mending when she heard frantic knocking at her door.

"Who is it?"

"It's Edgar, Miss. A telegram's come fer ye. I picked it up from the post office this mornin'. Just now able to bring it by."

She bolted to the door and let the messenger boy enter.

"My heavens, who would wire me? 'Tis such a costly—"

The boy thrust the message at her, eager to be given his coin and sent on his way.

"But of course. Let me fetch my bag."

She paid him and proceeded to read the message.

It was from Toni.

DALTON STOOD IN HIS CLASSROOM, evaluating his students' latest science projects. The girls had each been assigned an animal that inhabited the terrain and were asked to study its habits and behavior and create casts of its tracks. A final quiz would task them with identifying what animals created which footprints, based on a series of prompts.

While his heart swelled with pride at their creativity and ingenuity, he couldn't stop thinking about Bea. The girls liked to chat during lunch about having seen their teacher wandering the garden or up on a hilltop or prowling the kitchen for a midnight snack, but Dalton didn't think any of these sightings had been based in fact.

Bea hadn't complained of her usual physical ailments right before a "sighting," and he'd briefly spoken to her nearly every morning for the past few weeks.

He knew she was considering leaving Henderson Academy, the attack on Headmistress Chambers's quarters weighing heavily on her mind.

As far as Dalton could figure, no one actually ever spoke to this double — couldn't or wouldn't communicate with it. It was like an apparition, gliding through space and time, silent, yet present.

However, the claw marks, the stabbed dress, and the overturned furniture had taken some power, some energy, which he hadn't known the double to possess.

Unless it was maturing, coming into its own as a physical being.

The thought frightened him. He put his grading book in his top desk drawer, locked up behind himself, and began walking to the women's faculty living quarters to check on Bea.

He approached her room and rapped gently on the shut door. Hearing no sound, he knocked a little harder. He risked the termination of his employment for being caught entering her room, but he pushed the door open and went inside.

He saw Bea strewn on her chaise lounge, a piece of paper on the floor next to her. Unsure whether to send for smelling salts or read the note, he decided on the latter.

VOLKOV DID EXPERIMENTS.
CHLORAL HYDRATE. HYPNOSIS.
UNCLE RECEIVED £50.
HE FOUND ME OUT. ON HIS WAY. DANGER.
ANTOINETTE BISSETTE

Dalton's hands shook as he read the telegram. Had Toni meant their uncle Hugh was on his way *here*? As if just remembering Bea's prostrate form lay within reach, he knelt to her, gently trying to awaken her. He felt for a pulse, which was strong. He pulled a handkerchief from his breast pocket and gently wiped the perspiration from her forehead. He carried her to her bed and set her gently atop her quilt. He re-read the telegram, only then noticing the time stamp on the message: 1885 Sept 5 AM 8:27.

Dalton pulled out his timepiece. It was nearly eight o'clock at night. Toni must have sent the telegram the moment Hugh left for the train station in Dumfries. He would have reached Glasgow by early afternoon easily.

"Maybe I could send a telegram to the train station there . . . but there just isn't time," he said to Bea, but more to himself. How far was Glasgow to Inverness? He looked about the room and located a stack of books on her desk. He grabbed the atlas and flipped through its pages. About 275 kilometers between the two towns. Figure in stopovers for mail and refueling. He'd have to hire a coach the rest of the way.

Dalton glanced at the clock on her side table. Hugh could arrive at any moment — unless he was already here.

* * *

BEA WRAPPED her woolen coat around her more tightly as she made her way to Headmistress Chambers's office. As she approached, she heard the headmistress in a heated discussion with a man.

Uncle Hugh.

So, he had come to confront her with what she now knew. Without even knocking, Bea burst into the room, her eyes locking on her uncle.

"Miss Bissette, please do not barge in here like a herd of sheep."

"Go to hell, Agnes. This doesn't concern you."

Agnes tried to utter a reply, but fell silent. Bea walked her to the door, opened it, and sent her on her way. She locked it behind her.

"Good evening, Uncle. So nice of you to come visit me all the way up in the Highlands. Impromptu holiday, is it?"

"Bea! So wonderful to see my favorite niece. How's the new job treating you?

"Oh, the girls are perfectly charming, and I love teaching. Of course, splitting into two personalities running about the academy has led to so many rumors about me: I have special powers. I'm a witch. I'm a ghost. What do you think I am, Hugh?"

"Sweet girl. That's why I'm here. I've spoken to your sister, and we both think you're gravely ill. These delusions and the headaches are epilepsy-induced, no doubt. I think you should come with me."

He grabbed Bea's right arm and twisted it for good measure. She winced in pain, then swung him around in a circle, throwing him against the wall, smashing into a painting that teetered askew. He rubbed at his bloody nose.

"That deaf dumb sister of yours! Caught her going through my desk drawers. Found my ledger. So I let the Russian try a few things on you. He wanted to see how the mind responds to stress and stimuli. All for the sake of science, it was."

"How long have you known about my two personalities?"

"Oh, you mean the boring, weak, everyday Bea, then the other Bea who lets me touch her—"

"Shut up, you shite! The very thought of your hands or breath on me turns my stomach. But you're a little slow minded on this, aren't you? It's not just a split personality the doctor induced. It's a physical one, too."

"What the devil are you talking about? Though I have to say I don't mind this roughhousing from you. It's rather arousing."

He lurched at her, putting his hands around her throat.

Bea tried to pry his fingers and wiggle away, but his grip grew tighter. As the two struggled in Chambers's office, Bea looked about the room. Near the window stood a bronze statue of a falcon. She rolled onto the desk, sending Hugh on top of her briefly until she shook his greasy, sweaty form from her body. As he thudded to the ground, she picked up the statue and lobbed it at his skull. As he lay still, she reached for a kerosene lantern that sat on a table across the room. She poured the kerosene in a circle around her uncle, reached for a box of matches from the drawer of the desk, and lit one.

"This ends tonight."

* * *

DALTON LEFT BEA'S ROOM, shutting the door behind him. He shouted her name as he walked up and down the halls, asking a few teachers if they'd seen her. Satisfied Bea's double was somewhere else on campus, he rushed out the door, down the steps, and headed toward the administrative office. The acrid smell of smoke and flames shooting from the top of the building made his feet pound the pavement harder as he rushed into the fray.

Bea shut the door behind her, with Uncle Hugh still unconscious on the carpet. She heard Dalton call her name from the front entrance. "I'm coming," she said, as she rushed out into the cool evening air.

"What the hell happened, Bea? Was your uncle there? Did you see him?"

"Yes. An unfortunate accident. I couldn't do anything to help him."

Dalton glanced up as the flames licked the old stone structure. When he looked back to Bea, she was gone.

* * *

AFTER THE FIRE that claimed the life of her uncle — and caused considerable damage to that part of campus — Bea decided it was time to move on, pick up her sister at home, and relocate to someplace a little less exciting.

The constabulary had declared the fire accidental. Bea told the authorities she had pushed her advancing uncle away as he tried to sexually assault her. Headmistress Chambers had been surprisingly kind throughout the whole experience, but Bea didn't want to be haunted by the remnants of that night.

Suitcase in hand, she bid the group of students who had assembled outside her carriage farewell, kissing each on the cheek. Dalton hung back from her admirers, watching the scene with curious eyes. After Bea's disappearance at the scene of the fire, he ran with all his might back to her room. Upon opening the door, he discovered she was gone. Had the two Beas again become one?

As Bea grabbed her skirts to position herself inside the carriage, Dalton ran to her, putting a hand in the air to signal her to halt.

"Goodbye, Dalton. Thanks for everything."

"No trouble at all, Miss Bissette. Happy to help put things to rights."

She hesitated for a moment, then whispered in his ear, "Vincit qui se vincit." She conquers who conquers herself.

AUTHOR'S NOTE

Inspiration for "Splitting Image" comes from the legend of Émilie Sagée, who was allegedly a French teacher working in 1845 at a boarding school in present-day Latvia, who had the ability of bilocation. The story was first told by Scottish-born author and spiritualist Robert Dale Owen in his 1860 book *Footfalls on the Boundary of Another World*.

As the story goes, Émilie would never personally catch a glimpse of her double, but it scared those around her who did. She was fired from a total of eighteen positions because of the eerie encounters students and staff had with her double. While historians are unable to confirm that Émilie existed, it makes for an intriguing premise.

* * *

Sara Jordan-Heintz is an award-winning journalist, editor, and historian.

She serves as editor of the horror anthology series Behind the Shadows, *released by Inkd Publishing.*

She is the author of the biographies Going Hollywood: Midwesterners in Movieland *and* The Incredible Life and Mysterious Death of Dorothy Kilgallen. *She has written hundreds of articles for newspapers and magazines, many republished through the Associated Press and USA Today Network.*

Her novella "A Day Saved is a Day Earned" was published in the Rod Serling Books inaugural anthology Submitted For Your Approval, *edited by Anne Serling.*

Her fictional stories, heavily inspired by film noir, The Twilight Zone, *and everyday observations, have appeared in* 101 Words, Red Planet, 365 Tomorrows, Friday Flash Fiction, Blink Ink, The Mambo Academy of Kitty Wang, Better Than Starbucks, Potato Soup Journal *and* Shady Grove Literary.

Her work was published in the Brilliant Flash Fiction anthology Branching Out, *in Inkd Publishing's debut anthology* Hidden Villains, *in Savage Realms's horror anthology* Symphony of the Damned, *and in Sweetycat Press's anthologies* Movement: Our Bodies in Action *and* Jewels in the Queen's Crown: The Best of the Best.

The Mambo Academy of Kitty Wang nominated her short story "Sardines" for the 2021 Pushcart Prize for Best Small Fiction and the Best Microfiction.

She most enjoys writing speculative fiction, human interest stories, and pieces meant to provoke deep feelings and opinions in their readers. She lives in Iowa with her husband Andy Heintz, also a writer, their young daughter Louisa, and tuxedo cat Madeline.

THE UNIVERSE IN HER EYES

MADELYN LOPEZ

I think time is catching up to me.

In a way, I feel like I'm deteriorating, shedding layers of myself like sand in the wind. Maybe I'm trying to find a relation to the cold gray color painting the sky right now as if I were a distant cousin. The sky is falling asleep, and my mind is turning on itself, folding and folding until I can't understand myself anymore.

Or maybe I am trying to decipher a way to ask for sympathy. I don't deserve it. The reality of my world is that I am a murderer. I kill people. For my own pleasure, to inflict pain upon those who more than likely never have done anything to be worthy of some sick ending like premeditated torture. I take people's souls with no judgment in deciphering their lives' work simply to fulfill the act of death that so many fear.

I have never felt bad about it. The concept of dying, of killing, is something delicate. It takes a skilled person to know the right tactics to lure prey and convince them of trust, especially in a world where so many people like me are walking around.

But this is the first time I have felt wrong about my actions.

I killed her because I wanted to. At least, that's what I have been telling myself. She was so innocent, so pretty with her long chocolate curls that fluttered down her back, so endearing the way she swayed her hips and giggled at the sky. She didn't care about the symbolic political understandings people spend their lifetimes stressing over. She only cared about herself in the most beautiful way possible. Her life, her family, and her values. That was where her motives stood.

I loved that about her so much that I ended up hating her.

Her eyes never fluttered shut, which is something I have strangely become accustomed to. I've learned that the human body likes to watch, even in pain. And sometimes, people end up watching for far too long.

But *her* eyes. They haunt me in my sleep. They follow and watch me in my dreams, forge shadows with claw-like hands, webbed together in a gangly pattern. They are millions of branches that mimic the patterns of spiderwebs in the night.

There was a void in her eyes, a galaxy of stars that danced with each other like lovers on a ballroom floor. Yet they still watched, those stars peering over their shoulders to spot me looking at them. It was almost as if they wanted me to know that someone, something, had finally noticed all the awful things I had been doing.

Target marked. Karma bestowed.

Even now, reflecting as I sit on the edge of the beach, our beach, I can't help but feel like I had done the unthinkable after killing someone like her. It's ironic, I know. I have been doing the unthinkable for years. It is an unsettling feeling, knowing the force of fate has caught me.

It is even more unsettling knowing that her eyes still

watch me in the sea, the sky, and the darkness behind my lids when I close my own eyes.

* * *

"Isn't the sky the most beautiful thing in the world?" Mya Morgan whispers as she twists her hands through her hair, her curls like waves intertwined among her fingertips. She is quiet today and keeps mentioning how the clouds are shifting, just like the colors in the window next to us. Mysterious Mya, entirely distracted by the way things move and float around her. "I think it is. Look how it's dark blue over here but almost gray in that spot . . ."

"Is that so?" My eyes are still distracted by the way she is moving her hands, so fluid and calm in a way I wish I could achieve. Mya has a steady pattern of distracting me with the most mundane actions. She is intoxicating, a bubble of salt air and sea breeze. Beautiful and utterly — utterly distracting.

I can't take my eyes off her.

I never want to take my eyes off her.

"Az, are you even paying attention to me?" She is waving her hand in front of my face, her sharp, sparkly white nails turning into a blur of stratus clouds across my vision. Her voice has a forced labor laced throughout it, as if she is trying to keep her vocal cords in line. "Earth to Azrail . . . Did you get enough sleep last night? My boy is drifting again."

I didn't sleep last night. I was too busy walking down the street and into the alleyway behind this very coffee shop where Mya and I met. It is my favorite place to visit when my mind refuses to let me rest.

Last night, however, I wasn't strolling around for the sake of reminiscing about our friendship. I wish I were. I would be in a much better mood. I wish my nights could be spent only ever thinking about her.

Last night, I was fixing a particular — situation. A mess of a particular situation. A particular blond-headed mess that looked a lot like Mya's ex-boyfriend covered in too much dirt and blood than I would like to relive.

I fucking hated that guy.

I didn't kill him because he dated Mya or because he was the one who broke up with her. If anything, I should have thanked him because he was the reason Mya and I met in some small fraction of the universe's plan.

I killed him because it was convenient. He was someone on my list I had been pondering about, who had sparked my interest once or twice in passing. And the few times Mya spoke about him only confirmed my suspicion that he was the definition of arrogant, a soul-sucking inhabitant of this world. He would not be missed, nor would the world be in shambles without him. He checked all the boxes I needed to feed my mind, hands, and fingertips. Though, if I had known what a complete disarray going after someone his size would make, I would have waited for the weekend.

I'd like to think that being here and now with Mya, after a night like that, would give me a sense of peace, like the wash of a wave on a hot summer day. It is odd, the most bizarre thing to be granted to someone like me. No one has ever been able to bring me so much comfort, not even my own family. She is a gift wrapped in teal ribbons and pearly smiles — the best thing to ever happen to me.

Lately, I can't shake the idea that Mya is also the *scariest* thing to enter my life. I'm not the best person to be comfortable with. Maybe it's because I don't know how to comfort people. With Mya, it's different, like a string of seaweed curled around my ankles and wrists, drawing me in. She is the only person I want to be myself with.

It's hard to be myself when I have so many secrets — secrets that could get me locked in jail for the rest of my pathetic life.

I sigh, running a hand through my hair. I desperately need a haircut. The short brown curls gifted from my mom's side are slowly turning into cyclones all across my head. "I slept last night."

"Hmmm . . . for how long?" Mya doesn't look amused, her arched brows moving questioningly, probably regarding the bags underneath my eyes. "Two hours? Thirty minutes?"

I was expecting her eyes to start dancing at me, to laugh at me in their usual chaotic pattern. They have a habit of doing that when she knows she is right.

Mya has these beautiful blue eyes that turn a translucent green in the sun. Comprehensive and full of curiosity, they are the most significant thing on her face besides her lips. They look like globes spun in the water, as if she belongs in a place that isn't supposed to be on land. It was the first thing I noticed about her when we met.

And today, I can't keep my heart from sinking when I realize they have a silver ring around them.

IT WAS a Sunday morning when we met, and the seagulls were brushing their feathers along the ship-lapped panels of my local coffee shop. I had a habit of going there to get some studying in, just like the rest of my university. It was obvious why we all collected there; it was the closest spot to the beach, with windows like archways to lead people to the sound of the waves. The music, soft tapping of the fingernails on keys, and brushing of pages of books made the world slow down into a stream of movements and echoes, an escape and a perfect atmosphere to drift into a place where my mind could thoroughly think.

It was contrary to the mess happening in my head.

So, the studying I did there wasn't academic of any sort; it was the studying of human interactions. For me, the coffee shop was unofficially named the hot spot for innocent victims to meet their demise with a steaming cup of caffeine and the curly-headed boy in the back of the room.

I'd killed about five people from this coffee shop alone just by watching their patterns. It was deadly for them to do the same thing every day, to give me the perfect map into their lives to figure out where and what they would be missing out on when they were dead.

After figuring out their patterns, I'd switch up my leave time, stroll out of the coffee shop with my iced caramel macchiato in hand, ignore the missing person signs plastered to the coffee shop's front doors, and watch how their brains found their way to their destinations. Most of the time, students returned to their dorms or apartments. On infrequent occasions, I might find myself following someone to class. I hated when that happened because then I would pull some *actual* stalker shit like hiding in a bush or at the back of some ancient auditorium.

Once I have all the information I need about each victim, I conduct the rest of my work with only the stars as my witnesses.

My work takes careful construction, eloquent execution, and thorough planning. The art of life must be understood before granting things death. I never use the same strategy twice and always let their bodies flow out into the ocean when I am done. To me, that in itself feels like forgiveness, a silent farewell into our planet's most unknown territory. I never get attached to my victims nor make myself known in their lives besides helping them see the light granted to us at the end of our journeys.

It's an equation that can be filled out with a variety of numbers. Ironically, as much as I calculate and curate before acting upon my thoughts, I never remember the specific details of my killings. How I decide to end their lives is always a mystery until my head spins into its regularly scheduled programming. It is like an out-of-body experience, a blur in the simulation. It is an escape to get away from my own body by ripping someone of theirs.

For no particular reason did I kill other than to experience silent bliss.

"Can I sit here?"

The girl who stood behind the chair across from me interrupted my thoughts, the scuffling of her shoes ringing in my right ear. She was holding an alarming number of books in the crevasse of her sweater-covered arm, one looking too cartoonish and flirty to be a textbook.

I had seen her before in passing and in the coffee shop's blur of shadows and shapes. From my observations, she usually sat with the blond surfer who ordered an iced matcha with a few squeezes of pure-made chocolate sauce daily.

Yes, the same thick sauce in iced coffee or across innocent vanilla ice cream. Even I, the most despicable human to walk the earth, would never order that.

I had never seen her up close, however. I never had the chance to see her face so clear and bright. She had her hair tied back in a ponytail, chocolate curls cascading down the smooth, sun-kissed color of her back. Piercings lined the shell of her ear, and this sparkly substance rested in the corners of her eyes.

Her *eyes*.

Those eyes. Oh, her eyes were huge, wide, and curious, like the width of Saturn's rings. Her lashes curled at a startling angle, the color of her irises swirling in the pattern of seaweed floating through the ocean, chaotic and vibrant. She looked absolutely unreal, a blinking painting watching me as I desperately tried to turn my brain back on.

Her teeth moved to hold her bottom lip, her canines sharper than the average, but somehow, they weren't puncturing the soft flesh of her mouth. She was nervous. There was no denying that.

"Uhhh . . ." My mouth had fallen open slightly, while those eyes of hers squinted with amusement at my reaction before returning to their worried state. The girl peered over her shoulder, the books in her hand slipping slightly as she pressed them closer to her body.

"Please."

"Don't you—?" Those words caught in the back of my throat, burning the flesh inside my neck's collum. "You usually sit with that guy over there."

My lack of denial must have registered as approval because she sat, her movements slow and calculated, as if she were scared I would reach across the table and yank her into oblivion. I could have. I'd done it to other people before.

"I do. Well, I used to." Her voice skipped for a second, debating whether to tell me the truth or not. "We broke up."

There are always certain aspects of human interactions that I absolutely hate. One is the idea of sympathy. As someone who hates sympathy, I never can decipher the motive behind what people are expecting when they lay out something negative that happened in their lives. Are they *hoping* for sympathy? Or do they hate it just as much as I do? And if they do, then what exactly am I supposed to say? Obviously, something caring, but coming from someone like me, that is a difficult task in itself.

I was too lost in thought to think of a socially acceptable

answer. Instead, I muttered that simple word I believed someone like her more than likely wanted to hear. "Sorry."

"Such a heartfelt apology, as if it was your fault." She rolled her eyes playfully, her lashes brushing underneath her brow. I must have had some dumbfounded look on my face because she quickly corrected herself before shifting in her seat. "I'm messing with you. I really don't expect you to give a shit about my love life. I just needed a place to sit that wasn't with him or the weird girl that talks to the shells on the windowsill."

This girl seemed to be as observant as I was, yet I didn't really respect her comment about the other girl with the seashells. I liked her. She made me feel like I wasn't the craziest person to walk the planet. Misery loves company. "What about the lady with the suitcase?"

"Amy? She likes her peace and quiet."

I arched my brow at her, leaning back in my seat to fold my arms across my chest.

She marked each of my movements, her glass eyes sending signals to her brain. I wondered what she was thinking and calculating behind her thick skull, how she was pairing each of my responses with her previous assumptions about me. The girl brushed a rogue chocolate curl behind her ear and added, "Also, her space — look how many papers are all over that table right now."

I hummed, ". . . and I don't love my space."

She laughed at the comment, a fluffy cloud-like sound that could have stopped the world on its axis. What a creature, a human with immortal confidence. "I honestly didn't expect you to talk. I was expecting a nod of the head and pure awkward silence until I left for my class in an hour."

There was a beat of silence before she spoke again, her nails moving to open the textbook before her. They were another thing about her that was permanently carved at a daring angle, like a bird's talons, but somehow perfectly fitting for someone like her. When she finally found her spot to continue her educational embark, she informed me of something I would never forget, not until the end of time. "My name is Mya. Mya Morgan."

* * *

MYA BECAME my life after that interaction. It was *normal*. The most normal thing I had ever experienced. Lucky for me, it was also something that stayed normal.

Every Monday, we sat at our table in the back next to the window and drank iced coffees until she left for her class. She would text me throughout the week, and sometimes, we would meet up at the beach if the weather was nice.

The days we met at the beach were always my favorite because they gave me more time to get to know her.

On those days, Mya would wear these tight sundresses that flowed around her ankles, catching and wrapping around her legs in a cocoon of floral patterns. She would lean back against the sand in those dresses and talk about her family, particularly her sister. Her hair would spin in the wind, and she would whisper her dreams of becoming a marine biologist to the salty air, which was why she chose to attend a college close to the beach. We talked about nothing and everything. Fluid like the water, there was never a dull moment.

However, Mya's stories always had a sense of mystery to them, as if she were holding back from telling me everything. Whether it was not to come off super upfront or because she wasn't entirely sure where we stood, I honestly couldn't blame her. I never told her the details of my life and very rarely mentioned my family. I kept my distance from her, a safe six feet, to let her know I was there, but not enough to let her feel like she could fully let herself fall with me.

Even if I desperately wanted her to.

Even if I had already fallen myself.

I never asked her out. I couldn't because I knew the consequences of letting her get too close. With the details I had collected about her life, I knew my secrets wouldn't be something she would appreciate. But my heart still wanted her to see every sick and twisted knob in my head, to thread her sweet laughs throughout my memories until my mind no longer thought of the awful things I was capable of. I wanted to tell her everything, to map things out so she could help me decipher my life.

I didn't want to deal with the hurt of her leaving me.

I didn't want to deal with it so much that I became obsessed with it.

"Are you going to meet me at the beach later?" Mya cleared her throat, her eyes darting back to the window, searching for colors again.

I wanted to know what was wrong with her, but part of me felt I would be overstepping. We were close, but close in a sense for company. Not for feelings.

"For sure. I can do that." I shifted, bringing my elbows up on the table before me.

She didn't respond right away like I hoped she would. Usually, she would tell me a time and ask me to bring food or water if I had the chance. Yet, she stayed in that fixed position, her canines peeking out between the slit in her lips as she pursed them together.

I couldn't take it anymore, the awkwardness that usually didn't exist when she was around. I picked the safe route, the careful and strategic way to get the immediate answer I needed. "Are you okay?"

She nodded then, and her eyes returned to look at me.

They swirled knowingly, speaking to me in mocking tones. It looked as if there were smaller eyes within her eyes, tiny twinkles watching to see what I would do next. Her following words were muffled, a mixture of sadness and what sounded like anger moving throughout them, "Just thinking. Meet me at eight."

I said nothing after that, and she left for her class three minutes later.

* * *

I MET Mya Morgan at the beach about five minutes before eight. She had changed into a sheer white dress, barely enough to cover her tan complexion. The straps were thin across her shoulders, and the fabric danced dangerously close to the upper part of her thigh.

We sat close to the shore, the water moving in slow motion as it brushed the tops of our bare feet. Mya seemed to be in a better mood than that morning, considering she started talking about her class as soon as we sat down. They had discussed the different types of aquatic tail fins, shapes, and angles. She spoke about it like it was common knowledge, though I never knew how much a tail could affect how well a fish could swim.

Around ten thirty, she got up abruptly, the dim glow from the lighthouse next to the coffee shop causing her shadow to chase after her. She ran toward the water, her dress flowing behind her. We never went into the water; for some reason, it was an unspoken agreement to avoid it. That day, Mya had other plans.

I wished she would have stayed on the beach.

"Come dance with me!" Mya yelled back to me when the water was up to her mid-thigh, the white color of her dress becoming transparent.

I averted my eyes.

"The water won't hurt you. If it does, I promise to protect you!"

I had two options in that situation: I could sit on the beach or take the opportunity to spend time with her. Usually, I would have taken the boring route. But that day, my heart took control, the shadows dragging me toward her and into the water.

We danced then, chaotic movements without music, as we drifted further into the ocean. Mya's laughter filled the air as she flung her arms toward the sky, her body merged with the sea, and her fingertips arched like a halo above her head. The water she disrupted returned to the ocean in the form of tiny rain droplets, just for us. At that point in time, I didn't care how disgusting my clothes felt against my skin or how out of character my actions were.

I felt free. I felt at peace.

It was when Mya stopped in the water, her back turned toward me, that my world seemed to return to its usual state. There was a sense of hesitation in her movements, as if she were wondering what to do next. Her hands came up and around her neck, dragging her weighted wet hair across her right shoulder before she peered back at me and wondered, "Why haven't you asked me out?"

I had been expecting this conversation, but not yet. Maybe that's why my words were broken when I spoke, the most fragile they had ever been. "Because I can't."

"You can't, or you won't?" Mya's hands were in her hair again, and she seemed to be floating toward me. Her eyes were moving so fast, searching my face for an answer.

"I won't."

She didn't seem to like that response, her hands falling from her hair and into the waves of her dress. "Is it because of your sleeping habits?"

I fucking sucked at this. I knew that because I let the first thing I thought of rush out of my mouth without even thinking of the consequences. "Yes."

She nodded, her body drawing closer to me to the point where her chest was almost against mine. I had to step back, my feet slipping against the mushy substance at the bottom of the ocean. I wanted her to drop the subject, move back into the sea, and disregard me for the rest of my life. I wasn't ready for that conversation, especially not when she muttered her following words, "The sleeping habits that make you walk around by the coffee shop at night."

"How do you—?"

"I've seen you. From the beach," Mya interrupted, the green color in her eyes turning to stone, hard like jade.

I had to laugh. I couldn't help it. My breath puffed so hard it made the dry baby hairs across Mya's forehead scatter. Even they were running away from me, "So you make fun of me for my sleeping habits, but don't sleep yourself."

She whispered something that sounded a lot like *I don't need to.*

I sighed and ran a wet hand through my curls. I wanted to leave; for the first time since knowing her, I wanted time away from her. My brain wanted peace, not to think about her feelings or how pretty she looked drenched in the ocean, but my heart wanted to explain. "Look, Mya, you're lovely, and I really think that one day someone would—"

"Don't start with the bullshit, Azrail. I want to know why." Her words were mean and ruthless, contrary to the shore's soft moonlit waves and brushing sounds. I had never heard Mya sound so irritated.

I hate when people get snippy with me; it makes the creature that rests in the center of my stomach stir to life. It immediately made my subsequent response flow from my mouth in the same cold demeanor. "Why?"

"Tell me because I know why. I want to hear you *say* it."

I didn't know how to respond to that. My head started getting hot, and there was a ringing in my ears. I was beginning to forget where I was and why I was there. There was a feeling in my chest that felt heavy, an animal screaming to get out, get out, *get out*.

"Tell me why you walk around at night. Tell me why you watched that poor girl who sat behind me at the coffee shop for a month, and then suddenly she was gone." Mya's eyes were glowing, flashing with anger and vengeance in a way that almost didn't look human. "What about the runner with the pink shorts who would stop by to get her vanilla latte? You two missed the same day, and then she never returned. Tell me why I watched you— I watched you—" Her voice broke, and all the sirens in my head started to echo. She saw me. Where the fuck was she? In the ocean? I couldn't think of another place where she could have been hiding. "Last night, I saw you dragging his—"

"Mya! Shut up." She was starting to annoy me, my head moving a thousand miles per minute. Did anyone else see me? Was she alone, or was she with her friends? I knew she had friends she regularly hung out with and roommates who filled the rest of her personal life. Did they all watch the twisted events I carried out?

What the *fuck* do I do?

Her eyes flashed at my words, hurt brewing behind those pieces of seaweed. "You're telling me to shut up? When you do the shit that you do?"

"Leave then, Mya!" I hated raising my voice. It strained my vocal cords in a way I wasn't used to. My head was spinning, the edges of my vision blurring in the corners. "Is that why you wanted to come out here? Is that what you wanted to tell me? To get me to confess everything and then break my fucking heart?!"

There was a flash in her eyes, a flicker of hope at the confirmation of my feelings before they turned angry again. Distant and far away waves like the ones over by the edge of the world, "That's not what I want."

"Then what do you want, Mya?" My hands flew up in exasperation just as the statement escaped the column of my throat, the water splashing us in a chaotic storm of rage. She flinched when the water droplets hit her. My fingers crushed together over my head as I closed my eyes and tried to calm my brain.

One ... breathe ... two ... breathe ... thr—

"I want you to stop!" Mya's hands suddenly flew to push my chest, her fingers feeling like claws against the bones protecting my heart. She was strong, much stronger than I anticipated, and when she pushed me again and again, I almost told myself to take it. "I want you to stop fucking hurting people!"

I don't remember much after that.

I don't remember what she yelled over the roaring in my ears, her voice cracking like thunder in the sky. I don't know how it felt when her nails scratched down my chest; I'm pretty sure she broke skin then.

I don't remember what I was thinking when my hands flew to her shoulders, pushing her down into the water. I don't remember how I got the bite marks down my arm, though they looked awfully like her sharp canines. They were paired with scratch marks, similar to the ones across my chest, as if her nails were ripping at my skin all the way down until they lost strength.

I only remember how heavy she became in the water and how her eyes were still open.

For the first time since my mind had started to make my hands move without warning, I had a revelation, something I had never told myself after these situations I kept finding myself in. Maybe it was how her eyes were still trying to search mine, full of accusation. It repeated in my brain like a prayer, a plea to God to please forgive me.

I didn't mean to. I didn't mean to. I didn't mean to.

* * *

Time was catching up to me.

I knew that because I felt like someone was following me while walking back from the beach to my apartment. I'd had that feeling since I killed Mya three days earlier. Time felt physical, no longer metaphorical.

My mind kept reverting to how her hands felt across my chest, sharp and intentional; I always knew her hands would feel that way. Some sick part of me dreamed of the moment she would finally touch me. I was wrong to fantasize about something that ended up being the worst thing to ever happen to me.

Mya's hands felt ethereal, beastly but bony underneath her flesh. She was so powerful, too powerful for someone her size. My brain couldn't seem to comprehend the fight she put up when I pushed her below the surface of the water.

As if it made her stronger.

It was stupid. The places my thoughts were starting to go sounded like some backward fantasy, just like how my mind had begun to turn her eyes into something they weren't. They weren't watching me. They weren't stars, and they weren't lovers on a ballroom floor. The life in Mya's eyes went out the second she died.

Mya was dead because I killed her.

She was dead, floating into the ocean's depths, never to be found.

At least, that is precisely what I had been telling myself to keep my head from rolling off the deep end.

I didn't mean to. I didn't mean to. I didn't mean to.

It felt good to tell myself that. Every time I would replay the half of what I knew happened that night, it only solidified that thought into the stone of my metaphorical verdict. I had to remind myself that Mya had hope for me. She would have forgiven me if I had told her I would stop hurting people. She would still be alive.

I liked to think that she would have even helped me figure out my life. That we would have been able to start something, something permanent. Something I will never be able to have the chance to experience again.

Maybe this was her lesson all along: to truly stop hurting people. She knew I would have no choice but to stop if I killed her. She knew I needed her to breathe.

These are the things I had to trick my mind into believing to forget her eyes. The way they stared at me, watched me. Whenever I blinked, I saw them dancing chaotically, laughing at me like they did when she knew she was right.

What I would do to see that look on her face just one more time.

* * *

I THINK her eyes held my universe.

Six days.

It has been six days since I killed Mya. Three since I last sat here at the beach.

Today it is quiet, and the sun has already fallen into the ocean to sleep. The seagulls have floated away to their homes, their heads hanging with exhaustion, and I am desperately trying to find a sense of calm in the world of the waves.

I've spent the past hour waiting for the world to tell me what to do with my life, for the water to take care of all the problems I have caused. For some reason, my body feels drawn here, to the exact spot where Mya and I sat talking about the different types of tails a fish could have. Lunate, truncate, rounded, *forked*—

Before I know it, my head hits the sand beneath me, and I have to force my eyes to stay open. I still feel her hands drifting up my body and back down my chest, her teeth grazing my arm, her canines threatening to puncture my skin. No pain or revenge is laced through her actions, only sweet caresses made up by my mind. Only peace. Like the wash of waves on a hot summer day.

I revel in it, the phantom feeling of her overtaking my mind.

There is a moment when I could have sworn I heard a rustling to my left, waves hitting the ocean in slow motion. The sand seems to freeze, the universe pausing to grant fate the time it needs. I don't care whether there is anything there. I only care about feeling connected to Mya, even if it is all in my head.

My vision begins to fuzz the same way it does right before my hands start to move on their own. My ears heighten to the sounds around me, following and narrowing in on that slight echo to my left. I keep trying, grabbing, and pulling at the thought of Mya. I just want her; I only ever want to think of her.

It is then that the most beautiful face flickers across my vision, her eyes like seaweed, before I am yanked into the ocean.

* * *

Born and raised in San Antonio, Texas, Madelyn Lopez is a Latina debut writer pursuing her MA in English and a certificate in Creative Writing. She is slowly starting to share her writing with the world and is proud to say that Inkd Publishing's Hidden Villians: Betrayed is her first official publication.

During her childhood, Madelyn always admired reading and writing. In many cases, these activities were, and still are, her creative outlet. However, she first realized her love for sharing her writing during her freshman year of high school when she took a creative writing class. Since then, Madelyn has been writing short stories in her free time, covering various topics to test her skills.

Over the years, Madelyn has dabbled with gothic and fantasy elements in her writing, focusing on dark features to portray her messages. These genres have become her favorite to write, providing many opportunities to add layers to her writing. Besides being intrigued by eerie themes, she enjoys reading other pieces of work in her free time to get inspired. These pieces range from classics to more recent gothic fantasy works.

When Madelyn is not reading or writing, she likes to bake and hang out with her friends. One day, she dreams of owning a bakery with her sister and writing books on the side. That is far in the future, though, so for now, she is happy with sharing her short stories and working on her first novel.

TUCKERIZATIONS

Thanks to the patrons and authors who helped us Tuckerize a couple stories.

Patrick Dugan awesomely agreed to Tuckerize Andy Mays for Kickstarter patron Dino Hicks in his story, "The Nightengale's Curse."

Mike Jack Stoumbos took on Kickstarter patron for the Tuckerization of April Baker. Mike added not only April as a first name for one character, but found another to use her last name. Check out "Bartholomew's Bluff" to find his work.

Thank you to Patrons and Authors!

ACKNOWLEDGMENTS

Hidden Villains: Betrayed emerged from the suggested theme by Editor-in-Chief Robyn Huss, who agreed to edit our third Hidden Villains anthology. An editor with powerful developmental and grammatical skills, she retains the author's voice while polishing every story. Robyn works with authors on multiple passes to bring out the best in every story.

Thank you, Robyn.

With over 300 submissions, Inkd Publishing would like to thank Heather Lewis, Heather Norris, April Davis, Tony Cioffi, Kalyani Poluri, and Kevin Davis for their relentless hours helping Robyn read through all those stories. Thank you for your tireless work.

* * *

Producing anthologies can run into the thousands of dollars between editing, covers, and payments to authors. This year we would like to thank our Kickstarter supporters for helping to defray some of those costs.

Please join us in thanking the following for helping to make this anthology and future anthologies possible.

Kickstarter Patrons:

Adam Rajski, Aimee, Alexandra Corrsin, Algie Lane, Allison Charlesworth, Amanda Eschmeyer, Amber Derpinghaus, Angela Lucio Kulig, Anna Walton, Anthony Cioffi, April Baker, April Davis, Ashleigh Floyd, ASHLEY, Audrey McMahan, Billye Herndon, BretonNS, Brian Wassom, Caleb

Miller, CB Campbell, Christina Henggeler, Clara Egan, Colleen Feeney, Connie Shaut, Craig, crystalbrier, Dave Beever, David 'slick' Sellers, Dennis M. Myers, Dino Hicks, Dylan Humphreys, Edward Shafer, Ek, Erika Bester, Erika Hurley, Eve Weaver, Isaac 'Will It Work' Dansicker, Jackie Wanke, Jared Nelson, Jason Patrick Edwards, Jesse Lopez, Jessica Arden Cline, Jessica Enfante, Jessica Meade, Joelle Reizes, John Hartness, Joshua McGinnis, Joy Kristen Allen, Kalyani Poluri, Karen Phillips, Kathryn, Kenyon Wensing, KLGaffney, Krista Fehrenbacher, Kyle McLaughlin, Lauren Miller, Leslie, Luna, Madelyn Lopez, Mary Schmelter, Megan Hilldore, Michael Axe, Michael Barbour, Michael Feir, Michael Guishard, Mindy, Mordy gofman, Mustela, Patrick Dugan, Per Møller Jensen, Rina Wesel, Ronald L Weston, Ronald Miller, Rosemary Williams, S.D. Huston, Sara Jordan-Heintz, Scott Maynard, Seamus Sands, Stephanie K. Clemens, Stephanie Writt, Steven Byrd, The Creative Fund by BackerKit, Thomas Tellefsen, Tim Lewis, tonel, Tyler Hulsey, Virginia Keister, Zack Fissel, Zimmie

Thank you! Thank you!

Please visit us at InkdPub.com

Inkd Pub supports Multiverse, a fabulously diverse and inclusive convention in Atlanta, GA. We attend many fandoms and comic cons; however we especially love the mission and direction of Multiverse.

Please visit their website and learn more.

www.multiversecon.org/

ALSO BY INKD PUBLISHING

Hidden Villains by Robyn Huss - our original anthology with David Farland as lead author

Hidden Villains: Arise by Robyn Huss - with Jody Lynn Nye as lead author

BEHIND THE
SHADOWS
An anthology of thrillers, horror, and suspense stories.
EDITED BY SARA JORDAN-HEINTZ
INCLUDING STORIES BY
HEIDI HUNTER, SCOTT BRENDEL
AND LMG WILSON

Noncorporeal by A. Balsamo - our spooky anthology

Books are available in paperback and eBook; please visit us at
InkdPub.com to find locations. Join us on Facebook to keep up to
date.

Sign up for our newsletter at our website for open call announcements, Kickstarters, and launches.

Inkdpub.com

UPCOMING FROM INKD PUBLISHING

The next edition of *Hidden Villains* will continue with the theme of

Criminals

We welcome your submissions on this theme and hope you will follow us on Facebook, join our mailing list, or just check our website regularly for updates and submission dates.

Janci Patterson has agreed to pen the lead story for *Hidden Villains: Criminals*.

We have two new anthologies added to our annual lineup: *Yay, All Queer,* our LGBTQ+ anthology, and *Impulse,* our explicit romance anthology.

www.ingramcontent.com/pod-product-compliance
Lightning Source LLC
Chambersburg PA
CBHW032339310726
48973CB00007B/1774